THE ALTERED
MANUSCRIPT

ELLEN
TAYLOR

DIVERTIR
PUBLISHING
Salem, NH

The Altered Manuscript

Ellen Taylor

Copyright © 2021 Ellen Taylor

Cover image by
Kenneth Tupper

Published by
Divertir Publishing LLC
PO Box 232
North Salem, NH 03073
http://www.divertirpublishing.com/

ISBN-13: 978-1-938888-30-4
ISBN-10: 1-938888-30-8

Library of Congress Control Number: 2021952987

Printed in the United States of America

Dedication

Thanks Daniel for your support, and thanks Mike for helping Junior get out of trouble

TABLE OF CONTENTS

CHAPTER 1

BREE THREW OPEN the front door and bolted toward the bus stop. "Homework!" her mom shouted behind her, waving a fistful of papers in the air.

Bree skidded to a stop and turned around, kicking up freshly fallen snow as she ran back. The bus roared past right as she snatched her homework. She groaned and dashed back toward the street waving her arms. The squeals and shrieks of the old bus coming to a stop shattered the still morning air.

Her homework remained tight in her fist as she ran up the bus steps. The crystal blue eyes of the bus driver short-circuited her brain as he smiled at her, and garbled noises came out of her mouth that did not sound intelligent. He tipped his cowboy hat, and Bree used the moment to hide her face in her homework as she sped past him. One day his blue eyes wouldn't disarm her so much. Once she was safe in her undeclared spot, she used the moment to calm her breathing and rub the wrinkles out of her homework against the brown pleather seat.

The window felt cool as she rested her head against it. Her short dark brown hair stuck to the condensation. Another storm loomed over the mountains, ready to dump more snow on the ground. Last night's snowfall must not have been enough.

The bus made another stop, and Bree's best friend Holly walked on with books clutched tight to her chest. The bus driver didn't receive Holly's usual not-so-secret backward glance today. Instead, her eyes focused on the floor until she slumped into the seat on the other side of the aisle from Bree. With trembling fingers, she pulled the hood of her coat over her shoulder-length blonde hair.

Bree cleared her throat in an exaggerated way. "What's this?"

Holly looked over sheepishly as Bree looked at the empty space between them and cocked her eyebrow. "Um..."

1

"Get your body over here." Bree stuffed her homework in her bag before hugging it close to give Holly more room.

"I thought with everything that happened at the party on Saturday—"

"Forget what happened." Bree tilted her head to the side to let her friend know the space next to her was still empty.

"After all the drama I caused, you still want to be friends?" Holly asked.

"You didn't cause the drama. Aubrielle did."

Holly sighed and moved over to sit by Bree. "Thanks."

"It's what I'm here for." Bree grinned. "On to more important things. How do we get a hot cowboy bus driver to pay attention to some sixteen-year-old sophomores?" A good chat about the bus driver's hotness would distract them from the weekend drama.

Holly tapped her finger against her chin. "I thought about this last night. If a major disaster happens right now, we'll be trapped in this bus for a couple of hours. We can play the part of damsels in distress, and he'll save us, because he's awesome. Then we'll have the in we need to get to know him better."

Bree suppressed a giggle. "If we wait for a natural disaster to happen before we talk to men, we're going to be single the rest of our lives."

A new kid got on the bus, which cut Holly's chuckle short. They watched him sit in Holly's old seat. He turned to the girls with a shy smile, making Holly perk up. Bree suspected it was because of the undivided attention from a boy with curly dark hair.

"Hello," he said.

Out of her peripheral vision, Bree saw Holly lick her lips as she studied this new kid. Dark curly hair, sun-kissed skin in the middle of winter, vibrant green eyes; nothing drew Holly's attention faster to a boy than green eyes and dark curly hair. In fact, thanks to all the sleepover chats, Bree realized this new kid somehow possessed every physical feature on Holly's dream-boy list.

Bree cleared her throat. "Hi. Are you new?"

"Yeah. I moved in over the weekend. My name is Reggie."

"Holly." She thrust her hand out. "That's my name. And this is Bree."

"Glad to meet you." Reggie shook her hand.

"You have soft hands."

The urge to whack Holly's foot was strong. Holly meant well, but her pre-school-aged flirting sounded creepy coming from a sixteen-year-old.

"What brings you here, Reggie?" Bree's plan was simple—make sure

Reggie didn't feel so uneasy he'd bolt as soon as they reached school. It had happened before.

Reggie shrugged. "My dad got a new job."

"How old are you?" Holly asked.

"Sixteen."

"No car either, huh?" Bree asked.

"I have one, but my dad wanted me to ride the bus for a bit. See places, learn the route, and meet kids my age."

"You have a car?" Holly sounded like the bus driver offered to give her a back massage and feed her peeled grapes.

The urge overcame her, and Bree whacked Holly's foot with her own before smiling at Reggie. "I hope you like it here."

Reggie smirked, as if he knew something Bree didn't. It felt like someone took an eggbeater and began to churn her innards together.

"Oh, don't worry." The look in Reggie's eyes was anything but nonchalant. "I will."

§ § §

"Stop!"

I didn't mean to scream. The microphone could pick up the word even if I whispered. My hands trembled as I took off the headset, staring at the two computer screens on my desk. One screen held the text of my story, while the other played out the scene, now frozen in time.

My palms started to sweat. I closed my eyes and took a deep breath before opening them again. The boy named Reggie still sat there, watching Bree too close. He didn't belong. I didn't create him.

My legs trembled as I backed away from the two screens. A million nasty possibilities raced through my mind until I forced myself to stop. I worked hard to get the narration device. I did research to prove I wasn't a target. It was all in vain. The Rogue Narrator had entered my story.

CHAPTER 2

M Y FEET CARRIED me back and forth in my little office. *Maybe this was a horrible trick.* I looked back at the screen where Reggie smiled in a far too knowing way. My knees weakened. I took a deep breath, and slowly let it out as I slumped back into my office chair. My eyes glazed over and landed on the little black box, the narration device, connected to the desk computer and my laptop. The truth of the situation washed over me.

I was in deep trouble.

The narration device was an amazing accidental discovery thirty years earlier when scientists were researching virtual reality. What they discovered changed entertainment forever. I could narrate a story, and the finish project would produce a book, an audiobook, and rough footage for a movie which faithfully followed every word. Directors could still take the rough footage, edit it down, and stick a soundtrack to it. However, those loyal to the book would still have a copy in its raw form.

My cell phone rang. I jumped, startled out of my reverie. "Hello?" I asked, putting the phone to my ear.

"Hello. This is Samantha, Vince Boyle's head secretary."

I braced against the wall to keep myself upright as my pretense of control slipped away. My heartbeat rang in my ears. "The Rogue. He's in my story, isn't he?"

The question was superfluous. For all the amazing things the narration device could do, no one dreamed a mad genius could create his own twisted device to enter other stories and wreak havoc in them.

Samantha sounded professional. "Yes. The Guardians request you stop narrating until you discuss your situation with them. How soon are you able to get here?"

The Guardians were the narration government. They made sure people did not abuse the narration device. They had been trying to catch

5

the Rogue for years. To even meet them, despite my troubling circum-stances, would be an honor. I almost said I was ready right then before my eyes wandered to my sweatpants and baggy t-shirt. I didn't plan on going out in public today, let alone meet the four most influential people of my career.

"I'll be ready in thirty minutes."

"A cab will pick you up at the front of your apartment. Bring your narration ID."

I hung up and began making myself look presentable. Today I needed my lucky floral skirt with a white tank top and my green cardigan with quarter-length sleeves. I gave myself a good once over to figure out what needed the most work. Most of me looked great without too much work. My hair, on the other hand, always needed extra attention.

My black hair refused to be curled. By the time I finished curling my hair, the curls would already start falling out on one side. Doing nothing wasn't an option either—it was ridiculously thick, and despite it not being able to curl, it often looked like a tangle of weeds fluttering every which way. I hated my hair, but not enough to shave it. One of my elastic bands broke in the process of wrestling my hair into submission.

In a record-breaking time of twenty-five minutes, I walked out of the small apartment owned by the Guardians into the warm, early summer air. I sat on the front step, gripping my narration ID. It would have snapped in half if it wasn't made of heavy-duty material.

The small apartment building was one of three others, all owned by the Guardians. I lived on the ground floor and was the only narrator on the lot. The Guardians kept junior narrators near their headquarters while they narrated in case we ran into problems. They usually involved simple things, like the narration device shorting out. Or big things, like the Rogue.

The taxi arrived. I got up, hurried across the soft lawn, and slipped into the back seat.

"Guardians headquarters?" the driver asked.

"Yes please." The first of the rebellious strands of hair snuck out. I tucked them behind my ears. The prepaid drive was short, giving me no time to calm my fears.

The two-story marble building towered over me. It wasn't large, but still commanded respect. I rubbed my arms to keep the nervousness at bay. I'd visited the headquarters once before when I won top honors for a writing contest in high school. This time was different.

I climbed the stairs, walked past the pillars, and opened the metal doors. Two secretaries at the front desk were making calls. One called and canceled an appointment in less than ten seconds. They rearranged the Guardians' busy schedules to accommodate my current situation. The feeling of being an inconvenience started to nag at my soul.

"May I help you?" The brunette secretary sounded professional while she scribbled something down on a notepad.

"Yes, um, hi." I tugged at the bottom button of my cardigan. "I'm the narrator."

"Ah yes." She gave me a look of pity. "Identification please?" I handed it over and she scanned the code. "They're waiting for you in the conference room. Go down this left hall until you reach room 116."

"Thank you." I took back my ID, happy my voice sounded normal. I glanced up at the second-floor balcony where the Guardians' had their offices before heading to room 116. My green flats echoed through the empty marble hall, making me want to tiptoe the rest of the way.

I opened the door and peeked inside. With a name like 'conference room' I'd pictured something grander—a spacious room with dramatic drapes over windows to make it look warm and inviting but still holding a theatrical feeling. What I found instead was a simple square room with a simple, raised rectangle table. The Guardians' names were on little plaques in front of where they sat. My breath caught in my throat. These four people were the best narrators, voted into their position because of their skill and experience. In my dream of dreams I wanted to be one, but I needed to survive my current situation before running for Guardianship.

The one older woman in the Guardians beamed at me as though we were long-lost friends. Her wrinkles were a reflection on how much she smiled in life. It gave me the courage to walk into the room. She was at the end of the table on the right. She had to be at least seventy but dressed smartly for her age. Her hair was more gray than black. Kind brown eyes watched me with concern behind simple glasses. Her plaque read 'Grace Alvarez' and my soul brightened. I didn't often read poetry, but hers was optimistic and moving with a touch of humor.

The three men in the Guardians didn't see me walk in. They were working on various electronic devices. I stood there, trying not to scratch the back of my leg. A fold-up chair faced the Guardians. They probably wanted me to sit, but no one offered the chair to me. Grace squinted at the other Guardians, but they didn't look up. Vince Boyle, the Chairman of the Guardians and owner of the nicest looking plaque, studied his laptop before comparing it to some documents in a folder. I tried to clear my dry throat, but it wasn't enough to announce myself.

Grace saw my distress and coughed. The other three looked up. She gave them a gentle look of chastisement before smiling at me. "Take a seat, dear."

I tiptoed over to the chair and sat down. "Hi!" I said too loudly.

Grace chuckled. Vince, who sat next to Grace, lowered his notes. He placed his hands on top of them and peered at me over his thick glasses. I shrank under his gaze.

Everything about Vince the Chairman was big. Portly figure, beefy hands, and big eyes made bigger by his thick glasses. His sandy blonde hair thinned at the top. He had a tattoo on his forearm he must have gotten when he was younger, because it stretched to the point I couldn't recognize the design. That or the tattoo artist needed to be fired.

"Hello, Miss, um." Vince moved his laptop and opened the folder underneath with my narration information.

"Just call me Junior." I tried hard not to sound annoyed.

He grunted. "We are here to help you, since your story has been infiltrated by the Rogue."

"I figured that out," I mumbled, though not quietly enough. Vince paused to give me an ugly glare. I made a mental note that this man didn't understand sarcasm. My sweaty palms squeaked as I gripped the bottom of the chair.

"I have a few questions." Grace looked at a sheet of paper and positioned her glasses closer to her eyes. "You are a recent college graduate?"

"Yes. You delivered the narration device to me a week before my graduation." It seemed strange to believe the delivery came a month ago.

"Your application says you did not take any classes from the Rogue, at the time called Professor Andrews. Correct?"

Lying didn't come easy for me. My mind held fast to my line of logic, which kept guilt from playing across my face as my knuckles turned white. I didn't *technically* take a class from Professor Andrews. "No. I never took one of his classes."

Vince grunted again. I assume it meant he approved. "We are close to the Rogue's whereabouts. With your story distracting him, we will soon catch him."

"There has to be another way." I looked at the other Guardians. "I don't want to continue narrating."

The silence returned, but with more edge. Devin, one of the other Guardians, glanced at Vince to see his reaction. The other Guardian, Jim, gave me a sad smile. Jim was in newspaper articles and press conferences for something tied with the Rogue, but I didn't remember why. His dark brown hair was cropped short, and his dark brown eyes focused on me. His suit coat was tailored to make his thin body look more muscular. He was the youngest of the Guardians—I guessed late twenties or early thirties.

"Junior." Vince lowered his glasses down the bridge of his nose, completing the condescending look. "You signed a contract before we gave you the narration device. Your story belongs to us. The Rogue is almost caught. We demand your cooperation."

"I don't want my characters in more danger. It's been, what, three years since the Rogue started this? What's taking you so long?"

Vince's blue eyes darkened.

Devin raised his eyebrows. I couldn't tell if he was impressed or if he also saw me as a young, ambitious narrator with too many demands. He had light brown hair, his eyes were a deep shade of blue, and he looked in his mid-forties. He took minutes, but I knew his mind wasn't on the meeting.

"It sounds like you want to use my characters as bait," I said before Vince spoke again. "I need to know they'll be safe."

"You signed a binding contract." His kid gloves were off. I touched a nerve. "It states in times of emergency, the Guardians will do what they see fit with your story."

"Which is?"

"Have you narrate it. The Rogue is focused on you, and if we get anyone else to narrate your story, he will leave."

"That's what I want! Give my rough draft to a professional! Get the Rogue out of my story! I'll watch closely to make sure everything goes well." I desperately wanted to narrate it myself, but if I did, my characters would be in danger. Having someone else do it was the best option.

Vince glared at me. "You will narrate it, because this is the only way to find the Rogue!"

I clenched my fists to control the anger surging through me. Before I could retort, Grace placed a hand on Vince's arm. "Stop scaring the poor girl. She's going through enough as it is."

Was I scared? Possibly. I had a hard time keeping my emotions from my face.

"I know it's tough. I know you're afraid. Some of us don't like the idea of using you or your characters as bait." Grace's eyes flickered over to Vince before she returned to me. "This way seems barbaric, but it's produced the largest success rate. Of all the Rogue's infiltrated stories, three turned out unsuccessful. Many narrators have characters with beautiful endings to their story despite the infiltration."

The odds did sound nice, but the rumors swirling around about what happened to the three unsuccessful stories made me hesitant. Was it worth putting Bree at risk?

"We will not leave you alone. We'll give you the aid of a Guardian to protect you and your characters," Grace said.

It took me a moment to answer. "Okay." I didn't like it, but I'd agree to it. "Who's helping me?" My eyes begged Vince to choose Grace.

"We will send our most qualified member." Vince nodded in Devin's direction. "Devin will help."

Devin glanced up from the work he tried to do secretly under the table. "Um, sir? Could we talk?"

Jim and Grace exchanged uneasy glances. Vince's eyes narrowed. "What."

Devin cleared his throat and gestured toward the back of the room. He had the decency to give me a smile before taking Vince by the shoulder and leading him to the far-right corner. Maybe he hoped we wouldn't eavesdrop, but it didn't work. The room was small, after all.

"My schedule is booked for months," Devin whispered.

"You've protected narrators before."

"At the cost of my other work. I'm swamped. Either I search for the Rogue with Grace, or I protect Junior. I can't do both anymore."

My lips pressed together as I glared at the table. Grace looked uncomfortable. Jim went back to his work. I folded my arms and tapped my fingers against my skin.

"Everything will be fine, dear." With Grace talking, I couldn't overhear Devin and Vince's discussion. "They'll work something out."

I continued to tap. "And yet the Rogue keeps getting away."

"Believe me," Jim said, talking for the first time. "You don't need to lecture us on what the Rogue has done."

"My main character is sixteen years old." I straightened in my chair and leaned forward. "I've heard what the Rogue does to the main characters of failed books."

Jim winced.

"Well, you have two choices in front of you," Vince said as he and Devin returned to their seats. "There's a small chance the Rogue will get your main character, or you can stop narrating, and after a month all your characters will be thrown into limbo."

I held Vince's stare for three seconds before turning away. His version of tough love took a chunk out of the respect I once had for him.

Narrators didn't talk much about the limbo world, let alone joke about it. Every college class about narration drilled it into students about the limbo world. After a month of no narration, the device shuts down, and the characters enter the limbo world. The world was discovered ten years after the accidental discovery of the narration device. Characters ceased to exist in limbo, and no one had found a way to make them re-exist. It was more than cruel. It was inhumane. Only the Guardians saw the limbo world. For the most part, they didn't like to talk about it. Apparently, Vince considered it okay to use it as a threat for narrators who didn't do what he wanted.

As long as I narrated once every month, the device wouldn't shut down. Even the worst Rogue rumor didn't compare to condemning my characters to limbo.

Vince nodded, convinced he had my cooperation. "Devin, what's your opinion? Who should help Junior?"

Devin didn't even glance at the other three Guardians. "Jim will help."

11

Jim withered in his chair. "What?" The look on his face added another twist in my stomach. I already felt skittish with the Rogue in my story; I needed a Guardian who felt more confident. Why couldn't Grace help?

Devin looked surprised at Jim's reaction. "What do you mean 'what'?"

"No." Jim gathered papers into a folder as if he was going to leave. "No," he repeated as though we didn't hear the first time. "This is not a good idea."

"Jim, you'll do fine," Grace said.

"You and Devin have dealt with the Rogue before," Vince said.

Jim turned to Vince. "You've met him before." At first, I didn't understand. Then I remembered when Vince won the Chairmanship by a close election his opponent got angry, sought revenge, and was now better known as the Rogue.

"And we all know how well that went," Vince said. I heard a hint of sarcasm. Maybe Vince only understood his own.

"We all know how well it went with me, too." Jim shivered. "There's too much history. I can't."

"If you think *you* have too much history, then explain why I have all Rogue responsibilities," Devin said.

"Because you're successful at it."

I fought the urge to wave at them to remind them of my existence. What they talked about eluded me, but I didn't like the sound of it. Jim's posture stiffened as the seconds ticked on.

Grace gave him a loving look. "Take the project and put the poor girl's mind to rest, Jim. She doesn't want to hear us arguing."

Jim glanced in my direction, finally remembering I was there. "Fine." Jim's eyes darkened. "I'll take the assignment."

A muscle in my jaw twitched and my eyes narrowed. Did he call me an assignment?

"Good! It's settled." Vince rubbed his hands together. "Junior, Jim is now your Guardian buddy."

"Is that how I address him?" I didn't hide my sarcasm this time.

"Ask him any questions you have." He plowed right over my remark, and I pinched my lips together. "Hopefully we won't need another meeting like this, and we'll soon have the Rogue in prison."

"Great." I pretended to share in his enthusiasm.

"Do you have any more questions?" Vince asked.

I shook my head submissively.

"Meeting adjourned until further notice."

CHAPTER 3

JIM STUFFED FOLDERS and his laptop into his briefcase before heading over to me. As he came closer, I noticed a small scar on his upper lip. I stood up as tall as I could, but Jim still towered over me. He had to be six feet, if not more.

"Hello." There was no fluctuation in his voice.

"Hi." I tried and failed to make up for his lack of enthusiasm.

Jim handed me a business card. "This is my phone number. Write yours here." He pulled a small notebook and pen from his suit coat pocket, where I scribbled my phone number. It disappeared from my hand as he swiped it and stuffed it back in his pocket.

"I expect reports every Monday, Wednesday, and Friday. Continue your narration. I'll monitor your story in my office, but I can't be there every time you narrate. If you have any questions, you have my number." He was already halfway out the door.

I grabbed his coat sleeve. "Wait! What do you want in your reports?"

He glowered at the door, but the rest of him tried to look civil. "Everything. Keep me updated on how the story follows your original outline."

"It's already messed up. A boy I didn't create started talking to my main character."

Jim's lips pressed tighter together. "I'll look into it. I'll also alert Dr. Webb's secretary to set up an appointment."

I let go of his sleeve. "Who's Dr. Webb?"

"She's a therapist trained to help patients cope from negative experiences with the narration device."

"I don't need a therapist. I'm fine."

He broke his gaze from the door and met my eyes. "And we want you to stay that way."

Was it common to start people off with a therapist as soon as the Rogue entered their stories? My teeth started gnawing on my bottom lip.

Jim started for the door again but paused, rubbed his forehead, and then turned around. "One more thing. Check with me before you do anything stupid."

This had to be the worst meeting I'd ever attended. I folded my arms tightly across my chest. "I don't do stupid things in my stories."

At least he noticed my defensive position. "I don't doubt you. However, I've read a few of the infiltrated manuscripts, and there comes a point when, in desperation, the narrator did stupid things."

I unfolded my arms and let them hang loose at my sides, but my hands remained balled into fists. "Maybe they did stupid things because their 'Guardian buddy' was too busy trying to get out of the assignment."

Jim gave me a look I didn't understand. When he opened his mouth, I anticipated an apology, but his phone buzzed in his pocket. His mouth closed as he pulled it out, looked at it, and waved me away. "I have to take this. Get back to narrating. Let us do the rest." He left the room, phone to his ear.

Jerk!

"Are you alright, dear?"

I spun around to see Grace standing behind me, looking concerned. "Why does it seem like Jim doesn't want to help me?" I asked.

"He's been through a lot these past few years. The stress makes him prickly. The Chairman too, come to think of it. I'm afraid our first impression hasn't been the best."

My fingers found the sleeve of my cardigan as I played with the hem. "I didn't give the best first impression either. I'm just..." My mood couldn't adequately be described, so I went to my default reaction of smiling.

"These boys have been in the trenches with the Rogue for so long they forget a little compassion goes a long way. You'll see, Junior. They may seem prickly now, but they'll sacrifice everything for your safety. They were elected Guardians for a reason."

The tension in my body relaxed at Grace's words. No wonder she was a poet. "Why couldn't you help me?"

Grace gave me a side hug. "You'll find out soon enough, dear. Protecting a narrator takes someone more young and fit."

The air escaped my lungs as I remembered my situation. "How bad will it get?"

Grace's smile faltered before it came back less sincere. "Not as bad as some, I'm sure."

The secretary got a cab for me under Grace's direction. I insisted my apartment wasn't far, but she wouldn't hear of it. What Grace said haunted me. Was I in for a tough time? Could I trust Jim to help if it became hard? I thought about Jim all the way home. I tried to believe he'd sacrifice everything to keep me safe, but he admitted he had made mistakes—mistakes which caused serious problems.

The chair in my office squeaked as I collapsed into it. I scowled at the computers, the screens still frozen in time. Reggie wore his creepy grin, and Bree looked innocent but confused. My attention again turned to the device.

My line of sight traveled back to Reggie, and my thoughts turned to the Rogue. He broke many narration laws, and if he wasn't stopped my characters would be in danger. How was I supposed to fight a guy who wouldn't follow the rules? Could I skirt around the rules without putting myself or my characters in danger?

Laws were vital for the narration device. The device was revolutionary and extremely dangerous. In the early days, anyone could order a device and narrate stories. A group of five scientists wanted to test the limits. The experiment ended after three days—four of them died, and the fifth ended up in a coma. Distribution was shut down and didn't open again without the Guardians in place. The rules and regulations became so strict that a person had to graduate from college with a degree in Narration before they could even touch a device. Even then, the Guardians came out with fresh rules every few months. The device was powerful, almost too powerful, and I agreed with the laws. If it wasn't for the public outcry all those years ago demanding laws so they could keep using the narration device, it would have been destroyed, and no one else would have been able to use it. The laws protected us and helped us use an amazing device. So how was I supposed to fight the Rogue?

I clamped the headphones over my ears and adjusted the microphone close to my mouth. One of my other characters needed to become co-main character so the Rogue wouldn't focus all his attention on Bree. It'd make my story more complex than I anticipated, but what choice did I have? If I wanted to protect Bree, the other character needed to be an adult. It might be confusing to have an adult main character in a story about teenagers, but I had to make it work.

My first thought was Bree's mom, but I felt uneasy. She was older, but they were mother and daughter. Even without the Rogue putting them in danger, my original outline had them going through a lot. No, I couldn't give this responsibility to Bree's mom. I needed someone else, and I didn't have much of a choice. It had to be Allen.

This kind of responsibility on Allen was a gamble. He was a good man, but his soul was still fragile. If the Rogue got to Allen, it could destroy him. I massaged my forehead. As much as I hated Allen being co-main character, Bree's mother would be worse.

I pulled out a notebook and jotted down a rough outline for the next scene. An unplanned scene was difficult to narrate. The story could be thrown off if I wasn't careful. If I narrated in short bursts throughout the coming week, it should be okay.

Allen's office popped up on one of the screens. I double-checked everything. The device knew about Allen's character, but I wanted to make sure it didn't miss anything, down to the titles of the books on the three bookshelves inside his office. When I was satisfied, I situated the microphone again before I took a deep breath.

"Resume."

§ § §

Allen Simmons leaned back in his office chair reading the material for his class the next day. It was almost five o'clock on a Monday. From his window, he saw a small, back alley path to the library. It seemed a fitting view for an English professor. After a time, he found a new perk to his office view.

The math building was across the lawn from the English building. The door of the math building opened. He peeked over the top of his book and watched as Sadie stepped out of the building. She secured her red coat around her as she braved the winter storm.

Tomorrow marked the three-week anniversary since he bumped into her, a holiday only he celebrated in his quiet office. Allen knew this woman was different. It had been years since he felt a connection with a woman from a simple greeting. A casual bump into each other turned into an hour-long conversation at the coffee shop on campus. Now she reduced him to a lovesick teenager, waiting to catch glimpses of her from a distance and quietly celebrating the days since she came into his life.

The more practical, professor side of him shook his head, disgusted. The professor side of his brain wanted to beat some logic into the lovesick teenager and not rely so much on emotion. The final piece of his mind, the previously married side, wanted to remind him how relationships could hurt, and hurt deep. The three imaginary figures were in a constant state of war since he bumped into Sadie. The lovesick teenager demanded he march down and ask her on a proper date. The previously married side reminded him there were years of dust on that set of skills he needed to brush off. The professor nagged at him to keep studying for his lesson tomorrow and worry about Sadie another day.

Allen dug his fingers into his forehead and massaged his head until his fingers got tangled into his light brown hair. Why did love have to be so stubborn? He opened his green eyes and rested them on the lesson plan he had forgotten about the moment Sadie walked out of the math hall.

Someone knocked, and Allen expected it to be a student. He opened the door and instead saw a pile of boxes.

"Sorry," the distressed man behind the boxes said. "Could you point me to office 301 N?"

"301 N? We're office neighbors. I'm 301 M. Here, let me take some of those for you."

"Thanks."

Allen took a few bulky boxes, uncovering a man a head shorter than him. The man's black hair was short and receded a bit, and he had dark brown eyes that looked almost black compared to his pale skin. While the man unlocked the office next to him, Allen found himself with all the boxes. He struggled with the added weight, but didn't want to show it.

"I'm Riley Nelson, by the way. Visiting Faculty."

"Allen Simmons." Riley opened the door, and Allen unloaded his armful of boxes on an empty desk.

"Thanks for your help," Riley said.

"Yeah." Allen shook Riley's hand. Riley quickly dropped his hand, moved to the desk, and started opening the boxes. Allen headed toward the door. "If you have any questions, let me know."

"I do have one, yes. Who is she?"

Allen walked over to the window, and every muscle in his face stiffened when he saw Sadie walk back into the math building. She must have forgotten something.

"Who?" Allen wanted to make sure Riley meant Sadie.

"The woman in the red coat walking into the building."

"Her name is Sadie. She's in the math department." The lovesick teenager gasped at the audacity of uttering her name to another man.

"Sadie."

Allen bristled, but tried to keep his face neutral. He did not like the way her name sounded coming from Riley. The lovesick teenager almost strangled the professor side for giving more information. The professor told the lovesick teenager he was being polite. The previously married part of him remained quiet in the corner.

"Well, someone's got to teach it. Am I right?" Riley had a light and humorous tone to his voice. Allen did not find it funny. "Any idea if she's single?"

"I don't think so." The lovesick teenager said that bit. Before he felt too embarrassed for lying, he turned around and headed out the door.

"Thanks for your help, Allen."

Allen didn't answer as he returned to his office and opened a book, reading a couple of passages he planned to use in his class. Reading calmed his nerves, though most of what he read sailed over him.

It was three minutes past five before he realized what time it was. He snatched his coat and shoved his arms through the sleeves. Spring would never come with how much snow had fallen today. Even though February was the shortest month, it always seemed to last so long. Winter had a firm, icy grip over everything.

The last button on his coat slid into place right as he pushed open the door. The scene before him froze his heart more than the bitter wind did. Riley was talking with Sadie. The look on her face revealed a mild discomfort as she answered a question Allen didn't hear. She was so pretty. Not too thin, short black hair, and beautiful brown eyes. The smile on her face was so warm it melted the coldness around his heart, until he realized she was looking straight at him. His heart sputtered as he tried to smile back, but he didn't know if the muscles in his mouth obeyed. This time his mind panicked. Sadie was smiling at him, and he needed to smile back now so she wouldn't think he was ignoring her. All the heat in his body rose to his cheeks as his mouth made a semblance of a smile he hoped wasn't creepy.

Why was love so self-destructive? He turned and lumbered down the path leading to his car. The professor stuffed all self-deprecating thoughts in a box and demanded he think of tomorrow's lesson. It was the safest place for his mind to go.

CHAPTER 4

MY FOREHEAD WAS inches from the screen as I stared at Allen frozen in the process of walking away. Allen's introduction scene seemed short, but it took a whole week to narrate. I kept stopping to contemplate how to best get his character across. This man was dear to me, and I wanted to nail his introduction.

When the Rogue's character entered, I stopped the narration during the middle of a conversation and waited a day. My logic was the Rogue could only narrate when I narrated, so if the Rogue wasn't at his device, I could get his character away from Allen. I chose a late time of night to start narrating again, but the Rogue must have had an alarm on his device or something to alert him, because his character responded as soon as I started up again.

My cell phone rang, which made me jump. I grabbed it and saw Jim was calling me. "Hello!" I overplayed the enthusiasm so he wouldn't notice my annoyance.

"Why is Allen a co-main character? You're not following my instructions."

"Wow. Really? Crushing my work before giving it a chance?" If Jim wouldn't pretend to be civil, then neither would I. It took Jim a week to notice I introduced Allen as a co-main character. Why did it take a week?

"You promised to talk to me before you did anything stupid."

My cheeks burned. "You think what I'm doing is stupid?"

"At best it's an unwise decision. You are not following your outline and rough draft."

"Let me get this straight." My blood started to boil. "You want me to tell you every little decision I'm going to make?"

"Yes," was Jim's quick reply. "If it's not in your original outline."

I held my breath to keep from screaming then slowly let it out. "Fine." My voice was flat. "Sorry." I meant the exact opposite. Did he realize what it meant? Eventually my story would be nothing like the original outline. Soon I'd have to call every time I started the device.

"Why did Allen become a co-main character?" Jim asked.

"I don't want them focusing on Bree, so she and Allen will share the load. Allen can protect Bree if things go south." Jim took a breath to start talking, but I didn't want to hear him. "These are my characters. It may not mean much to some narrators, but I'm protective of mine."

"Okay, okay." Jim sounded exasperated. "Calm down, Junior. I realize you might be a little on edge."

"A little?" I couldn't believe what came out of his mouth. "A *little*?"

There was silence on the other end. I tapped the edge of my desk to keep my temper in check. The sun came from behind the early summer clouds, warming my office and adding more heat.

"The stress is getting to you. You might need a few days away from the device," Jim finally said.

"I can't."

"Your characters are fine in the frozen state. They can't do anything without you narrating."

"This is important. I need to solve it." My voice sounded panicky. I stopped tapping the desk and began to pace around my small office.

"The Guardians have worked on this for three years. Do you think you'll solve it in a week?"

I glared at the wall. Part of me wanted to like Jim. He was, after all, in charge of my welfare. "I deserve to know what happens to stories when the Rogue enters them."

Jim responded too quickly. "You've heard the rumors."

"I need more than rumors. What's the Rogue's battle plan, the things he did in previous stories? This isn't a story anymore, it's war."

The sigh I heard on the other end didn't sound exasperated—more like Jim dreaded answering my question. "There's a reason the public doesn't know the truth."

"I'm different from the public now."

"It will freak you out because you're going through it."

I shook my head as I paced faster. "Don't protect me, Jim. Tell me."

He breathed in and out. "It's not my place to decide whether I can tell you." Jim sounded less angry. "But I will ask Vince."

I used my other hand and tried to hug myself. "Do you have any suggestions of what I should do next?" The phrase took a blow to my pride on its way out. Why did I have to go to him for ideas?

"Technically, he hasn't done anything yet, so we can't either."

"He's placing *his* characters in strategic places throughout *my* story." I didn't bother hiding my sarcasm. "That's all."

"Junior, it's fine."

A flood of anger rushed to my brain. "I have to get back to narrating."

"You have an appointment with Dr. Webb next Monday at one."

"I don't need a therapist."

"Dr. Webb can help you with your anger. Take a break for a couple of hours. When you get back, follow your original outline."

I glared at the phone, disgusted. He was supposed to help, not treat me like this. "Fine, Guardian buddy."

Jim hung up without saying goodbye. I pushed the phone far away right as my stomach rumbled. Much to my horror, Jim was right. I needed a break. My phone went off again. For a wild moment, I thought Jim called back to apologize. Nope. Different number.

"Junior! Hello! How are things going?" Devin asked.

"Devin?" I groaned for my answer.

"That doesn't sound promising," he said. Before I chickened out, I told him my whole conversation with Jim.

"Don't be hard on him. This is his first time dealing with the Rogue since…" Devin trailed off. "It's not my place to tell." Devin seemed like a guy who wouldn't tell other people's secrets, but it still made me curious. "I'll chat with Jim and sort things out. By the time this is done, you and Jim will be great friends."

A laugh had no trouble escaping me. "Maybe if he wasn't so bossy."

"Jim copes with stress by becoming a control freak. It's something I've noticed as we've worked together, though I don't condone his actions. He's a pleasant fellow when he's not stressed. I'll talk with him."

I sank into my chair and rubbed my forehead. "Thanks. I'll get back to narrating."

"Good luck."

I hung up and placed the headphones back over my ears, ignoring my stomach for a bit longer.

§ § §

Bree sat down at the neon red cafeteria table and unwrapped the cellophane from the school's salad. With a decision between a hamburger, pizza, or mashed potatoes and gravy, she felt safest with a salad. Not because it was healthier, but because she had lower expectations of what it should taste like.

Holly slammed her tray on the table. Bree jumped and squeezed ranch all over her tray instead of the salad. "Holly, what—"

"I'm done." She sat down with a huff. "Done!"

"Done with what?"

"Have you seen them?" Holly used her spork to point at another table across the cafeteria where Aubrielle and the senior football quarterback were making out.

"Wow," was all Bree could say. "They've...they've gone pretty fast since the party."

Holly sat down and looked at the couple again before facing forward with a sad puppy dog face. "That could have been me."

Bree glanced again at the couple and saw the sheen of slobber on them, even from across the cafeteria. She suppressed a gagging noise and instead patted Holly's hand. "I'm sure the Stud will grow tired of her and move on."

"No wonder they nicknamed him Stud." Holly clearly wasn't listening. "Hot men are my Achilles ankle."

Instead of chortling, Bree said, "Heel."

The sad puppy face barely registered confusion. "Huh?"

"Heel. The phrase is Achilles heel."

Holly shook her head, stabbed her yellow newspaper-colored potatoes, and mixed them into the lumpy gray gravy. Bree watched them pool together, and her stomach started to churn.

"Disgusting," Bree said.

"I know." Holly looked behind her again. "Ugh. They're all over each other."

Bree reached out and grabbed Holly's wrist. "You're going to break your spork, and I'm losing my appetite."

The physical touch must have jolted Holly to the present, because she finally noticed the liquid mass on her plate. Grumbling, she threw her spork down. "I'm sorry."

"Hey, it's okay." Bree attempted to scoop the ranch back onto her salad. "A lot happened since the party this weekend."

Holly looked at her mush. "She had no right to sell us out. I thought we were friends. Crazy what people will do for the attention of a boy."

Bree nodded, glancing over at Aubrielle and Stud before she grimaced and returned to her ranch. "Karma is on our side."

A frown creased Holly's face as she watched Bree continue to clean up her ranch. "Are you not mad at all?"

"Of course! Aubrielle broke our best friend confidentiality agreement and spilled your secrets. I'm livid!"

"Stupid sleepovers." Holly rubbed her head. "They make me such a blabbermouth."

"What's wrong with being a blabbermouth?" a new voice said. Bree and Holly whipped around to see Reggie with his lunch tray. Holly turned bright red and forgot how to speak.

"Nothing," Bree said for her friend.

"Can I sit here?" he asked. Holly moved her mouth, but nothing came out. "I'll take that as a yes." He sat down with a smirk in Bree's direction.

"Reggie is in my biology class," Holly blurted out. Her face deepened to a maroon color.

"Are you taking biology, Bree?" Reggie asked.

"I took it last semester."

"Too bad. It would have been fun to all have a class together."

The silence between the three of them gave Bree a sick feeling. "Well, I think I better go. Nice seeing you again, Reggie." Bree grabbed her tray and dumped her untouched salad before leaving the cafeteria. Her eyebrows furrowed in thought. Instincts screamed at her to be as far away from him as possible. But why? Other than her gut feeling, nothing else seemed wrong with him.

Reggie had scooted closer to Holly, and she smiled at him. Bree hadn't seen a smile on her for a few days, since the party when Stud took notice of her. It was right before Aubrielle, far more subtle and flirtatious, took Stud away. She wanted to check on Holly but didn't. She had nothing to go by. Besides, when Reggie looked at Holly, Bree didn't feel uncomfortable. It was only when he looked at her.

The lunch hour opened up for Bree, and she had no idea what to do with it. A group of girls passed, many of them whispering about Holly. Bree overheard them talking about how Holly boy-hopped from Stud to the new kid. It put a knot in Bree's stomach.

CHAPTER 5

DO YOU NOT talk to other people, or am I an exception?" Dr. Webb asked.

I sat in a way too comfortable chair, wearing out the armrest by tracing a circle over and over with my finger. My lips twitched in a smile. Dr. Webb seemed like a nice lady. She had dark hair with a few grays intermingled. A notebook was poised in front of her, a pen resting on the pages, though her hands were clasped together, not reaching for the pen.

"I've never had a therapist before. It feels weird," I admitted.

"It's nothing to be ashamed of." I bit my lip in response and looked away. "How are you holding up?" she asked.

"Good." Dr. Webb cocked an eyebrow. I spoke too quickly and felt heat creep to my face. "I know, lying to a therapist is pointless."

"A therapist is not a mind reader." She picked up her pen and wrote a note. "But I did know you were lying."

I felt more relaxed. Even though she made it a joke, I still couldn't help but think she could read my mind. My emotions played across my face like a book, and Dr. Webb's profession was all about reading people.

She looked at me again. "I was one of the first to study the impact of what the narration device could do to a person. I'm well-trained to help."

I didn't want to look her in the eye, so I studied her office instead. It was on the second floor of a twenty-story building in the central part of the city. The Guardians' headquarters were in a quieter part. Dr. Webb had a single bookshelf full of psychology books behind her desk. A few fake trees were scattered around the room, though a real plant sat on her desk because it looked dead.

"Still don't want to talk?" Dr. Webb asked.

"I don't know what to talk about. I feel like I'm okay."

Dr. Webb wrote something down. "I need to know something about you. How do you view your characters?"

I frowned. "What do you mean?"

"Some narrators view them like rats in a lab. Others are detached from their characters because of what they have planned for them. Other's treat them like family members. Since science has no evidence your characters are equal to you or me, I cannot give advice on how you treat your characters. I simply accept how you view them and move on."

I swallowed. "My characters are more than family. They are my creations. I feel protective of them, like a mother hen."

Dr. Webb nodded. "I understand."

"I've calculated every trial and test they'll go through to help them improve. The Rogue is messing everything up. He could seriously hurt my characters."

Dr. Webb smiled. "All I needed was to hit upon the right topic to get you to talk."

The comfy chair called to me, and I leaned back. I knew the debates she meant about characters. Many of my college classes continued those discussions. It came down to my own principles and beliefs. These characters were mine. Even without the narration device, I felt a sense of protection and love when they were figments of my imagination. Because the device helped me give them a physical form, my devotion deepened.

"Let me make you aware of some things." Dr. Webb's voice brought me out of my reverie. "You are a strong woman, but the Rogue can over-power you if you don't take care of yourself physically. This means eating when you should and getting adequate sleep. This sounding familiar?"

My stomach rumbled as I nodded. Hopefully Dr. Webb didn't hear.

"Write down what you eat for breakfast, lunch, and dinner, and we'll review it at our next session. Find another activity not related to narration to give yourself a mental break."

"It's difficult for me to focus on other things when my characters are in trouble."

Dr. Webb nodded. "I understand, but sometimes it's good to break away from narration so you can return with a fresh perspective."

"It would help if I didn't have to do everything."

A frown appeared on Dr. Webb's face. "What do you mean?"

"I feel like the Guardians don't care."

Dr. Webb opened her mouth to say something and then closed it again. She looked genuinely surprised. "I work for the Guardians. Sure, they can be intimidating, but Devin is excellent at what he does. You're in good hands."

"Devin passed me off to Jim."

The surprise turned to astonishment. "Oh, he did?" She looked at the ceiling, the frown still on her face. "That's unusual."

"Devin's too busy catching the Rogue."

"It's a good sign, right? It means he's getting closer."

I folded my arms and looked out the window. "Or he's behind on his other assignments."

There was silence as Dr. Webb blinked a few times before fiddling with the notebook on her lap. "Get to know Jim. It will put your mind at ease. He's the youngest Guardian ever, which comes with an impressive resume. Devin has done a lot with the Rogue, but Jim is a great substitute."

I gave one last calculating look towards Dr. Webb before nodding. "I'll try."

§ § §

A week after my visit with Dr. Webb, I sat on the couch and stared at the ceiling. I tried hard not to feel anything. On my computer sat less than ten pages of my story. I narrated the last segment a week and a half ago. The worst case of writer's block ever.

Indecisiveness about whether to follow my original outline drove my lack of desire to pick up the headset. The clincher came because of my overactive imagination. One thought of Bree or Allen getting hurt sent my wildest fantasies playing out worst case scenarios, which made me want to narrate less.

If I could force Holly not to have a crush on the Rogue's character I would, but it was impossible. Holly was boy crazy. While hacking into my device to put his characters into my story, the Rogue saw my characters' profiles. He figured out what Holly liked in a boy. Even Bree picked up how Reggie was *everything* Holly physically loved about boys. If Holly wanted to change, she would have to decide for herself.

My phone made a sad ding as I lost my twelfth card game. I started another game without much reaction when Jim called again. He was in the habit of calling every hour, which started to grate on my nerves. Dr. Webb suggested I get to know him, but she did only suggest it.

I didn't do any narrating for the past week and a half, so I didn't give Jim any reports. He owned a portable screen which let him watch my narration, or the lack of it. Whatever he wanted to talk about couldn't be good.

The phone stopped ringing. It gave me enough time to calculate my next move before Jim started calling again. With a long groan, I answered the phone.

"Hullo?" I relayed through my voice how much I didn't want to talk to him.

"Hello, this is Jim from the Guardians."

My fingers rubbed the bridge of my nose. "I know."

"I want to inform you Devin is not happy."

"With you or with me?"

Jim cleared his throat, his way of relaying how much he didn't appreciate my answer. "Are you going to narrate today?"

"No. I don't feel like it."

"You have two and a half weeks before your characters enter limbo."

"And a few days before then, I'll narrate." I straightened my shoulders, proud of how resolved I sounded. My smile widened the longer the silence lasted.

"Devin gave me permission to do whatever necessary to get you narrating again."

"Are these tactics illegal?"

"I didn't reach Guardianship by breaking rules, Junior." He did seem like the guy who loved rules. "You will come to headquarters, and we'll have a chat." It sounded like a threat.

A chuckle threatened to burst out of me, but I stared at the wall in confusion instead. "That's your plan?"

"I've been given permission to answer many of your questions." It sounded tempting, but I also felt annoyed it took Jim so long to get permission. "I'll meet you here in fifteen minutes. If you take a cab, I will reimburse you."

The chuckle broke free as I leaned against the couch. "And if I refuse?"

"Then I'll come and pick you up." The silence lasted long enough for him to add more, but nope. That was his threat.

"I expected something more intimidating from a mystery writer."

"I'll see you in fifteen minutes." He and Vince were masters at ignoring my snarky remarks.

He hung up before I unloaded the things on my mind. I whispered curses as my fists clenched. Everyone who knew Jim spoke so highly of him—Vince, Dr. Webb, Devin, even Grace. Did they see what I saw?

My phone returned to the card game. I started playing again to push Jim's resolve. Two minutes into the game I realized the full implication. If Jim came to get me, and my suspicions told me he would, I might go to headquarters in sweat pants and my comfortable plaid, button up shirt I wore exclusively in my apartment. I moaned, tossing my phone on the couch, and headed to my room to get dressed. At least my hair was fixed. It was always half the battle.

Fifteen minutes later I walked out of the taxi and into headquarters. Once again, I passed over my ID. "I'm here to see Jim."

The secretary scanned my ID and tried contacting him. "I believe Devin wanted to talk to him. I'll take you to his office and let him know you've arrived."

"Thank you."

We walked down the hall and up a set of stairs to the second floor. Though intimidating at first sight, the building was small compared to other buildings in the city, with two floors and a basement. On the way to Jim's office, I saw the door ajar to Devin's office. Jim must have been there, because no one answered when the secretary knocked on Jim's office door. After a pause, she opened the door and ushered me inside.

"Wait here until he returns."

I thanked her again and waited until she was back at her desk downstairs. It was rude, but I had to hear Jim and Devin's conversation. They still might refuse to answer my questions. As soon as I got close to Devin's office, I heard his voice.

"…is as frightened as you are."

"I'm not afraid of the Rogue," Jim said. The desk faced the door, so I didn't peek inside in case they caught me.

"Frankly, Jim, you're obnoxious toward everyone now. The Guardians know you act like this when you have too much on your plate. Junior deserves to know your pleasant personality, too."

My back pressed against the wall, and I started to feel guilty. This sounded more private. Did I think everyone talked about me and my problems in this building?

"You enlisted me to do this. This is how I fulfill assignments."

"You need the Guardians as much as Junior does. It's your assignment, but we can help. It's how I got through the Rogue problems I faced."

Silence permeated the room before Jim let out a breath. "How bad will it get for Junior?" There was the smallest catch in his voice. My eyes widened a bit.

"It's hard to predict. Though there might come a time when Junior's life will depend on you. She needs to be able to trust you."

My lips clamped together to stifle the gasp inside me as I backed away from the door. Their conversation didn't include the questions I wanted answers to. If I listened any more, I'd freak myself out.

Yes, characters got in trouble, but I forgot about the danger for the narrators. The three unsuccessful narrators disappeared without a trace. It was still a small possibility, as possible as Bree dying, but something I needed to consider. I could disappear and not be heard from again.

CHAPTER 6

I SKULKED BACK to Jim's office and sat in the chair across from his desk. Jim would come back when they finished and maybe act nicer. For now, I resigned myself to hear the information they wanted me to hear. My active imagination always assumed the worst.

Studying story structure helped me to know an office desk hinted at a person's personality. Maybe I could pick up clues by looking at Jim's. It disturbed me that his desk was so clean. I thought maybe he cleaned it recently, but the thin layer of dust proved otherwise.

Two baskets rested on his desk. One was labeled "to be completed" and the other "completed." Most of the papers were in the "completed" section. A mug of coffee waited for his return, resting on a coaster.

On either side of his computer stood two pictures. I bent over to look at them. What I saw surprised me. Jim didn't wear a three-piece suit or pose with a high-ranking leader in either picture. He looked relaxed.

One picture depicted a younger Jim with his arm around an even younger man in graduation robes. Jim, sporting jeans and a worn-out T-shirt, beamed at the camera with a glimmer of pride in his eyes. They had to be brothers. The younger one had lighter brown hair and mischievous green eyes, but both had the same square face and nose. I tried to do the math in my head. Jim was about ten years older than me, and it looked as though his little brother in the picture was five or six years younger than him. I hated to admit it, mainly because I still didn't like Jim, but his brother was handsome. He could pull off a bulky graduation gown.

The other picture looked recent. Jim held hands with a pretty woman. Whoever took the picture caught them naturally. It was a simple walk in the park. They were both smiling, she at the camera and he at her. She had auburn hair and hazel eyes. The way Jim looked at her, I could tell she was his girlfriend. I never saw a ring on Jim's hand, but if Jim still looked at her the way he did in this picture, her girlfriend status would soon change.

Jim opened the door and I jumped, feeling like a child caught with a hand in the cookie jar. His frown of worry turned into a frown of annoyance. "I'd appreciate it if you didn't touch my stuff."

My hands shook as I placed the pictures back in their spots. As I walked away from the crime scene, his little brother's picture dropped on the ground, making me wince. Jim rubbed his temples.

"Sorry," I mumbled.

He walked behind his desk and picked up the picture. He situated the pictures back in their spot as I plopped down in the chair. His fingers lingered on the picture with his girlfriend—brushing a little dust off the frame—before he sat down and faced me.

Jim sat stiff and straight, still wearing his three-piece suit, his tie secured to his throat and not a single button undone on his vest. I glanced down at my jeans, T-shirt, and sneakers, feeling under-dressed. Better than my sweat pants, though.

I waited for the inspirational chat. He did, after all, place a lot of hope it would change my attitude. His fingers interlocked and he smiled, but I could tell a businessman's smile from a friendly one.

"My purpose is to help you get back to narrating. The Guardians realize you are in a peculiar situation."

I fought down the desire to crack a joke. "I'm glad."

"We want you to be as comfortable as possible without stopping narration altogether. I've gotten permission to tell you anything you want to know about the Rogue."

Excitement played across my face as I leaned closer. "Anything?"

"To a point."

"Of course." I leaned back in the chair and looked away. "There's always a catch."

"Ask, and I'll let you know if I can tell you. Whatever you hear from me can't leave this room."

It wasn't long before I found myself tracing a circle around my knee with my fingertip. I missed the ridiculously comfy chair in Dr. Webb's office. "How will this make me feel better?"

"We won't treat you like other narrators, or the public, and definitely not the press." Jim leaned back and almost looked less like a businessman but kept his stiff posture.

He made an attempt to be nicer, I'd give him that. Maybe he tried too hard. I looked away, feeling obligated to be nice back. Once again I glanced at the pictures on his desk. The Jim before me couldn't be the same guy in the pictures unless he truly did have an elusive kind side.

I asked the first question nagging me since this whole thing started. "Are the rumors true about what the Rogue does to the main character?"

Jim's smile waned. "I thought you'd ask." We sat in silence, my fingers again tracing an agitated circle. "Junior," he started but faltered.

"Is Bree in danger?"

Jim sighed. "Yes."

"Could she die?"

"Yes." I winced and looked away. Jim looked apologetic. "What rumors have you heard?"

My fingertips felt warm as my circles became more vigorous. "The narrator keeps the story going after the Rogue invades so they don't doom their characters to limbo. Most of the time the narrator is lucky and manages to overcome the Rogue and finish the story. Not always how they want, but their characters are okay. On rarer occasions, the Rogue wears them down until one of the Rogue's characters...kills the main character. Then the narrator disappears and is never heard from again."

Jim tried to remain neutral, but I could see flickers of anger in his face. So it was true! I didn't like my options—fight a mental war with the Rogue or doom my characters to a fate worse than death.

"There's something else you should know," Jim said. He studied me to make sure whatever he shared was something I could handle. "The Rogue doesn't have the power to kill any of your characters." Jim licked his lips before he continued. "Hurt them, yes, but not kill them. Because you created them, only you have that power." He looked solemn, and I didn't understand why.

"But what about the manuscripts of the missing narrators?" I furrowed my brows in thought. "If the Rogue didn't kill the main character, then..." Jim didn't move. He waited for it to click in my mind. "Then the narrators killed their main characters?" I didn't recognize my voice as it squeaked out.

Jim nodded. "In a way, you give them permission to die." He watched my face again. My fingers turned to ice.

"Why? How? I don't..." My emotions didn't know how to express themselves into words. Thankfully Jim understood.

"The Rogue gets them in a situation where killing your main character is merciful."

My mouth hung open. "She's sixteen!" I said the phrase a lot lately, but it didn't change how much it scared me.

Death itself wasn't necessarily a bad thing. In Jim's example, the pain they felt disappeared, and they entered a waiting state. The real pain was the repercussion on the other characters when a character died without sufficient planning. For me, killing off a character took days to plan, making sure the death wouldn't break the other characters. Death took time to cope with, but it was possible. When the story came to an end, the characters would reunite. If death came unexpectedly, it could haunt the other characters forever. The bitter feelings might not resolve, even when the story ended and they meet up again. Death brought a permanent change, not only to the dead character, but to the other characters too. Narration taught me how much anger could morph and twist characters. Some narrators expected that outcome. I did not want it.

Dark times loomed in my future, and I had to prepare for a fight.

Jim looked at me with such sympathy in his eyes. It surprised and consoled me. "Can I read the other infiltrated manuscripts where the character doesn't survive?" I asked.

"No. Devin doesn't think it's a good idea. I agree." I stared at Jim, sinking further in my chair. Jim took a sip of his coffee before focusing again on me.

"What about the other manuscripts? The success stories? Why don't they get published?" I asked.

"It's up to the narrator, and so far, none of them want to. Many of them claim it's not their best work. Others don't want a reminder of what happened."

"Has the Rogue ever hurt a sixteen-year-old girl before?"

"The Rogue doesn't care what age she is, or gender." Jim stared at his desk, not looking me in the eye. "To him, Bree is a character in a story, not on the same level as you or I." He kept an eye on me through his peripheral vision. I stared at the wall, feeling overwhelmed.

"It doesn't sound like the man I remember," I said.

Jim paused and then focused on me. "What did you say?"

My face turned red, and I looked at the ground. "He was famous for teaching about characters. The better the narrator knows them, the better the reader will."

Jim waved his hand in front of him to stop me. "That's not what I meant. Do you know the Rogue? Personally?"

I looked down at my hands. My fingers found their partners and clung on for dear life. "Yes."

Chapter 7

JIM STARED AT me, mouth open.

"I don't know him anymore, though." I still couldn't look Jim in the eye. "He's changed."

"Junior." He sounded sincere. "We believed you were different because you never took any of his college classes. Did you?"

It took a lot to tear my gaze from the floor. "I never *technically* took a class from him. But he did teach me. Since I was sixteen." Jim still gawked at me. I had to look away again.

In high school I won a writing contest. I kept going up the divisions of the contest and managed to get the highest award. It was my first time feeling I could do something with my talent. One of the prizes included coming to headquarters for a tour. My story was also published in a journal. Professor Andrews took notice and sent me an email. He said I had skill, and he always kept an eye out for young talent. We started corresponding for a few years. I graduated from high school and was accepted into the college where he taught the higher division classes. I was so anxious to learn from him, I asked if he could start teaching me right away. He laughed, but to my surprise, agreed. Professor Andrews was already living a secret life and was unmasked as the Rogue two years later.

"Junior?"

My relationship with Professor Andrews was something I kept to myself. Everyone focused on the evil things he did, but I felt like I lost a dear friend. "He was my mentor."

Jim's eyes widened. "Your mentor?" There was nothing to do but nod.

"The number one guy on the Guardians' most wanted list taught you everything you know about narration?" It sounded bad when Jim put it that way. I hesitated before nodding again.

"I need to send an email." Jim pulled his chair to his computer, sounding both angry and amazed. "He was your mentor. The Rogue Narrator."

"It was before he was revealed as the Rogue," I couldn't help but say. I had to defend myself.

"Were you friends?" Jim tapped away at his computer and glanced at me when I didn't answer. "Were you close?"

I nodded again because I didn't want to verbalize it. Ever since his dealings came to light, I tried to call him the Rogue. It helped separated the friendship I had with Professor Andrews. A few nasty rumors pinned him with unsolved murders, which I refused to believe.

It hurt to think about Professor Andrews, and it hurt to think he knowingly attacked my story. Emotions ripped at my throat as I leaned back in my chair. My mind flickered through memories of my mentorship with him. I was fooled, like everyone else. There were signs, certainly, but I never made the connection. Three days before the Guardians unmasked him, I remember going to his office to discuss my latest short story.

Professor Andrews greeted me as I sat down. He pulled out my story from his desk. "Jaw dropping, as usual."

"You must have something big to critique," I said.

He laughed. "Am I that predictable?"

"I can read you like a book."

"Okay. You've got me. For the most part, my corrections are minimal, on the grammatical level. Grammar can detract from the story if you're not careful. But if you change one character, it will strengthen everything in your story."

"Who?" I pulled out a notebook and pen from my backpack.

"Your villain."

I cocked my head to the side. "My villain?"

"Yes. He's got potential but could be much stronger. It's something I've noticed in all your writing. You're afraid to make a strong villain."

"I guess." I clicked my pen and began to doodle on my notebook to help my creativity. "It's difficult. You taught me that, to make characters stronger, I have to understand them, and, well—"

"And you're afraid to understand a dark and twisted mind," Professor Andrews finished for me. I nodded. Professor Andrews gave me a smile I didn't understand at the time. After a pause, he asked, "Why do you think we love to hate villains?"

He was in lecture mode now. I stopped doodling. "Sorry?"

"Why do we love to hate bad guys?"

My mind grasped for ideas as I stared down at my page. "Because narrators have this tendency to make bad guys super-hot."

Professor Andrews chortled. "You always make me laugh, Junior. Tell me a list of villains you love to hate. From books, not um, visually." It seemed random, but I rattled off my top five villains.

"Why do you hate them?"

I shrugged. "Because they're a nice balance for the good guy. Is my good guy too good?"

Professor Andrews shook his head. "We love to hate villains because we see qualities of ourselves in them."

Though I wanted to ask for further clarification, all my voice managed to squeak out was, "Sir?"

"It's human nature." He leaned back with his arms crossed. "Truly amazing villains are ones masking the fact that you're reading about yourself. The awful things we do are magnified in these characters, and we feel a sense of elation when they are defeated. Locked away. Destroyed."

"Or redeemed and forgiven," I added.

"Yes."

The pen twirled in my hand. "So it's like a part of us has been cleansed because of what happens to them?"

Professor Andrews smiled. "Exactly. I know you won't like this, but here's your assignment. Find the ugly in you and magnify it. Write a villain you relate to, and he or she will truly stand out. Become the villain."

With some trepidation, I jotted the assignment down. "Anything else?"

"No, that will be all."

I took the bundle of papers and stood up. "See you next week?" I asked.

He nodded. "See you next week."

The air conditioning in Jim's office switched on. It sounded like a dull roar, throwing me back into the present, and I flinched. I stared at my hands so Jim wouldn't see how much I struggled to keep my emotions in check.

After Jim finished his email, he turned back to me. "Why didn't you tell the Guardians he was your mentor?" Jim's anger beat out his amazement for dominance in his voice. "You could have saved yourself a lot of heartache."

"I didn't think he'd come for me." My voice, on the other hand, was soft and humble. "I thought he went after people in his class who didn't vote for him to be Chairman."

"You thought the victims were people who didn't vote for him?"

"Well…yeah."

Jim never called me stupid, but the look on his face did. "We gave an announcement not long ago. Anyone with any past contact with the Rogue was strongly encouraged not to apply for a narration device."

My forehead began to sweat despite the air conditioning being on. Yes, I heard the announcement. More importantly, I heard the words "strongly encouraged not to" instead of "forbidden."

I never should have assumed I was immune. Everything my characters would go through would be my fault. As fear settled in, I folded my arms and hugged myself tightly. Jim grumbled about something and turned back to his computer, but then stopped.

"Wait, the vote was almost eight years ago. You weren't old enough." It took him a while to make the connection, and I fought to keep my eyes from rolling.

"I told him in person I would have voted for him if given the chance. He had some brilliant ideas about changing the Guardianship laws to include more checks and balances."

Jim nodded. "It was his strongest point. Vince is thinking about implementing those." He glanced at the pictures on his desk. "He had such good ideas about laws. Seems strange he wants to fight them now." Jim returned his focus on me. "Is there anything else we should know?"

"Not that I can think of."

Once again Jim sat in a business-like manner, but the look on his face didn't seem business-like anymore. I became self-conscious of how I slouched, so I tried to straighten my back without him noticing.

"Junior, we need to stop this guy, and you need to continue narrating to help us out. We get a signal when the Rogue narrates alongside your story. It takes our best experts to pinpoint his location, and often we don't get there in time. We don't want to wait two more weeks before you decide to narrate. We'll lose our trail."

Part of me felt defeated. The sooner they caught the Rogue, the sooner I could fix the damage to my story and make it normal again.

But I was scared for my characters. Even if the Rogue didn't kill them, he could still do a lot of damage before he was caught. Jim's attitude made it seem like the meeting was over. I got to my feet and headed for the door. My fingers lingered on the door handle, and then I turned.

"I have an idea for my story."

"What is it?" Jim took out one of the papers from the box labeled "to be done" and glanced over it. He looked busy, but I needed to talk to him.

"My characters are created to react around my outline. I need a character more flexible to handle an altered outline."

It made Jim pause. "You want to add another character to your story?" He sounded hesitant.

"Yes."

Jim's eyebrows furrowed together, which caused wrinkles in his forehead. It made him look ten years older. "How would this character handle the different outline?"

"My main characters have weaknesses and vulnerabilities I planned to use in my original outline to give them character arches. The Rogue knows what they are and will use their weaknesses against them. It could destroy them. I need a character whose weaknesses won't be so dangerous when exploited who can protect the others, if it ever came to that."

The silence from Jim lasted an eternity before he nodded. "Stick this new character in the background for now. Bring him or her out when I give the okay."

My mind reeled with ideas. I turned back to the door, ready to go, when a thought struck me. "The Rogue got in Devin's manuscript, right?"

Jim nodded.

"Can I read it?"

He glanced at me with a hint of a smile. "I don't have control of his manuscript, but I can ask him for you." Jim took out a small notebook from his breast pocket to make a note.

"Thank you."

This time I had the door open before another question popped into my head. "Jim?" He grunted to let me know he was listening. He took a break from typing to take a sip of his coffee. "Why haven't you told me about your dealings with the Rogue yet?"

Jim choked on his coffee. Coffee almost hit his suit, but nothing seemed to mess it up. He wiped his mouth with the handkerchief in his pocket. "You must not get the news." Jim put the coffee back on his desk and pretended like he didn't just choke on it. He also acted as if he already answered my question.

"I..."

After the Guardian's unmasked Professor Andrews, I failed my semester miserably. Everyone close to me thought it'd be a good idea to travel abroad and clear my head. Whatever Jim referred to, it must have happened during my time abroad when I refused to look, read, or listen to anything to do with the Rogue.

My feet carried me outside to the waiting taxi. For some reason, when the driver asked me where I wanted to go, I said the public library. He nodded and drove the four miles to the beautiful brick building. My mind began to wander.

I felt driven to narrate. This fulfilled my life-long dream, and I felt honored it came at such an early time in my life. The warning signs were there, but I made the brash move to seize this opportunity, no matter the consequences. It seemed fate wanted to cash in on my reckless decision.

The taxi pulled up to the library. I paid, got out, and jogged to the air-conditioned library. My eyes wandered the shelves and found where my book would sit if it ever got published before turning my attention to the public computers. My laptop was hooked to the narration device and couldn't be used for anything else until I finished my story. Besides, the internet in my apartment was awful, and I needed to do a lot of research.

This new character was taking shape already inside my head. Because all the characters the Rogue put in my story were men, I decided to make him a man, too. Being a family member was a must. It couldn't be weird if he needed to hang around Bree's house all day.

Maybe Bree's grandfather? I frowned. It shouldn't be someone too old or frail. He might need to fight. Though it'd be endearing, I needed someone in good physical condition who could also care for and protect Bree. It couldn't be her father, because her mother was single and going to date soon if the Rogue didn't mess things up. I settled on creating an older brother for Sadie, therefore an uncle for Bree.

Bree, Allen, Sadie. What was another name that fit well with that group? Michael was a good name for an uncle, but I knew too many

Michaels. It'd be strange. Pulling up a baby name website, I scrolled through them in hopes one called out to me. A few did, and I took out a pen to write down the names. I searched for paper but couldn't find any. Cursing under my breath, I wrote the names on my palm.

My finger hesitated on the mouse button as I almost logged off the computer. Curiosity got the better of me, and I pulled up a new search window. I typed in *Jim Solomon Rogue Narrator* and hit enter. The first couple of links looked promising. They were newspaper articles from the same time I was abroad and purposefully ignoring everything about the Rogue.

My eyebrows shot up as I read the article. Jim's younger brother was one of the three unsuccessful narrators who disappeared without a trace.

CHAPTER 8

WITH MY CURIOSITY fed and feeling more compassionate toward Jim, I headed out of the library. A warm breeze whispered through the pine trees, and I decided to walk back to my apartment. It gave me time to flesh out the character. I wrote down the many characteristics I wanted to see in him, again on my palm. It must have looked silly to see someone writing on their hand as they walked down the street, mumbling to themselves.

When I got back, I planned to transfer the characteristics to a notebook to be sure they were as vague as possible. If the Rogue could hack in once, he could hack in again. The more I fleshed out the character, the more some names didn't feel right. I kept crossing them out until I had one left.

As soon as I entered my small apartment, I went straight to my office. I pulled out a notebook and transcribed his personality from my arm, did a quick sketch of him, and made the final touches to his character before I put on the headphones and adjusted the microphone.

"Narration code 0807, addition of character."

Both the computer and my laptop screens went white. I put in the basic information. His name. Male. Thirty-four. Almost six feet tall. Blonde hair, but not too blonde. Similar facial features with Sadie so they'd be recognized as siblings even if they had different hair color.

"And brown eyes," I said to finish off the physical features.

The character's blank eyes turned brown. He was exactly as I pictured him. I pushed the microphone away from my face, which put everything on a soft pause. The orange juice in my glass was halfway down my throat before I realized I'd grabbed the glass and taken a drink. *When did I pour this*? It couldn't have been today. I pushed the glass farther away from me and went over my list again. When I finished, I brought the microphone back down.

"Loyal to his family." I made a check mark next to the characteristic on my list. "Bit of a goof. Other people don't get his humor, but he doesn't care. He and Sadie are close as brother and sister. This character was there during Sadie's rough years of raising Bree." I tapped my chin and nodded. Time to add my fail-safe, something to guarantee the security of my novel against the Rogue.

"Narration code 1013, personal note about this character not known to him. He has a secret weapon he does not realize." I picked up my notebook to say this word for word. I worked this paragraph multiple times to make sure it sounded super vague. "He was created with this, and it will appear when I say the code words 'now is the time.' He knows he was born with it, and it will help him throughout this story. Some of the abilities he can already use, but he doesn't know his full power."

I slid the microphone up again and studied the character with a frown. Hopefully he'd never use the full extent of the power, because if he did, it would drive him insane.

The familiar sensation of ideas stirring my creativity lifted my writer's block. Possible scenes tumbled into my mind, but first I had to interview this new character to solidify his personality and the secret weapon. Through the interview, I got to interact with my characters before they entered the story. It was my favorite thing about the narration device, because it was the closest I could legally be in my story. Bree's interview filled me with excitement to be able to chat and interact with her. This character's interview filled me with trepidation.

Once again I brought the microphone down. "Place new character into the interview room." I checked my watch. For a main character, the interview took at least a couple of days, but I didn't have the time. I had to power through this interview and hope it was enough.

The white screen faded. He floated in nothing until a chair materialized beneath him, and he sat down. Slowly his eyes focused, and he looked around the room, taking everything in. When I closed my eyes, I found myself in the room with him. It was a strange sensation. I couldn't feel my actual body slouched in the office chair, my head probably resting against the desk. This me in the interview room was the only version I felt. Again, scientists tried to explain the structure and matter narrators had while in this interview room, but all I knew is it felt real.

My character looked at me, surprised. "What—" he stopped. He glanced at his hands as though realizing they were there.

"Your name?"

He frowned in thought. "Josh."

I beamed. "Great."

We had a nice chat, the kind I learned to do in college. Josh took a while to talk in complete sentences. He told me about his memories I placed in him, and I felt like I learned more about him. He remembered certain ones, specifically how he helped Sadie and Bree. We talked ever so quietly about the power he had. He'd forget as soon as he left this room, but it was vital he understood it.

Four hours later, I sat back, feeling satisfied. "I think you're ready."

Josh scratched the back of his head. "If you're sure, then I guess so."

"When I leave this room, you will have no memory of me."

Josh frowned. "Why not?"

"It's the law." I sighed. "But I'll still watch over you."

Josh looked sad. "I'll miss you."

A smile couldn't help but trickle across my face. "No you won't."

"Will I ever see you again?" Josh asked.

This time I patted him on the shoulder. "All will work out. Promise me you'll protect the others."

"I will."

My eyes closed, and I felt myself pulled from the virtual world. I opened my eyes and was back in my office. "Save additional code."

When I lifted the microphone, I took some time to reorient myself. The interview room always made me a little dizzy. The clock on the wall indicated it was about dinnertime. Lunch eluded me, but I felt too excited, so I rode the adrenaline and decided on another scene to narrate. I brought down the microphone again.

"Prepare next scene." The interview room holding Josh dissolved into another freezing outdoor scene. Bree looked out the glass door of the high school building.

"Resume."

§§§

The sun was out, but the cruel wind kept everyone bundled up. Bree wasn't excited to leave the warm school. She planned on waiting inside for her bus to arrive until she saw Holly. More importantly, Holly without Reggie. Bree opened the door. The wind made her gasp, but she tried to ignore it as she ran toward her friend.

"Holly!" she called out. Holly stopped and turned.

"Hey, what's up?" Holly smiled. "Reggie brought his car today. He said I could ride home with him if I wanted. I think he likes me. Can you believe it! Someone with perfect eyes likes me!"

It was then that Bree noticed Reggie leaning against a new black Toyota in the parking lot, watching them. He was too far away to hear anything, but the way he watched them unnerved her. She bit her lip and turned back to her friend. "I don't like him."

"What?"

Bree had forgotten her gloves and rubbed her hands together to keep them warm. "You know I'm always the cautious one, but I'm often right. This guy is bad news."

Holly frowned. "He's the sweetest guy I've ever met."

It took a second for Bree's heart to stop pounding. This could end up in a fight. "He says hi, talks with you, and owns a new car. It doesn't automatically mean he's the sweetest guy in the world."

"It doesn't mean you should automatically dislike him, either."

Frustration surged through Bree, but she fought it down. "I know what I feel. Promise me you won't get involved." The wind picked up and hit her face, giving her the odd sensation of feeling both cold and hot at the same time.

Holly's frown deepened and a flash of anger flickered through her eyes. "I know what this is."

Bree didn't know what to expect. She never saw Holly with such a look of anger. She usually listened to Bree.

"You don't trust men. They're your Achilles ankle for a different reason."

Humiliation flushed hot in Bree's face. "First of all, Holly, it's Achilles *heel*. Second, I don't distrust men. Hesitant, maybe, but not distrusting."

"Because of your dad, you've become a man-hater."

"What? No, I—"

"Some of us might want a relationship with a boy, Bree."

Bree heard herself growl. She knew she needed to be compassionate.

The second to last thing she wanted was to drive her friend away, but the absolute last thing she wanted was to see her friend in a bad relationship.

Holly shook her head. "Not all relationships end in disasters."

"They might if you assume he's a knight in shining armor because he has pretty eyes." The wind carried their conversation to eavesdroppers who turned and listened. Bree zipped her coat up to keep the chill away and hide her face.

Shifting her books from one hand to the other, Holly shook her head. "Think what you will, but I'll discover for myself what he's like."

"Holly," Bree started.

It was too late. Holly was already running toward Reggie. Bree struggled with the urgency to chase after Holly and force her on the bus. She went so far as to take the first step but stopped. Aubrielle and Holly teased and sometimes warned Bree about her need to control their lives. Aubrielle was already gone. She didn't want to destroy her friendship with Holly. Maybe Holly was right. Maybe Holly needed to discover for herself. Her heart ached, going through every worst-case scenario.

Eavesdroppers turned away, whispering. She didn't know if the whispers were about Holly or Bree's past. She didn't volunteer information that her mom's boyfriend left before she was born, nor was it something she wanted to remember. More people probably knew about it than let on. Scandalous things traveled fast.

Her ride home was lonely. Usually she kept the loneliness at bay, but the hole returned and situated itself back into her life. It crept across her mind like ice stealing over windows, spreading out in disjointed sheets to make her view of the world fragmented and foggy.

The bus driver dropped her off, and she didn't say thanks. Her shoes fell through the crisp outer layer into the soft, wet snow beneath. She opened the door, dropped her bag on the floor, collapsed on the couch, and draped her arms over her eyes.

A gentle snore emanated from the guest room across the hall from her mom's bedroom. She got up and tiptoed down the hall before peeking through the door. Her Uncle Josh was snoring away. He was in a car accident a couple of weeks ago. A cast was on his arm, and there were stitches in his hairline. It wasn't bad, but enough. Since her grandparents were gone, her mom didn't want Josh to be alone. He didn't complain. Josh's idea of fancy cooking was a grilled cheese sandwich.

It was always fun to have Josh over. She and her mom owed him so much. When her biological father refused to give any help, Josh and her grandparents supported her mom through the darker times of depression and rearing a child on her own. Because of their support, her mom went back to school, graduating from high school, college, and then graduate school. Bree always knew her mom was amazing, but hearing how she balanced two jobs, school, homework, and raising Bree at the same time, she wondered if she'd ever be as incredible as her mom.

Bree sank back into the couch and waited for the homework muses to make her want to do the stuff. The farther she sank into the couch, the more the muses didn't want to help. They started to inspire her right before her mom got home.

"Lots to do?" her mom asked.

"So much," Bree said, milking it.

Her mom smiled as she took off her red winter coat and draped it over the chair. "So how was your day?"

On a different day, Bree would say "fine" and that'd end the conversation about school, but not today. Bree sighed, which made her mom stop the jokes. Her mom had a gift of sigh reading and knew Bree's mood by the length, degree, and tone.

"What's up?"

Bree tapped her pencil against her homework, frowning. "Do you remember Aubrielle?"

"Remember?" She laughed. "You two and Holly have been best friends since the sixth grade."

"She went all cloak and dagger on us."

Her mom's smile faltered. "She did? Oh, Bree, I'm so sorry!"

It was all Bree could do to shrug like it wasn't a big deal. She pushed aside her homework. "Now things are different. Holly's not taking it well."

Her mom walked over to Bree and sat down next to her. "You need something to get your mind off this?"

"Well, I tried to do homework, but it's not going as planned."

Her mom patted her hand. "It never does."

Bree wanted to be done talking about herself. "How was your day?"

"Good. Taught some classes, fended off a new guy who wanted to ask me on a date."

"The usual, then?"

Her mom laughed. "Men don't often ask me on dates."

"And those who are successful never last. Is it because of me?"

Her mom gave Bree a quizzical look. "Of course not, dear. It's because of me."

A smile stretched across Bree's face. "Well, whatever the reason, I'm glad it's just the two of us." Bree's heart started beating faster as she saw her mom's eyes glaze over as she bit her lower lip. She was thinking about someone. Someone male? Was it possible? "Mom?"

Her mom blinked and returned to the present. "Right. Dinner."

They never talked about dinner. She frowned. First Holly, now her mom? Bree felt her heart sink into her toes. She and her mom were always there for each other. She didn't want anyone to come between their relationship, especially a man. Didn't her mom learn from last time? They heard Josh groaning in the guest room, and then the door opened.

"Josh?" her mom asked. "Do you need me to get you anything?"

He stumbled down the hall and leaned against the wall, looking exhausted but pleased with himself. "I'm fine, Sadie. I'll get my pain meds and go back to sleep."

"Let me help."

He got up from leaning against the wall and headed toward the table. "Don't get up."

Her mom frowned. "I'm already up."

A strange chuckle left him. "Yeah."

"What medication do they have you on?" her mom asked with her hands on her hips. Whether he heard her or not, Josh didn't give an answer.

He staggered through the kitchen until he got to his medicine on the counter. Bree suppressed a smile as Josh tried his hardest to open his medicine. The cast covered up a lot of his palm, and his fingers stuck out like useless twigs. He tried to get the lid off, but the childproof cap was merciless and refused to give up the jewels inside. Josh's face showed a lot of concentration. Her mother snatched the medication from his palm and popped open the lid.

Josh mumbled thanks, then something about how stupid it was to not be able to open pain pills with a cast. He swallowed the pills, his pride, and then ambled back to the guest room. Her mom shook her head. Josh was more than her mom's brother. He was her best friend.

55

§ § §

Bree and Holly automatically dropped their voices when they passed through the doors into the school library. It was their lunch break, and Holly wanted to see if the library had the book she wanted. They ambled through the shelves. Bree stopped cold when she heard two students walk by saying Holly's name among the whispers. Maybe the girls weren't talking bad about Holly, but it was better to be cautious.

"I don't think the book is here." Bree grabbed Holly's arm to move her away from the whispers.

"Nathaniel Hawthorne. I know my alphabet. It should be right about..."

"And did you hear what happened at the party?" one of the students whispered as they moved closer. "Holly tried to steal Stud right from under Aubrielle!" Holly's eyes went wide. She turned toward Bree with the lost puppy look Bree was used to seeing now. Bree glared at the bookshelf, trying to calm the anger inside her.

"What?" the other student asked, chomping away at her gum. "Awful! Who would do that to Aubrielle?"

"Come on," Bree whispered. "Let's go." Holly leaned closer to listen.

"This is not a good idea," Bree said. Not only was she afraid of Holly's mental health, but if she heard any more gossip, she might end up punching the two girls. Holly placed her finger to her lips.

"I don't know how they stayed friends for so long," the other student whispered. Her voice was high and annoying. "Aubrielle said Holly played around with guys since Junior High." Holly's jaw dropped. She turned to Bree and mouthed *I did not!*

The rumors were out of hand. Anyone close to Holly knew how abysmal her flirting skills were. It shocked Bree to the core when Holly's flirting seemed to work on the quarterback at the party, because no other boy stayed long after Holly started talking. Bree turned to walk out and punch one of the girls, but Holly grabbed her arm and shook her head. Any attempt to try to shake Holly off only made her tighten her grip. Both froze when they heard a new but familiar voice.

"What are you two talking about?" Reggie asked the gossiping friends.

Bree parted some books to see Reggie. She and Holly exchanged glances.

"Reggie, right?" the gum-chomper asked. "You're new, so let me give you some advice. If you meet someone named Holly, stay away. She's a slut."

Holly bowed her head as Bree curled her fingers into a fist. No one called her friend a slut. She tried once more to shake Holly's grip, but she shook her head, tears of shame in her eyes. Bree didn't like Reggie, but Holly did, and the two gossiping friends ruined her chance.

"She's my neighbor and a sweet girl. Leave her alone," Reggie said. Holly perked up, surprised. It was Bree's turn to drop her jaw. Maybe she was wrong about him.

Taking advantage of Holly's slackened grip, Bree broke free and ran over beside Reggie. "Holly and I heard every word. Stop passing nasty rumors." The two girls stuck their noses in the air as they left.

Holly joined Bree and Reggie. "Thanks guys. This means a lot."

Reggie walked closer to Holly, placing a hand on her shoulder. "I know desperate gossip when I hear it."

When Bree saw Holly wrap her arms around him, she hesitated, afraid it would scare Reggie, but Reggie hugged her tightly. Bree wanted to drop her doubts and cheer her friend on, ready to apologize for what she thought of Reggie. Then she saw Reggie turn to her. He stared at Bree and sneered. Bree winced, feeling childish for doing so. His cold manner towards her was the polar opposite to his treatment of Holly. The uncomfortable feeling returned full force in her gut.

CHAPTER 9

M Y CELL PHONE rang a few sentences after Reggie came into the scene, and I had to focus. I didn't like him—he didn't act like a typical sixteen-year-old. Professor Andrews admitted he could never create believable teenagers, and Reggie seemed more of an adult psychopath.

The space between calls got shorter and shorter until it rang constantly. Finishing the scene was my top priority, so I turned off the ringer and continued narrating. When I finished the scene, I removed the headset and retrieved my phone. I didn't need to look at the screen to know it was Jim.

"Junior!" He wasn't happy. "Why didn't you answer?"

"I had to finish narrating. Can't you track my story in your office?"

Silence came from the other end. "It's seven at night."

My eyes darted to the clock. "Oh."

"I don't think you understand how dangerous this is."

I shrugged, even though I knew he couldn't see me. "Sometimes I get distracted."

"When I call, you need to answer. You are under my protection, and I thought..." He trailed off.

"Thought what?"

The tension built the longer he didn't answer before he let out a breath. "I thought he had you." The concern in his voice stunned me. I swallowed and looked at my desk.

"Sorry. I didn't want to lose my focus." It sounded lame the moment it left my mouth, but Jim didn't say anything. Part of me didn't want him to worry. Ever since our conversation, he seemed more protective.

"I asked Devin about his manuscript." Jim returned to his business attitude. "He doesn't want you to freak out about what you might read. I agree."

I grumbled with annoyance. They wanted to protect me too much. Reading a manuscript where he defeated the Rogue could have helped me. "Fine." My voice sounded prickly and unwelcoming. It surprised me.

"How's your story?" Jim asked.

The topic was one I wanted to avoid, but I couldn't avoid it forever. "One of the Rogue's characters is becoming friends with Holly, and the other is trying to date Sadie."

There was silence as Jim thought this over. "Have they done anything violent to them?"

"No, but I don't like them in there at all."

Jim grunted. "Agreed."

I put my head against my desk and closed my eyes, feeling the weight of the situation. The evening summer sun shone right through the window, and I shielded my eyes from the light.

"Junior?" Jim asked after a while. "Are you okay?"

The worry in Jim's voice was clear. "Fine." I tried to make it sound convincing. "I'm fine." The happiness was too thick in my voice.

"Junior, you need to take care of yourself. If you need me for anything, don't hesitate to call, no matter what time it is."

A few pebbles were brushed off the weight on my soul.

"Is there anything I can get you? Do you need any food?"

"No, I'm okay." The Rogue was in my story, trying to destroy my characters. Eating felt trivial in comparison. I rested my head against my sweaty palm and waited. Words eluded me.

"Hang in there, Junior. Everything will be okay."

I bit my lip as heat stung my eyes. His words were hollow. "I'll get back to narrating."

"Alright. Call if you need me, and *answer* when I call. It makes me nervous when you don't."

"I will."

After saying our goodbyes, I hung up the phone and rubbed my head. I looked at my screen and saw Reggie's smirk. Instead of putting on the headset, I got up, walked out of my little office, and headed straight for my bedroom. Maybe I'd wait until tomorrow before narrating.

I collapsed on my bed and curled up in a fetal position. The first of the tears slid out my eyes, and I tried to ignore their existence.

§ § §

The hot cup of coffee in Allen's hand was the only thing keeping his fingers warm. Even with gloves on, the icy snow sucked the warmth from his hands. He held his books in the other, although he was afraid they'd break his frozen fingers and fall to the ground. With a head bent from the falling snow, he stared at the ground. As soon as he thought how awkward it would be if he ran into someone and spilled coffee on them, he saw a pair of shoes coming up to him. Both of them stopped in their tracks, and Allen's fantasy never became a reality.

"Sorry," he said.

"It's okay. No one can see anything in this freak snowstorm."

It was her. Allen looked up to see Sadie. "Oh." He tried not to appear too happy. "Hello, Sadie."

She smiled at him, which caught him off guard. "It's good to see you again, Allen."

"Are you off to teach a class?" He struggled to control the lovesick teenager in his head and pretended he didn't already know her schedule.

"Yes. Statistics."

An involuntary shudder ran through him, prompting a questioning look from Sadie. His brain scrambled to think of something to say. "Well, someone's got to teach it." He felt awful stealing a line from Riley but was surprised when she laughed.

"Yes, someone does."

Now that Allen had her attention, he didn't know what to do next. An awkward pause sprinkled over them. He tried to find something to say, but nothing came.

"I see you're reading Chaucer. Teaching him in one of your classes?" Sadie asked.

"Yes." Allen was glad she thought of a conversation as he glanced at the book in his hands. "Yes, I am."

"I guess someone has to teach him, too."

It was so unexpected it made Allen laugh. It was a pleasant realization to know the woman he liked could make him laugh. "So, I was wondering something," Allen said.

"Yes?" Sadie asked.

His heart quickened, and his whole body felt warm from nerves. Was he really going to ask her on a date now? "I was wondering if, um, sometime this week..." Why couldn't the lovesick teenager be more eloquent in speaking?

"Yes?" Allen thought he saw excitement in her eyes. Was she excited at the prospect of a date?

The final question was there, ready to stumble out of his mouth when Riley appeared out of nowhere. "Hello Sadie," he said.

Riley looked pleased to see them, but more pleased to see Sadie. The courage left and ice formed in Allen's stomach. It had been a week since he helped Riley move, and he didn't mind the absence. Defeated, he bent his head and looked at his coffee. He wouldn't ask Sadie with Riley standing next to them.

"Hello Riley," Sadie said. There was something plastic about the smile she gave Riley.

"You look stunning today. I think the snow enhances your beauty."

"It doesn't matter how pretty it makes me look. It's cold, icy, and I'd rather be inside instead of walking around in it." Allen grinned at her bluntness but tried to hide it as Riley glared at him. Riley turned back to Sadie.

"There are some activities which only happen in the wintertime. Like ice skating. Come ice skating with me tonight. I know this nice place, not too crowded. Small. Intimate."

The lovesick teenager bristled. It didn't take much to ask a person on a date; why couldn't he have been a tad faster? Sadie rubbed her shoulder, looking uneasy. It was the reason Allen did not excuse himself to leave for his class. If Riley was not afraid to flirt so openly with Sadie while he was here, he didn't know what he would say if he left. The thought made his skin crawl.

"Thank you for the invitation," Sadie glanced around campus as though looking for a physical escape route. "But I—" Her eyes rested on Allen. "Allen already asked me on a date tonight."

Riley turned to look at Allen, who took half a second to realize what had happened. His mind froze as the professor and the previously married side of him both glanced at the grinning lovesick teenager for help.

"With you?" Riley looked like he was going to laugh. "You're going ice skating with Sadie?"

Sadie gave Allen an anxious—and dare he hope excited—nod.

"Yes. We're going on a date." Allen tried to make it sound final.

"Tonight," Sadie added.

"At six," Allen threw in.

"He'll pick me up at my house."

"Then we'll go out to dinner."

Sadie's face lit up. "And ice skating. Because I really do love ice skating."

A trickle of panic hit Allen's chest, but he didn't want to stop the momentum. "Even though I haven't gone for a while and might end up making a fool of myself."

"And I will find it adorable and not judge you."

"But it will be the big, indoor skating rink, because I don't know any others." Allen nodded, feeling overwhelmed at what transpired. A goofy grin was definitely on his face, but he didn't care.

"Great. I will see you at six." Taking out a pen from her pocket, Sadie wrote her phone number on his notes. "Call me and I'll give you my address," she added before glancing at Riley. Turning away from Riley, she looked back at Allen, truly happy. "Thank you."

The double meaning wasn't lost on Allen. "See you at six."

Sadie gave him one last smile before she turned and left for class. Allen couldn't help himself. In the growing blizzard, he stood rooted to his spot and watched her go, the goofy grin still on his face. It was as if he was back in college instead of being a professor, and he didn't mind it one bit.

Riley cleared his throat. Allen's grin faded, and he saw darkness in Riley's eyes. It made him uncomfortable. "Nice move," Riley said.

"I asked her right before you came." The darkness deepened, but Allen held his gaze to show he wasn't afraid.

"Does she know?" Riley asked, his voice as black as his eyes. "About your wife and child?"

It felt like an invisible punch to his gut, causing him to take a step back. He didn't try to keep them a secret. Their memories still caused him deep pain whenever someone brought them up, and it wasn't something for a casual conversation. If the opportunity ever arose, he wouldn't mind talking about them with Sadie, but he would *not* talk about them with Riley.

"How did you find out?" Allen asked.

Riley shrugged. "I have connections. I'd hate for there to be secrets between you two. Your budding relationship might uproot before it even begins."

"What happened in my past is my business." Allen took a few steps away from Riley. "I'm not talking to you about it."

"Pretty women get hurt easily, you know. Especially pretty women like Sadie, with her kind of past."

White-hot anger filled his veins. His once frozen fingers curled over the spines of his books. Allen's eyes narrowed, and his protective instincts kicked in. What was Riley doing looking up their pasts? What weird game was he playing? He whirled around and faced Riley. "What are you doing here? Are you really visiting faculty?"

"Yes." Riley stared right back into Allen's eyes. The look wasn't pleasant, but Allen refused to back down.

"I could report you."

"And you'll get me fired." Riley gave a shrug. "But I'll let you in on a little secret. I don't need this job, and getting fired won't stop me."

"From doing what?" The sneer on Riley's face turned the surrounding snow to ice. "Stay away from Sadie. Understand?" Allen said.

Riley's sneer turned more twisted. "Perfectly."

With a quick turn, Allen made his way to the English building, refusing to look behind him. His hands shook for reasons other than the cold.

§ § §

My eyes kept wandering out the window of Dr. Webb's office as I went through the latest scene I narrated. Things were getting dark. Riley almost revealed the Rogue's plan. It scared me, but then again, it made me proud Allen didn't cower from him even when Riley brought up Allen's wife and child. It was still a tender spot for him, and he handled it beautifully.

"Junior?"

It jolted me back to reality, and I realized I wasn't paying attention to a single word Dr. Webb said. "I'm sorry." My muscles strained to move as I straightened in the comfortable chair. "I'm more distracted these days."

Dr. Webb nodded. "I understand. Did you write down what you ate this past week?"

"Yes." I reached inside my pocket, pulled out a folded piece of paper, and handed it to her. Dr. Webb unfolded it, glancing at my list.

"Those are some good, healthy choices for lunch." She turned the paper over. "Where is your list for breakfast and dinner?" My heart pounded as my face turned red, and Dr. Webb noticed. It was so embarrassing I couldn't keep eye contact with her. She looked at the list again. "In the past seven days, you ate eight times?"

"They were huge meals." My voice was quiet. They were huge meals for me, maybe.

The paper crinkled as Dr. Webb folded the list and handed it back to me. "Do you snack at all during the day? Before and after this meal?"

I shook my head, and Dr. Webb gave a calculated look. "You're a worrier."

"My characters are in danger. Mortal and psychological danger. I can't stop worrying about them, and when I worry, I can't eat. Or sleep."

She jotted something down on her notebook. "I remember. You treat them like family."

"It's so much more!" My voice was sharp. "I'm responsible for their development with the trials I give them, because I created them. If Bree dies, it will tear Sadie apart! I've invested so much into Sadie. I created her, and I know her well. It's to the point I'll feel her pain at losing her child, one she sacrificed everything for. Sadie would never recover. Her relationship with Allen would crumble because of it. And Allen is…" There was too much about how it would psychologically mess up Allen, so I didn't bother to try to use words. "They don't deserve that kind of life. I will do anything to keep Bree alive."

Dr. Webb gave me a solemn nod. "If you are willing to do anything for them, then eat more. Get adequate rest. As difficult as it might be, you need your strength to narrate. If you get exhausted, you will start making mistakes. I'm betting you don't want that any more than I do."

What she said was true; I had to admit it. Defeated, I glanced at my hands clasped in my lap. "I understand." It was a struggle to force myself to look at her.

Dr. Webb looked at her notes. "Junior, there's something I want you to consider. I'm sure the Guardians have already warned you that your situation might get harder."

There was a moment of silence. It took too much energy to speak.

"What are your feelings about antidepressants?"

I chewed my bottom lip and looked away. "They…work. For people. With depression." My finger inched to my knee. "Do I have depression?"

"Well, difficulty sleeping, lack of appetite, anxiety about the future, anxiety about your current situation. Those are some symptoms."

Tears formed in my eyes and threatened to fall. Even though this was a place to cry, I tried to fight the tears back anyway.

"The pills will help ease the burden, not take it away. It will be like giving you a weapon to fight against the anxiety. I'm suggesting them now because they take a week or two before they're effective. If you need the extra support the pills offer, I will gladly write you a prescription."

My fingers gripped my knees. "I feel like a failure."

"For needing antidepressants?" Dr. Webb asked.

Since speech was still a problem, I nodded. Dr. Webb smiled sadly. "You probably felt the same way when Jim suggested you meet with me." My eyes couldn't hold her gaze and I looked away again.

"Anxiety and depression are dangerous if they aren't helped, Junior. If you get a broken arm, you're not a failure for getting a cast. Antidepressants don't have to be a permanent solution. They are a help and an aide, and you should never feel like a failure for seeking assistance."

Even though Dr. Webb already knew my struggles, I still tried to hide the tear falling down my cheek, flicking it away. "Okay. I'll take them."

CHAPTER 10

BREE STUFFED HER math book in her bag and closed her locker. Her feet went into autopilot as she walked down the hall to class. The sounds of a fight stopped her short. Down one of the side halls, she saw a crowd of students gathered in a ring.

"Stop it!" someone yelled from the center of the ring. It sounded like Holly. A terrified, fighting back tears kind of Holly. Before she could stop herself, Bree ran to the ring of students. Elbowing her way through the circle, she saw Reggie take on two seniors while another senior held Holly back with a laugh. In a second she was in the bully's face. "Let go!"

"Make me."

In a single motion, Bree had her bag off and swung it hard toward the senior, for once grateful for a bulky math book. He grunted as it hit his side. When Bree went to hit him again, he let go of Holly and grabbed her bag. There was a slight tug of war before the senior won and tossed it outside the circle.

Holly went to help Reggie, but the senior laughed and grabbed her arm. "You still owe me something, you little—"

Bree didn't let him finish. The punch to his face was weak, but it got the senior's attention. Holly broke free again.

"You've got a feisty little friend." He straightened up to his full height, towering over Bree. She stood her ground.

"What's going on here!" a teacher yelled. The ring of students broke. Bree turned and noticed Reggie for the first time. He was in bad shape.

"What happened?" Bree asked Holly in a whisper.

"Reggie saved me." Holly grinned at her. "Like in the movies. He swooped in and stopped them." Reggie held a hand over his nose, his hand dripping blood as the teacher checked him.

"Stopped them from doing what?"

Holly clamped her mouth shut, looking uncomfortable. Bree wanted to persist, but a teacher came and escorted the group to the principal's office.

After telling the principal what she saw, he asked Bree to wait outside. When Holly gave her arm a reassuring squeeze, Bree felt she had no choice but to leave. She paced the floor as she waited for Holly so they could go to class together. It was weird to hear the normally boisterous halls so quiet.

Why did Reggie risk his life to help Holly when he didn't care? The image of his smirk couldn't leave her mind. If she figured out his plan, she could help Holly see how dangerous he was. Until then, she didn't know how to convince Holly to stay away.

The door of the principal's office swung open. Holly and Reggie walked out and met up with Bree. The three seniors stayed in the office.

"What's going on?" Bree asked.

"They're getting suspended," Holly said.

"What did they do?"

Holly started to explain, but Reggie shook his head. "It doesn't matter. They won't bother her anymore." Holly beamed at Reggie. It made Bree uncomfortable.

"Hey Holly, can I talk to you for a minute?" Bree asked.

"Sure, what's up?"

Bree glanced at Reggie. "Alone?"

Holly frowned, the flicker of anger returning to her eyes. "Okay."

Reggie reached over and squeezed Holly's hand. "I'll see you after school."

Holly giggled and waved. Bree waited until he turned the corner. The giggling immediately stopped when Holly turned to Bree. "What's going on?"

"I know you still think—"

"You have an irrational fear of men? Yeah, I do."

Bree raised her eyebrows. It was the first time she'd heard such sharpness from her friend. The drive to let Holly know her feelings made her continue, even though everything else warned her to drop it. "I know scumbags when I see them, and he is definitely a scumbag."

"Reggie saved me." Holly folded her arms. "Those seniors tried to force me to kiss one of them, and it may have happened if Reggie didn't stop them."

Her innards churned, making her want to punch the seniors again, but she had to focus. "I know it sounds ridiculous, but there's something wrong with him."

Daggers shot out of Holly's eyes. "Nothing is wrong with him! He saved me, and you didn't want him to. You wanted those seniors to kiss me!"

"That's not what I meant! I'm glad I hit one of them! Stop putting words in my mouth!"

"Reggie warned me about this. You have a crush on him, too."

It was so ridiculous Bree took a step back. "What!"

Holly's eyes darkened. "You're as bad as Aubrielle. You want him all for yourself."

Panic bubbled up inside of Bree. "No!"

"I thought you hated boys, but they must be your Achilles ankle too!"

So many things were happening at once. Bree groaned. "Heel! It's heel! How are you getting an A in English when you don't know this simple idiom?"

Holly let out her own frustrated cry. "What does it matter? It's all part of the foot anyway! Why are you so controlling!"

This conversation couldn't continue with both of them angry. Curling her fists in her pockets helped Bree control some of the anger. "I'm going to repeat myself slowly. I do not trust Reggie *at all*. I have been your friend since the sixth grade. You *just* met Reggie. Why do you trust him more than me!"

"I thought I could trust Aubrielle, too." Holly's voice was quiet, but still churning with anger.

Bree's body froze as her mind scrambled to say something. Did she already lose her friend? "There is something wrong with Reggie. I don't know what, but I feel it. Can't you feel it too? Don't you sense any red flags?"

The hesitation in Holly's face made Bree's heart swell with hope. Something inside Holly knew he was wrong, but she let her stupid infatuation get in the way. For a glorious moment, Bree believed Holly would come back to her side, but then Holly shook her head and walked away.

"You know I'm right!" Bree yelled after her.

"You're worse than Aubrielle. At least she had the decency to steal Stud from under me. You're trying to get me to hate Reggie before you steal him." Tears stung Bree's eyes, and she took a couple steps in Holly's direction.

"Leave me alone, Bree. I don't want to be around you anymore."

This couldn't be happening. In less than a month, she lost both friends to boys. It took everything inside her to just watch as her best friend walked down the math hall.

Reggie met Holly before she turned to go to class. They chatted, and Reggie leaned forward and kissed the top of Holly's forehead. Bree forced herself to go numb so she wouldn't freak out. With a trembling hand, she braced herself against the wall and slid until she hit the floor. Math class was the farthest thing on her mind. Maybe she could text her mom and claim some sickness so she could go home and do nothing.

"Hey." Reggie popped out of nowhere and startled Bree, but she refused to let him see her reaction. Instead she glared at him.

"Get away from me." She ignored his extended hand as she struggled to her feet and started walking toward math class.

Reggie followed. "It's not my fault."

"I have class." Bree held the strap of her backpack. If she needed to use it as a weapon again, she wouldn't hesitate.

"Why do you hate me?"

She turned and faced him. "Maybe because you ruined my life. I don't know who you are, but I know your friendship with Holly is insincere. What do you want with her?"

"I follow orders. That's all." He pushed past her as he walked to his class. Curiosity wanted her to demand what he meant, but her math teacher poked her head out of the classroom.

"Bree. Get in here, young lady."

A grumble escaped her as she walked into class. Holly refused to acknowledge her as she sat down. With numb fingers, she opened her notebook and began taking notes.

At the end of school, Bree stood in line for the bus, her hood up to keep snow from falling in her face. A familiar giggle came close by. Bree looked up to see Holly and Reggie walk hand in hand toward his car. When Holly laughed again, she turned away from Reggie and noticed Bree watching her. Her old friend stuck her nose in the air and turned away. Bree tore her gaze away, stared at the ground, and pulled at the strings on her hood to be sure her face, and more importantly her tears, were covered.

The bus pulled up and she got on, sitting in her regular seat. She leaned her head against the window, watching snowflakes tumble to the ground. The bus ride was long and awful. Dark thoughts plagued her. Aubrielle and Holly both left because they found boys. Couldn't Holly see Reggie had other motives? Couldn't Aubrielle see what she did hurt them both? Bree got up at her stop and walked down the steps of the bus with plans to barricade herself in her bedroom.

"Have a nice evening," the bus driver said, tipping his hat.

Bree didn't have the heart to return the small talk. As she stomped through the snow, she wanted more than anything for the world to disappear.

§ § §

I set the headset down and stared at the wall. The heavy weight in my soul glued me to my chair as mental exhaustion took its toll. A gentle knock came to my front door, which forced me to my feet. How long had I been staring at the wall? A bright ray of sunlight shone in as I opened the door and saw Jim. He smiled, but I noticed the worry behind it.

"I'm glad you're here. I need permission to make Josh part of the main ensemble. Bree's mom is at work, and Bree needs someone right now."

Jim's face fell, the worry more prevalent. "I read the notes from your last session with Dr. Webb."

"Does she email you everything we talk about?" I couldn't look him in the eyes as I said this.

"No, no. She only emails when she thinks the Guardians should be aware of something. In a way, we are responsible for you. Junior, you need to take a break from narrating. You've been at it for a while."

My initial response kicked in. "I can't. I need permission to—"

"You have it, as long as you stop for two days."

There was a heavy frown on my face as I scrutinized Jim. "First you want me to narrate more, and now you want me to take a break?"

"I've been following along in your story. You sound exhausted."

"I can't tear myself away when things are getting dark for them." I started to close the door, but Jim put his hand on the door to stop me.

"Yes, you can. The good thing about narrating is you can stop anytime, and your characters won't notice how many days go by. You need this time to get your strength back."

"I'm perfectly fine. Besides, it messes with my momentum. I have ideas I should use before my mind goes stale." Again I tried to close the door, but he was stronger than he looked.

"This is a logic puzzle, not a war." Jim forced the door to open wider. "You can stop as many times as you need and think things through. Or to stop and rest."

"But what about the Rogue?" My list of excuses were thin. I needed

71

to get back to narrating since I now had permission to bring Josh in. "Don't you need him to enter my story so you can track the beacon or whatever and find him?"

"The Rogue can wait. Your immediate health has me worried. I order you to take a break and come with me."

Jim grabbed my arm and gently pulled me out of the apartment. He locked the door and led me to his car. With the bright midday sun overhead I blinked multiple times. The heat made the blue sky look hazy. Jim opened the door, grabbed my head, and forced me into the car like cops do when they arrest someone. I stuck my foot out so he wouldn't close the door.

"I appreciate your concern, but I need to get back to my story."

Jim shook his head. "No."

No argument, just a no. I mumbled my annoyance as I stuck my foot back inside. When it came down to it, I didn't want to argue with the Guardians. He closed the door and got into the driver's side, backing out and driving down the road.

He didn't say anything. The scenery rolled by, and I watched that instead of talking to him. My fingertips grazed my forehead as I rested my arm against the door. Summer turned hotter, with the promise of more heat. It felt weird narrating a story in the dead of winter when everything outside my office window looked so scorching hot.

A stray lock of hair fell in front of my face. I tried to blow it back into place, but it fell, dangling over my nose. In the end, I grabbed it and tucked it behind my ear. Jim's car was the same as his office desk—unusually clean. Everything in it was necessary. Jim didn't seem like a clean freak; if he was he would have dusted off his dashboard.

"Since I need Josh, I'll stop narrating for a few days to make you happy," I finally said.

"Junior, why do you care so much about them?"

His question surprised me. I couldn't help but turn and look at him. "Care about my characters?"

"Yes."

"Wasn't my reply in Dr. Webb's notes?"

Jim tried hard not to look at me. "She said you believe they're family, and you feel responsible for them. But I'd say this is an obsession, not protectiveness."

Another building passed by. "If there was a way to finish this story and then go back and re-enter my characters so they'd follow the original outline, I'd do it. But I can't. This is my one shot to get my characters in the database and make a story. And it's going bad. I love my characters, and they have a ton of potential."

Jim stole a glance at me before focusing back on the road. I was torn on how I felt about the limitation. The device could only create them once. In a way, it made my characters more real. There could only be one Bree or one Sadie in the entire database. If I could recreate them, they wouldn't feel as real.

"You started with your best story?" Jim asked.

"I had to. You guys didn't want me to narrate my other stories. You said they still needed more work."

The frown deepened on Jim's face. The silence in the car made me uncomfortable. I thought I offended him somehow. After a bit of a drive, he pulled into a parking lot of a restaurant and stopped the car. I gazed at it curiously.

"Like I said, Dr. Webb sent us an email." He got out of the car and I followed. Jim looked gloomy.

"I didn't bring any money," I said.

"I didn't expect you to. I'll pay."

We walked into the restaurant. It felt strange walking next to a man in an expensive business suit while I wore cut-off jeans, a loose t-shirt, and flip-flops. After we ordered our food, we talked about trivial things. Jim tried too hard not to start a conversation about my story or the Rogue. Since it took up so much of my life, I didn't know what else to talk about. He tried some get to know you questions, which I answered. We talked about college since we both went to the same one, but he changed the subject there, too. It reminded me too much of the Rogue.

Halfway through our meal, I finally got the courage to ask him the real question on my mind. "Okay, what's going on?"

Jim looked up from his plate of spaghetti. "What?"

"Why are you doing this? You're being nice but look like you're in agony."

The corners of Jim's mouth twitched. "It's complicated."

"I'm a woman. I might be able to figure it out."

He forced a laugh, placed his fork to one side, and wiped his mouth with a napkin. "I'm curious to know where you were about a year ago."

"A year ago now?" I asked.

He nodded.

"I failed a semester of college because of Professor Andrews..." I swallowed to control the lump forming in my throat. Jim watched me carefully. "I traveled abroad to take my mind off things here," I finished.

"And I assume during that time you didn't research anything about the Rogue?"

"Nothing."

Jim nodded and gave a sigh which sounded like he had the weight of the world on his shoulders. "There's a reason why I didn't want to take this project." He didn't look at me and instead played with a spaghetti noodle on his plate. "The Rogue kidnapped two people I care about."

My jaw dropped. "Two?"

"Yes."

I turned away embarrassed. I knew the Rogue kidnapped his brother, but two of the three narrators who disappeared were connected to Jim!

"I saw what the Rogue did psychologically to my younger brother and girlfriend." There was a hint of bitterness in his calm voice.

And his girlfriend? The girl in the picture he looked so lovingly at?

"I watched from the sidelines as they withered away," he continued. "I felt helpless. Kyle, my brother, was kidnapped while he was out with friends, drinking, and Lydia, she..." he looked away. I stole a glance at him. His eyes were red, but he tried to control himself. "She was in the hospital when he abducted her. The stress got to her, making her physically sick. He kidnapped her right from under my nose. I stepped out for five minutes to get breakfast, and when I got back she was gone." His hand trembled as he ran his fingers through his hair. My stomach churned. There was a lot more to this obnoxious, pompous suit wearer than I thought.

"Kyle was first. Then Lydia. Back to back. It's been a year." He turned to look at me. The only sign of tears was that his eyes looked redder than before. "I resolved never to assist the Rogue's victims again. I didn't want to watch someone go through hell."

I realized what he meant. He was in the same position he never wanted to be in again. It was a huge deal he was trying to help me at all. It must have crushed him to lose two people he loved. Two people specifically under his care. As calmly as ever, Jim picked up his fork and returned to his meal, not looking at me.

My fork found itself on my plate. "Thank you, Jim. I understand now. It must be hard going through this again."

The look on Jim's face was more miserable than before. "You remind me of Kyle. And I am sorry. Trying isn't enough." He stared at the electric light of the fake lantern decoration on the opposite corner of the room. "I promised myself when I became a Guardian I would do what they asked and defend who I needed to. With what I experienced before, I've been too afraid to help you. I didn't want to get to know you or your characters. I didn't want to care, because I didn't want to get hurt. I was selfish. I may not get hurt, but you were getting hurt. I promise to be there for you more."

Jim finally gave me a genuine smile.

CHAPTER 11

BREE REMAINED CURLED in bed with a blanket over her head. Someone tapped on her door. She didn't move, pretending to sleep. The person tapped the door again. "It's Josh."

She didn't answer. Josh opened the door a crack. "Can I come in?"

Deep down she knew it didn't matter what her answer was. As though on cue, she heard Josh creep in and close the door. Josh might not worry as much as her mom would about the experience at school, but she still felt hesitant.

Josh sat at the edge of the bed. "When you don't come in and wish me a good afternoon, I'm entitled to worry."

"I'm fine." The covers muffled Bree's voice.

"Liar. What happened at school?"

Bree yanked the blankets off her head. Josh had blonde hair, different from her mom's dark hair, but they both had kind, brown eyes. Reaching out, Josh tried to ruffle her hair with his casted hand. She giggled at his attempt to make her feel better.

"There's a new kid at school. Maybe I'm way too judgmental, but I don't like him." Bree put a hand through her hair to straighten the mess.

Josh waited patiently. Bree distracted herself by looking at her fingernails and continued. "Today I'm sure he turned Holly against me. I have no friends anymore, and it's all that stupid boy's fault." Her voice caught.

There was a comforting smile on Josh's face as he patted her shoulder. Bree felt alone most of her life until sixth grade when she finally had friends. Maybe she was protective of her friends because she knew what it felt like to not have them.

"Sorry, Josh." She pretended to scratch her nose to mask wiping away tears. "I'm in a man-hating mood right now."

"Man-hater?" Josh asked. "Including uncles?"

"Uncles are different."

Josh's laugh was contagious. "Now, as for this new kid—"

"I know." Bree tugged the covers back over her head. "I'm too harsh."

"No." Josh sounded careful. "In this case, trust your gut."

It was such a strange reply, Bree didn't know what else to do but throw the blankets off again and look at him. "Do you think he's dangerous?"

Josh's face was serious for once. "Your mom says first impressions are usually wrong, and believe me, I do not want to contradict her. But if it feels wrong, be careful. Don't be rude, be careful."

"Do you know him?" Bree asked.

"I've heard of him."

"What have you heard?"

Josh traced Bree's signature on his cast, looking at the opposite wall. "Things." He sounded distant. Questions filled Bree's mind, but before she could think of one, he started speaking again. "Let me call up your mother, tell her you had a rough day, and she'll make some of her famous cookies."

"Thanks Josh." Bree snuggled deeper into her bed. "You're the best."

"I'm the best uncle you've ever had." He squeezed her shoulder before he left to make the phone call.

§ § §

Allen pulled into the driveway and checked his watch. Three minutes to six. Taking a deep breath, he forced his pounding heart to stay calm. This date was a way for Sadie to escape from Riley, nothing more. Allen didn't even put on his special cologne, mainly because he hadn't used it in over a decade and didn't know where it went.

When he called Sadie an hour earlier, she once again thanked him. Before telling him her address, she let him know she had a teenage daughter so he wouldn't be surprised when he came to pick her up. Allen thanked her for her honesty. He almost told her about his wife and child but stopped. If he was going to talk about them, it would be face to face, not over the phone.

The entire time driving to her house, Allen tried to do the math in his head. He didn't know how old Sadie was, but she looked younger than him. This meant Sadie must have been young when she got pregnant. He wanted to meet her daughter, but maybe on a different date. If there was another date.

Allen stepped out of the car and took faltering steps through deep snowdrifts before coming to the shoveled sidewalk. His gloved fingers brushed the snow off his pants before he knocked on the door. There were scuttling noises inside. Someone was talking in a distressed tone before the door opened and Sadie stood there, lovely but anxious.

"Allen, hi." Something was on her mind. "Um, please, come in. I've got to talk to my brother about something."

"Is everything all right?" he asked.

"Fine. Have a seat."

Sadie disappeared down the hall, and Allen heard hushed yet urgent voices. He pulled back the hood of his coat, brushing away snowflakes from his hair. He noticed pictures of Sadie and her daughter and took a step closer to study them.

"Josh, please, I—" Sadie said as she appeared in the room with a man who could only be her brother.

"Hello!" the man named Josh said when he saw Allen. Allen noticed Josh's stitches and that his outstretched hand was in a cast. Allen tenderly shook his casted hand. "I'm Josh. Sadie's my little sister. She's excited to go on this date with you."

"Great." Allen glanced from Josh to Sadie, wondering what he missed.

Sadie stood next to him, her lips pressed together tightly. "My brother got in a car accident a couple of weeks ago, and I don't think he's capable of looking after Bree right now."

"Ouch. Don't attack my babysitting skills." Josh put a hand on his heart in mock hurt. "She's sixteen, Sadie. She's not a child."

Sadie's lips disappeared as she pressed them even tighter. "She had a bad day, and the pain medication they have you on would make you sleep through the apocalypse. What if she needs someone?"

"I hardly need the meds anymore."

"If this is a bad time," Allen said, backing toward the door, "I'm sure we can resched—"

"No." The way Josh said it gave Allen the impression they were talking about something more important than a date. "Absolutely out of the question." He turned to Sadie and pointed a finger at her. "You will go on this date. You will enjoy being out of the house, and you will have a nice time with a good man." Allen didn't know how Josh assumed he was a good man since they barely met. He didn't know what to say.

"What's wrong with staying here for the date?" Sadie asked. "If you and Bree stay up—"

"No," Josh said again in a sharp but friendly tone. "My words are final."

Sadie slapped his good arm. "They are not."

Josh grabbed Sadie's shoulders and forced her to look at him. "You need to go on this date."

She gave him a scrutinizing look. "You're acting as if this is life or death. Seriously, we need to change the meds you're on." Josh about said something, but hesitated.

A timid voice came from the hall. "Mom?" The three of them turned to see Bree. Bree glanced at Allen and turned her attention towards Sadie.

"Go ahead, mom. I'm fine." She rubbed her upper arm, and Allen somehow knew she wasn't fine. "You made cookies. I'm feeling better."

Josh turned back to Sadie, a triumphant smile on his face. "See. She said it herself! Bree, come introduce yourself." It looked like introducing herself was the last thing on Bree's mind, but Josh seemed like a difficult man to say no to. She hesitated before walking toward them, not looking at Allen as she stuck out her hand.

Allen shook her hand. "Hello, I'm Allen."

"Hi. Bree." There was still no eye contact as she edged closer to Josh.

Josh nudged Sadie toward Allen. "Have a good time."

Still not sure about the situation, Allen tried to think of something. "Well, should we go?"

It was a long second before Sadie grabbed her coat and gloves. Allen helped her put on her coat and noticed she was glaring at Josh. "If you need anything, call."

Josh beamed at her as though she paid him a deep compliment. "Keep your phone off. It's rude to use your phone during a date."

After she put on her gloves, Sadie went over and kissed Bree on the forehead. "I'll be back later. No matter what Josh says, if you need me, call."

Bree nodded. "Don't worry mom. I'll be fine."

Allen opened the door for her, and they left the house.

§ § §

It took three sets of knocks before my sleep-deprived brain realized someone was at the door. I rubbed my head and felt my hair. After narrating last night, I decided a shower needed to happen. It also meant I thought I was awake enough to braid my hair, but only got halfway through one when exhaustion overtook me. The only curl which lasted in my hair was if I braided my hair while it was wet and left it to dry.

After another knock, my brain realized the correct response was I needed to answer the door now. I threw my bathrobe over my pajamas and stumbled to the living room. As I touched the doorknob, I realized half my hair would look wavy from the braid and the other half ridiculously straight. I refused to look in a mirror. It'd be better not to know how bad my hair looked.

I secured my robe before I pulled open the door. My eyes burned in the blinding sunlight. It took a few seconds before my eyesight returned, and I saw Jim and Devin.

"What time is it?" I asked, shielding my eyes. The frown on Devin's face deepened while Jim checked his watch.

"Almost noon," Jim answered.

I yawned as I leaned my head against the door frame. "I lost track of time last night. I went to bed at six."

Jim winced. "In the morning?"

Another big yawn kept me from answering right away. "Yeah." It took a lot to narrate those couple of scenes. I didn't want to narrate Allen and Sadie's date yet, since I wanted to finalize some ideas first.

"Junior, we have something to discuss with you," Devin said. He strolled inside my apartment like he owned the place. Technically it was the Guardians' apartments, but still. Jim walked in, turned, and gave me an apologetic smile. It frightened me.

"Can I get you anything to drink?" My mind struggled to remember my hostess skills as I walked over to the fridge. I assessed what I had to offer. "I have, um, milk. Some orange juice. Water. A lot of water. I could make some tea if you want."

"We're fine," Devin said curtly as he sat down. Jim joined him, quiet. I walked over with my own little glass of orange juice.

"Is there something wrong?" My fingers gripped the bottom of the glass of orange juice. Seeing their business suits once again made me want to finish braiding my hair. If I wanted to, I could cut an apple on the creases in Devin's pants. I pretended to scratch my hair so I could flatten some of the waviness.

"Junior, we want to ask you a few questions, and depending on your answers we may have to take you in for a hearing," Devin said.

I stopped drinking my orange juice and lowered the glass. "What?" The narration judicial system wasn't something I completely understood, but enough to know a hearing meant I did something wrong in my story.

"Answer them honestly." If Devin's pants could cut apples, then his voice could cut granite. I didn't feel thirsty anymore. My hands shook as I lowered my glass of orange juice.

"Ask away." I tried not to reveal how frightened I felt.

"Who is Josh?" Devin asked without hesitation.

"My story needed a character not bound by my original outline." I nodded toward Jim. "I already ran it by Jim."

"Is this true?" Devin asked, turning toward Jim.

Jim frowned. "She did. But I didn't realize how far she would go."

I matched his frown. "Wait, did I do something wrong?"

Devin pulled out a pamphlet from inside his suit coat, opened it, and handed it to me. "Read these three paragraphs taken from the contract you signed."

"And then?" I asked.

"Tell us if Josh is breaking these laws."

I took the pamphlet and skimmed through the paragraphs. Guilt played across my face, so I raised the pamphlet to shield myself. After I finished reading, I crafted what I would say.

"Well, if you're following this word for word, there might be…a few things…taken a certain way, which are not exactly what you might call law-abiding."

I glanced at them over the pamphlet. Their faces were stone-cold. They were nice enough not only to let me get dressed for the hearing, but to even let me finish braiding my hair.

CHAPTER 12

O NCE AGAIN, I stood in front of the four Guardians. Again I tried not to let them see how nervous I felt. My hands were folded in front of me so the Guardians wouldn't see how much they shook. The braids in my hair gave the impression I was ten years younger than I was, which might work for or against me.

"Good afternoon, Junior." Vince didn't sound cheery or happy.

"Afternoon." My tone matched his. Vince glared at me as he shuffled through his papers. I glanced at Grace who frowned at me. This was bad.

"Jim and Devin asked whether your character Josh is someone working within the laws the Guardians set forth. You mentioned he is not."

A small ember of anger burned in me which I quickly smothered. "For the record, I said he might not seem like a character who easily falls under those laws."

Vince looked at me over his spectacles in his annoying, condescending way. "Josh's character is breaking the rules." I gritted my teeth and controlled my temper. If things went badly here, I might forever lose the opportunity to narrate.

"This is from Devin and Jim's observations of your story." Vince pulled out a piece of paper. "'Josh shows signs of knowing more than he should. He might even be aware of Junior, the narrator. He knows more about the Rogue and the situation the other characters are in, giving him corruptive powers.'"

Jim got a betrayed look from me, but he shrugged. I got the message— he couldn't help me.

Silence settled in the room. My fingernails bit into my palm. All my hopes rested on Josh. If he stayed in the story, my other characters had a chance. Somehow, I had to get out of this hearing in control of my story with Josh still a part of it. Jim didn't look happy but wasn't angry like Devin or Vince. Grace's small frown deepened.

"What do you have to say for yourself?" Vince's voice was cold.

His coldness fueled my courage. "Without Josh, my characters will be led blindly to their doom."

"He broke the laws." Vince's eyes darkened. "Major ones."

"I don't want to wait for the Rogue to attack Bree." I unfolded my arms and tried to sit up straight in the chair. "There's been no news about how close you are to capturing the Rogue. In case you don't, I want to be ready."

"Junior." Grace's loving tone was a sharp contrast from Vince's condescending one. I winced. I couldn't fight Grace. "These laws are here for a purpose. Do you understand the consequences? Not just for you, but for your characters? Josh's power might corrupt him, and he could ruin your outline faster than the Rogue."

"I have full faith in Josh. I don't believe he'd get corrupted."

"Many people wish to think their characters are better than they are, but this power Josh has is dangerous. He might turn, and it wouldn't be pretty for your other characters," Grace said.

"I wouldn't have given it to him if I didn't trust him completely. He is loyal to his family, and he'd rather see them protected."

"What is this inside his code?" Vince didn't sound as sharp as before, but after the calm conversation with Grace, I felt attacked by him. "This secret weapon?"

"It's strictly for me and me alone." My heart pounded with adrenaline. So many thoughts raced through my head.

"So, it breaks the rules too?" Vince's voice was dipped in sarcasm. It made me want to yell, but I forced myself to calm down.

"Just because I want to keep it secret doesn't mean it breaks the rules." There I go, lying again. The code absolutely broke every rule the Guardians upheld. I promised myself to never use it unless my characters were in a life or death situation.

"I demand you tell us what it is," Vince said.

"No." Vince looked furious, but I didn't care. I stood up, my hands folded again, and my calm demeanor crumbled. "I don't know where you went to narrating school, but they taught me to think outside the box."

"The Rogue himself taught you." Vince said his name with deep animosity.

White-hot anger exploded in my chest. "Is this what it'll be like?" I pointed at the four of them accusingly. "Will you assume everything I do differently is a mark of the Rogue because he taught me? Yes, he's done evil things, but Professor Andrews was one of the best teachers I've ever had, and I wish you were more open-minded like him!"

I gasped as the anger finished pulsing through my body. It took a second to realize what I said. I might as well give them the form, signed and dated, to ban me from all future narration jobs. Grace's mouth hung open. Jim rubbed his forehead and glanced at me through his fingers. Devin stared at me, blinking a few times, and Vince looked positively fuming. My hands trembled. I curled my fingers into a fist, and my fist trembled. I stared at the floor, not wanting to look at them anymore.

"Do you realize what you just said?" Vince's voice was icily quiet. I didn't want to tell him my internal dialogue, so I remained silent. I pushed it too far.

Vince rose to his feet. "You are suspended from narration. Josh will be removed, and your story will be handed over to a law-abiding narrator."

It was over. I was milliseconds away from hanging my head and kissing my lifelong dream goodbye. Tears formed in my eyes.

"Sir." Jim spoke up for the first time, his voice calm. "I disagree. Junior needs to narrate her own story." The room became still. I looked at him, lightheaded, as I sank back into the chair.

"Explain." Vince sounded both curious and angry at the same time.

"If we are as close to capturing the Rogue as Devin and Grace reported two days ago, then it would be unwise to have Junior stop." Jim seemed calm, unlike myself, who had a thin line of sweat forming on my upper lip. "If a professional steps in, the Rogue won't pursue. We'll lose our trail, and we'll have to wait months before the Rogue finds someone else."

I blinked. There was some sound logic there.

Devin rubbed his forehead. "Jim's right, though I hate to admit it." With half of the Guardians on my side, I felt more confident. I flashed Jim a grateful smile, but he did not return it. My own smile faltered.

"Are you two suggesting we ignore the consequences of breaking the law?" A vein in Vince's neck bulged. "You're the ones who brought her here in the first place."

Devin glared at me. "As long as she isn't kidnapped, we can give her a proper trial when her story is finished."

"I agree with Devin and Jim." Grace's frown wasn't nearly pronounced. "We shouldn't waste all our hard work."

Vince glared darkly at me. Maybe this once he had to let go of some pride. He tapped his fingers on the desk in thought, resting his hand over the tattoo on his forearm. "I want Josh out of your story."

I found my voice. "He needs to be there for Bree." Vince almost shot me down, but I plowed through his beginning arguments. "I don't care if the book won't be published afterwards." Those words resisted leaving my mind, and they struggled and scraped at my throat before leaving my mouth. "It's not about that anymore." I closed my eyes as the truth of it settled in my soul. "It's about catching the Rogue now."

Jim cocked an eyebrow. Vince didn't look angry, which was a plus. "Are you aware of the dangers of keeping Josh in the story?" Vince asked.

"Yes."

"Are you prepared for the possibility of Josh turning corrupt and hurting or killing your characters which you claim he is loyal to?"

It was completely out of Josh's character, but I nodded anyway. "I am prepared for the possibility."

Vince shook his head. "As you said, it's not about your story being published anymore. It's about catching the Rogue. Keeping Josh gives you a slim chance of this book getting published."

I closed my eyes, nodding as a solemn shift happened inside my soul.

"Keep Josh then." Vince paused in thought. "But if you have ink-lings to do any more of these experiments which 'may or may not' break the rules, contact Jim first. And Jim, double-check it with me. We'll call a meeting to discuss the idea as a Guardianship to be approved by majority vote before she moves forward."

The desire to once again speak my mind came forward, but I kept my mouth shut. They gave me a second chance. A second chance which didn't feel like one, but I couldn't blow it.

"As for you, Junior, when you finish the story you will stand trial for your actions. Get her a taxi. This hearing is over." Vince seemed as happy to hear those words as I did. My shoulders relaxed. Somehow it happened. My story was still in my narration power, and I could keep Josh! I was in Jim's debt. The other Guardians started to leave. Jim walked over to me with his briefcase in one hand. I was about ready to thank him when he grasped my forearm.

"I'm taking you home." Jim led me toward the door, his fingers tightening over my arm. It made me gasp.

As soon as we got out of the conference room, I shook his hand off. "What's going on? I may be in your debt, but it doesn't mean you can treat me like a criminal."

Jim turned to me, a look of anger he somehow concealed throughout the whole meeting. "Do you enjoy walking on thin ice?" Jim's voice sounded as angry as Vince's.

I didn't want to hear Jim angry. His anger brought back my own, and I was aware of how much I was in Jim's debt. The last thing I wanted to do was compete in a screaming match with someone who saved my characters. I pressed my lips together to keep from saying anything that might get me deeper in the hole I dug myself into.

"Did you hear anything Grace said? These laws are there because what you are doing with Josh is *extremely* dangerous. His powers could corrupt him, and if he lets your name slip, your world will break down and everyone will enter the limbo world."

What he said was true, but the anger in his voice made me want to fight him. "I had little choice."

"So instead of giving your characters the possibility of not following your outline and maybe ending up miserable, you instead gave them Josh, the walking time bomb who might send them all into the limbo world? Or become corrupted and kill them all?"

"Josh won't do that!"

Jim let out a doubtful laugh. "How do you *know* he won't?"

"Because he wants to protect his family! He will keep his powers secret for as long as possible."

"And then what?" Jim shook his head and rubbed his forehead with his free arm. "You are a complete mystery to me, Junior. You sacrifice so much for your characters, putting your health on the line, yet you put in Josh who could destroy them all!"

I felt flustered and didn't know what to say. "He won't."

"You keep saying that, but he might."

"But he won't!"

Jim glared at me so darkly it took everything inside not to step back in fear. "Just like you knew the Rogue would never enter your story?"

I looked away, fighting the urge to slap him. Jim grumbled to himself, moving his briefcase from one hand to the other. "Do you know how much power corrupts?"

"Yes. The Rogue's characters have the same power Josh has. They're not slipping Professor Andrews' name in there."

"In case you forgot, Professor Andrews is the Rogue. The guy is number one on the Guardian's most wanted list. It's not smart to compare your ideas to his."

I hated Jim's sarcasm. I breathed a few times to calm my nerves. "Josh doesn't know my name. He knows my nickname."

"That's…" Jim paused as he realized what I said. "Genius," he finished. "Except the powers could still corrupt him."

I pushed past him and stomped out of headquarters. Yes, the powers could corrupt, but Josh was selfless. He loved his family. He'd never hurt them. The Guardians seemed so worried, but this was the one thing I was confident in. Josh would never hurt his family. I was outside before Jim caught up with me.

"Junior, stop." He still sounded angry. He grabbed my shoulder and turned me around, so I didn't have a choice. "Vince's order he gave you of talking to me before you do anything 'semi-law breaking.' You must follow it. To the letter. You'll be in more of a mess if you ignore it."

I wanted to tell him my thoughts in a logical, thought-provoking way, but my anger was still in control. It took all my willpower to stay silent. I learned from my experience in the conference room.

Jim noticed my silence and leaned forward, trying to pry it out of my eyes. "What are you planning?"

"I'm not planning anything. Things like this happen."

"What's that supposed to mean?"

I rubbed my temple with my finger and closed my eyes to calm myself down. "There might be a moment when I have to make a split-second decision. I won't use my precious time to ask you if it's okay." My voice turned sharp. "You and the Guardians don't get it. I'm trying to keep my characters alive!"

Jim dropped his hand from my shoulder. He looked at me, almost with guilt. "Junior, we're not entirely focused on catching the Rogue. We're worried about you, too." The anger disappeared from his voice.

I turned around and continued walking down the stairs until I got to Jim's car, no longer interested in having a conversation. He didn't say anything as he unlocked it. I got in, buckled up, and stared out the window the rest of the ride home. Jim tried to start a conversation a few times but never did.

As I closed my eyes, scenes from my original outline played before me. At the end, Sadie and Allen were married, with Bree basking in the love of her mother and new father. Bree would help Holly overcome her bully problem, and Holly would help her adjust to having a father. They would become inseparable. The trials they went through would make them stronger, but also make them happier. Bree and Holly were never supposed to break up their friendship. The Rogue also tried to get between Sadie and Allen. Luckily Sadie jumped in at the last nanosecond to get this date Josh struggled to make happen.

What would happen if it didn't end up how I wanted? My characters could get quite miserable. It's one thing if they chose to be miserable, but quite another if their situation forced them into misery. Especially if I could stop it.

Jim parked the car and we both got out. "Junior."

It was a struggle to control my breathing. Jim wanted to continue the conversation, and I didn't think I was calm enough for it. I remembered all he did for me, for my characters, for my health. Remembering them helped me lose my anger. "What?" I sounded a lot calmer.

Jim glanced around to make sure no one was near, then walked up to me. "Do you still want to read a manuscript the Rogue corrupted?"

My eyes widened, but I tried to keep the excitement hidden. "Yes."

Again, Jim glanced around. "I'll give you Kyle's. I'm going home this weekend to visit my mother. You must keep it safe. Don't let the other Guardians know you have it."

I threw my arms around him. "Thank you, Jim. I owe you so much."

"If you get out of this without disappearing, I'll consider us even."

I smiled as I broke away. "Then I'll do my best to be a model citizen until I hear from you."

"Good." Jim headed back to his car. I walked into my apartment and closed the door as a feeling of dread returned. Time for Allen and Sadie to go on their date.

CHAPTER 13

THE LAST OF the snow from Allen's hair melted as he and Sadie finished their orders and handed their menus to the waitress. Allen folded his arms and placed them on the table. Every time he tried to start a conversation, he stopped before he opened his mouth. Sadie stared out the window, lost in her own thoughts, and Allen knew she'd rather be home with Bree. Despite this, his brain ordered him to start a conversation.

"So, Bree had a bad day at school?"

She jumped and turned to Allen. Her cheeks flushed as though remembering she was on a date. "Yes, sorry." With a shaking hand, she picked up her glass of lemon water, took a sip, and then set the glass back down. Her finger absently traced around the edge of the glass.

"Don't be sorry. I'd be worried too."

"There's a boy at school giving her grief. Apparently this boy took her friend away from her." Her voice was quiet, but Allen sensed the protectiveness inside her.

"Boys can be trouble sometimes." He felt his heart go out to this girl, even though he barely met her. "That's rough."

"Bree doesn't make friends easily. I think she feels..." Sadie trailed off, which made Allen look up from watching her delicate finger trace the glass. "I guess I haven't told you about my daughter, have I?"

"No, not much."

There was a pause as Sadie opened her mouth, then she looked away as she took another sip of water before beginning. "Her name is Bree. She's sixteen. I had her when I was her age. A week before I found out I was pregnant, I broke up with my boyfriend. He concluded he must not be the father since I had a whole week to find some other guy and get pregnant."

Allen winced. "Wow."

"Yeah. Not bright, even for high school. I haven't talked with him in over a decade."

"And since then you've gone on to get a doctorate and teach at a university." A modest smile crossed her lips. Allen raised an eyebrow, looking at her in a new light. "Quite the accomplishment."

"Thank you." She broke his eye contact and went back to looking out the window. "It's hard though. Sometimes Bree feels like a mistake no one wants, and I try to express daily how she's my everything." Sadie's finger collected some condensation as it made its way around the glass. It was a mystery to him why watching her finger move around the edge of the glass was so captivating. She had such delicate fingers.

"I haven't seen Bree in the happiest of circumstances, but I believe you are doing an amazing job."

Sadie's lips twitched upward. "Thank you. And I'm sorry. I don't want to be one of those people who talk about their child the entire night."

"It's fine." Allen gave a reassuring smile. "I did ask about her, after all."

"What about you?" Sadie picked up her glass and took another sip. "I don't know much about you, either."

Allen tapped the table nervously. "I was married before." There was no soft way to put this, and he found he couldn't keep eye contact with her. "She and the baby both died five years ago. Complications with childbirth."

Sadie's jaw dropped. There was silence as the waitress came over with their food and placed it in front of them. Allen thanked the waitress while Sadie continued to stare at him.

"I don't know what to say." Sadie's voice was soft. "I don't know if there's *anything* to say, other than I'm so sorry you had to go through those experiences. That you're still going through it."

The utensils trembled in his hands as he began to cut into his chicken and potatoes. "Quite the heavy subjects we're talking about." He focused on his food, still refusing to meet Sadie's eyes. "Maybe we should talk about lighter things." Just as he suspected, he wasn't ready to talk about it in depth. Already it felt like he scraped at a fresh scab and felt it start to bleed.

"Yeah." Thankfully Sadie got the hint. "What made you want to be a college professor?"

He tried to smile as he talked about this much safer topic.

After dinner, they went skating, where Allen was impressed with her skills. He wasn't too shabby, though he took more tumbles than Sadie. By the sound of Sadie's laughter as they headed back to the car, he knew she loved it.

"I didn't know you skated so well," she said.

"I went all the time as a kid. Sadly, I'm out of practice. My hand can testify." Allen raised his injured hand.

"I'm impressed you kept moving after such a tumble." She turned and gasped when she saw his hand. "Your hand! I didn't realize how much it swelled up. I'll get you some ice when we get back to my place." Sadie brushed her hands over his swollen knuckles. He felt the fabric of her gloves against his numbing skin.

"I can always get some snow. Don't worry. This gives you a good story to tell Riley if he asks about the date," Allen replied.

She gave him a calculated look. "If I didn't want to go on a date with either of you, I could have gotten out of it."

A flutter of excitement swelled inside him. "So...you actually wanted to go on a date with me?"

"I said yes, didn't I?"

Stupid lovesick teenager. He couldn't control the grin on his face. "I mean, I didn't quite ask."

"No, but you were going to. I had a fun time tonight." Sadie looped her arm through his. "I didn't think of it as an excuse to escape Riley."

"Oh good." The lovesick teenager did a victory lap. They walked up to Allen's car. Snow began to fall again.

"'Scuse me," said a different voice. "Don't I know you?" He pointed a bruised and shaking finger at Sadie.

Allen and Sadie turned to see a short man stumble out of the parking lot. The hairs on the back of Allen's neck prickled. This man smelled drunk, and he didn't like the way he eyed Sadie.

"Sir, I don't know who you are. If you need assistance, I can call a cab for you." Allen was impressed with how calm Sadie sounded.

"Sadie." The man stepped closer. "You're the one *he's* after." The man kept moving forward at a slow pace.

Allen instinctively touched Sadie's elbow. How did he know her name? He glanced at her, but she looked as perplexed as him. "Who? Riley?"

"No." The man stepped under the streetlamp. The light revealed his mud-crusted clothes. "This man's name cannot be spoken here. If it is, the integrity of the world will crumble."

Allen took a step forward. "You need to go home."

The man's smirk ignited Allen's desire to protect Sadie. Allen placed himself in front of Sadie so the man looked at him instead. "I know you too, Allen. It's why *he* wants her." The man tried to look past Allen toward Sadie. "Because he knows it's how to get to you. Get to you, to get to *her*."

"What on earth are you talking about? Did Riley send you?" Allen's eyes narrowed. "If so, this is childish."

"No, but the same guy who sent Riley also sent me."

It took everything inside Allen to calmly lead Sadie toward the passenger door. "Get in the car and lock the doors." Since they stood by the passenger's door, he wanted to make sure she was safe inside before he tried to get in the car. Sadie fumbled for the door as Allen took a few steps forward.

"This is your last chance to walk away before we call the police," Allen said as Sadie got in and locked the doors of the car.

The man started laughing. "As soon as I'm arrested, I disappear." The man no longer looked drunk. He looked insane. "I am disposable. Servant of *him* to help capture *her*."

"You're not getting anywhere near Sadie." Allen found himself growling.

"Not Sadie. *Her*."

"Yeah, you enjoy talking gibberish." Allen raised his hands in case he needed to punch the man.

"I don't want to fight. I bring a message. Tell *her* we know about Josh, and we're up for the challenge."

"Stop talking nonsense! What's your real message?"

The man turned around and headed into the darkness. "Don't worry. The message is already sent." Allen blinked and the man blended into the night. A second later, Allen rushed to the other side of the car. Sadie unlocked the door, and he slid into the driver's side.

"Are you okay?" She sounded alarmed.

"Fine." Allen started up the car and backed out. "Are you?"

"He scared me."

"Did you hear his message about Josh?"

She nodded. "Let's get out of here."

Allen flexed his hands over the wheel and winced in pain. The whole time the drunk was talking to them, he forgot about his injury. It was badly swollen now. Allen drove quickly to her house, feeling like she would be safest locked away in her home. He was cautious, borderline paranoid, watching to see if any cars followed him too long or too close. It seemed like the drunk was done, but he wanted to make sure before he dropped her off.

"Thank you for a wonderful night," Sadie said.

"Sorry about the drunk at the end."

They got to the front porch and Sadie looked at him, hesitant and embarrassed. "Allen, there's something I want you to understand. Because of experiences I've gone through, with having Bree and everything, I don't get physical fast on dates. I want you to understand this, so you know how big of a deal this is for me. For what I'm about to do."

Before he said anything, she stood on her tiptoes and kissed his cheek. "Come in and I'll get you some ice."

Allen couldn't respond. It was a simple kiss, nowhere near the passion of most, but it still left his brain foggy. Sadie had the door open and pulled him into her house before he came back to reality. On the couch in the front room sat Bree and Josh, eating popcorn. They both looked up when Sadie and Allen walked in.

"A movie this late on a school night, Josh?" Sadie asked.

"It's why I'm her favorite uncle."

"You're her only uncle."

Josh chuckled. "Yeah."

With a roll of her eyes, Sadie walked into the kitchen. Allen watched her go with a small smile on his face.

"What happened to your hand?" Allen turned to see Bree peeking over the couch, staring at his knuckles.

"Slipped on the ice." It was difficult to wiggle his swollen fingers, but he wasn't sure what else to do. Bree shrugged and turned back to the movie. A thought struck Allen that maybe he should tell Josh about the drunk, since the message was about him, but he didn't want to scare Bree. Josh turned to look at him, his face neutral.

"Allen?" Sadie called from the kitchen. He headed toward her voice and Josh followed. As soon as Allen reached Sadie, she handed him a sandwich bag of ice. He thanked her and placed it against his knuckles.

"You two okay?" Josh's voice was a low whisper.

The thought still lingered to share with Josh what happened, but Allen was hesitant. Instead, Sadie leaned forward. "Do you know any alcoholics?"

Confusion flickered across Josh's face. "Alcoholics? No."

"He said he knows who you are and accepts the challenge, whatever that means." The confusion melted, and Allen thought Josh looked scared.

"Josh?" Sadie asked.

"Josh is a popular name." He put an arm around his sister and squeezed. "He must have me confused with someone else."

With a slap from Sadie, Josh's grip loosened. "If you know something, you should call the police. I didn't like him at all," Sadie said.

Josh let her go. "I told you, I don't know many alcoholics. At least, not any sober enough to give that kind of threat."

A particularly nasty look from Sadie made Josh give her a lame smile. Sadie picked up a cooling rack of cookies and offered one to Allen. He placed his hand on the table and situated the ice so it balanced on his knuckles before he took a cookie with his free hand, thanking her. "I'm going to check on Bree." She went to the front room.

With Sadie gone, Allen turned to Josh. "What are you hiding?"

"Nothing. I truly don't know who he was."

Allen craned his head to see Sadie leaning over the couch chatting with Bree. "Will they be safe tonight?"

"Tonight, yes."

"Is there anything I can do?" Allen asked.

Any semblance of a smile disappeared from Josh's face. "Keep an eye on her at work. Just in case." Allen had no idea what Josh did to get threats like that. True, it wasn't Allen's business, unless Sadie or her daughter were in danger. He hoped Josh knew what he was doing.

Sadie sat on the couch, eating popcorn with Bree. When they were situated, Bree rested her head against Sadie's shoulder. Allen took a small bite of the cookie. He stopped chewing from the shock. This had to be one of the most delicious cookies he had ever eaten.

A quiet laugh escaped Josh as he gave Allen a nudge. "She doesn't give her cookies to anyone unless she likes them. They are powerful."

§ § §

Bree was on her back, staring at the ceiling. It was well past midnight. Though she should be asleep, her mind refused to shut off. It terrified her enough to go to school. She didn't want to be scared to come home, either.

The bed rustled beneath her as she turned around, trying to get some sleep. Every time she closed her eyes, she saw the look on Allen's face when he watched her mom enter the kitchen. He loved her. Bree never got the uncomfortable feeling she did with Reggie, but the selfish part of her didn't want to share. She and her mom were fine without another man potentially ruining their lives again. What if he broke her heart?

Another twenty minutes went by before she had to talk. Throwing back the covers, she slid out of her bed and crept out of her room. The light in Josh's room was on, but she paid it no mind. She cracked open her mom's door. Inside she heard her mom humming. Bree froze at the door, the strangeness hitting her. Her mom was happy and *humming*.

Her mom stopped when she noticed the door opening. "Bree, come in. What is it?"

Bree hesitated so long her mom sat up and turned on the lamp. The sudden bright light made her blink multiple times. "I want to know...how was your date?" Bree asked.

"It was lovely."

There was another pause. It wasn't awkward, but Bree found she had a hard time trying to voice her concerns. "How was the guy?"

"Allen's a wonderful gentleman."

The sincerity was clear in her mom's voice. It was difficult not to pass instant judgment on the guy. She knew little about him and felt conflicted for wanting to hate him. He was, after all, barging into their lives. But he made her mom hum!

"Bree, what's this really about? Are you okay with me dating someone?" Her mom gave her the look. At least her mom knew how to start the conversation Bree was too scared to have.

"Yes, of course." After a pause, Bree asked, "Do you promise it won't be like Holly? Do you promise not to abandon me?"

"Bree, look at me." Her mom watched her close. Bree felt a tear fall down her cheek. "Why would I abandon you now? I'm your mother, and above everything, I will protect you. I'm making sure Allen is a good fit for my family, which includes you. He's respectful, and I like him."

It was a simple nod from Bree, but she tried with all her soul to believe it. For the most part, she did. She tried not to listen to the small, doubting part of her. "I think I'll go to bed now."

Her mom kissed her cheek. Bree walked back to her room. Before she entered, she saw a shadow under Josh's door and the lights turn off before she heard him go to bed. With a yawn, Bree figured she ought to do the same.

CHAPTER 14

SOMETHING MUST HAVE possessed Jim to knock on my door at six-thirty in the morning. I opened the door, again in my bathrobe, this time squinting in the early morning light. "Really Jim?" My eyes were still half closed, and my voice slurred from being woken up.

"I wanted to drop this off before I went into work today. I don't want the others seeing it. I read what happened on Sadie and Allen's date. Are you okay?"

Seeing the package in his hands made me feel more awake than if he had shot caffeine into my bloodstream. He hadn't offered it, so I didn't reach for it. I didn't want to look too eager.

"It shook me up a bit." I still eyed the package. "Devin called since you were out of town. He advised me to stop narrating until you returned. He wanted to talk about more security. He's afraid the Rogue is doing things earlier than expected." Jim nodded, not taking his eye off the package. I stifled a yawn, but it didn't help. Jim must have known I was exhausted.

"Is that your brother's manuscript?" Hopefully my cue would remind him to hand it over so I could start studying it.

Jim stared at me. "Yes. There need to be some rules. First, do *not* tell Devin. If he finds out, we'll both be in trouble."

My eagerness slipped away. From the sound of his voice, he was having second thoughts. "Is this your first time breaking rules?"

"Funny." The humor was noticeably absent in his voice. "Next, don't get overwhelmed."

"Too late." My fingers inched toward the package, but he pulled it farther away.

"I'm serious, Junior. The experiences Kyle went through were awful. Every other night I had to drag him out of a bar. He became an alcoholic because of what the Rogue did in his story."

I remained silent, feeling my stomach twist inside me. It hurt Jim to do this. He was afraid for me. "I'll take care of myself."

The hard stare Jim gave me made me drop my hands to my sides. "What have you done since Devin told you to take a break?"

My weekend consisted of pouring over notes and journal entries I wrote while under Professor Andrew's mentorship. I wanted to see if anything back then would give me clues as to who he became and what he might do. I made notes of the notes, and it consumed my time. I hugged myself, blaming it on the chill, but it was now the middle of the summer. The early morning was comfortably warm.

My lack of an answer didn't please Jim. I quickly thought of something. "I'm preparing."

Jim's eyes darkened. "You may think this only affects you, but don't you know what it's doing to the Guardians?"

"Jim, I'm fine."

"No, you're not. This has turned into an obsession. The more you cling to this, the more power the Rogue has over you."

He sounded like Dr. Webb in my last session. I felt embarrassed and ashamed to look at him, so I studied the door. My gut told me they were both right, and I was mortified to acknowledge it. I was destroying myself over this. Why couldn't I stop?

"You are withering away like Kyle and Lydia."

I swallowed, not sure how to react. It must have hurt to return home and see all the pictures, to see his mother, and to sit at dinner and have one spot remain empty. To think deep inside a part of him failed his brother.

Stuck in the middle of the dilemma, I didn't notice what Jim saw. He was right. I started slipping. My work came before my well-being every time. My clothes got baggier, and I didn't care anymore about sleep. My temper bubbled closer to the surface than usual.

"I'm afraid if I give you this, it will feed your frustrations." Jim looked at the package in his hands.

My mouth went dry. What Jim said made sense, but the package might hold clues to help me get past the Rogue. I feared losing the manuscript, but I didn't have a good enough reason for him to trust me with it. What he said came eerily close to how I'd act if he gave it to me.

"I promise if you give me the manuscript right now, I will put it on my desk and go back to sleep for a few more hours." I made sure to let him read my face so he knew I wasn't lying. He scrutinized me, but I didn't turn away.

"And what about after today?"

I was more hesitant. "I'll always eat something before I read it."

Jim gave me one more look before he reluctantly placed the package in my hands. "Just…be careful."

"Thanks Jim." My fingers closed around the package. Jim started down the stairs, and I almost closed the door when he called out my name. I stopped and opened the door again.

"I read over your story. This is around the time when…" He slowed to a stop. I waited. "My first order of business today is to discuss with the other Guardians more protection around the apartment. Keep sending reports and try not to go anywhere unless you have to. And let me know when you do."

"I will." I tried my hardest to not sound frightened.

"Devin expects you to start narrating now that I'm back, but wait until we've got the protection in place. Go back to bed."

I nodded. He smiled, but it was the kind of smile only his lips believed in. Stuffing his hands in his pockets, he left for his car and I closed the door. When I reached my office, I cleared off a place on my desk for the package. I untied the string around the paper. Jim's family must be traditionalists. A manuscript tied up in brown paper and string?

What genre did his brother write? I forgot to ask. My hands itched to pull out a fresh notebook and pen to start taking notes, but I made a promise. If I looked at the manuscript a second longer, I would open it and start working. Instead, I closed my office door and headed back to bed.

§ § §

For a week, Bree didn't see Holly on the bus. Every morning she was afraid she wouldn't see her at school either. She assumed Reggie wouldn't hurt her, but she still wandered the halls every morning, trying to pick out the familiar blonde hair. She caught glimpses of her friend, and saw her in classes, but Holly treated her like a stranger. Their friendship hung by an imaginary thread only Bree believed in.

Holly ignored Bree's texts. Giving up all contact was out of the question, but Bree also didn't want to be obnoxious.

It seemed impossible to close her locker without slamming it, even if she wasn't in a slamming mood. When she turned, she noticed something in Holly's locker. She slung her bag over her shoulder and peered into the small slits. Little papers stuck out of her locker, meant to tumble out the moment it opened. It was stuffed so full, Bree easily pulled out one of the pieces of paper and saw the word *slut* written on it. Her eyes widened.

"So you found our trap."

The paper crumpled in Bree's fist. Aubrielle was there, her arm wrapped around Stud. "This is wrong, Aubrielle, and you know it. She used to be your friend."

"Apparently she dropped you, too."

Bree winced and pretended the sentence didn't hurt.

"Have you seen her today?" Aubrielle laughed. "*Slut* isn't far off from what she's up to. Check the lockers downstairs. I doubt she's moved much. She's quite occupied, if you know what I mean."

Horror seized Bree, and she sprinted downstairs, ignoring the no running in the halls rule. She froze in her spot when she saw Holly making out with Reggie. "Holly!"

Holly jumped, turning from Reggie. She laughed when she saw Bree's face. "What's the matter, Bree? Jealous?" She almost returned to Reggie, but Bree took another step forward.

"Stop." Bree wanted to say something more, but fear stopped her sentence short.

"Mm, you are jealous." Holly returned to Reggie.

"Where's your boyfriend, Bree?" Aubrielle walked down the stairs, holding Stud's hand. "Oh, right. You've never been kissed. You still think they have cooties."

Anger and humiliation surged through Bree as she spun toward Aubrielle. "You don't know what's going on."

"Ah, it must be me." Reggie tried to pull away from Holly, but succeeded only after he peeled her hands off him. "You don't like me. I'd almost say you're afraid." He got closer and closer. Bree felt like a child, backing away with every step he took forward. She didn't know why, but it was instinctual. The look in his eyes scared her.

"Afraid. Like you were as a child." Reggie's voice was quiet, but impossible to ignore. "When your mom was jobless, no steady income, and you lived in your uncle's basement. The pipes hissed, and you thought someone or something would grab you in the night."

The room felt hazy, and her breathing increased. The wall stopped her from backing away from him, and she found herself trapped in a corner. She knew how childish those fears were. Thinking about them now made her groan at how silly she felt. However, Reggie knowing about them with unmistakable detail made her sick to her stomach.

"You can't possibly know that."

Reggie smirked. "So young. You didn't mention your fears to your mom, because every time she looks at you, it reminds her of the mistake you are."

Bree's eyes widened. These were not secrets she blabbed at slumber parties. They weren't even secrets she told her mom. Those insecurities she kept to herself. "You can't..." Bree couldn't finish her thought. Reggie reached out and took Holly's hand.

"No one wants you, Bree," he whispered as he walked away.

"Bye, Bree." Holly didn't hear anything Reggie said. She couldn't have. Their friendship may have been in question, but Holly wouldn't allow someone to treat her so nastily. Aubrielle snickered and walked away with Stud as though proud she created such drama.

Bree covered her mouth, hyperventilating, and staying in the corner Reggie backed her into. Her vision swam in front of her, and panic started to take control.

"Hey, are you alright?" a girl asked.

"Fine," Bree choked out before stumbling away and heading outside. The brick wall supported her as she pulled out her cellphone. Bree's hands shook as she called her mom. The phone rang, and Bree willed her mom to answer.

When no one answered, Bree glanced at the clock on her phone and groaned. Her mom was teaching a class and always had her phone off. Without hesitating, she dialed Josh's number, hoping he was off the pain meds and not sleeping.

After three rings, she heard a chipper, "Hello?"

She almost cried in relief. "Josh? Could you pick me up from school?" The fear she felt wasn't something she bothered hiding. After all, it might spur Josh to come get her as soon as possible.

"Sure, what's up? Is something wrong?"

Tears were running down her face. "I'm...I'm not..."

"Give me a minute to get dressed, and I'll be over."

"Okay." Bree's hands still shook as she ran her fingers through her hair. She didn't want to hang up. In a perfect scenario, he'd stay on the other end until he got here so she felt the security of simply knowing Josh was there. The late bell rang as she reluctantly hung up. As she sat in her first class, she did nothing but stare at the clock.

After an excruciatingly long thirteen and a half minutes, an office aide came with a note for Bree. She gathered her things and left, refusing to cry in front of her classmates. As soon as she saw Josh in the office, she choked him in a hug. Josh hugged her back.

"Take me home, please," she whispered.

Josh must have heard the fear in her voice, because he nodded without making a joke. It was a struggle for him to sign a paper with his casted hand, saying a responsible guardian took Bree home. In any other circumstance, Bree would have giggled, but not now. True, she already felt safer in Josh's presence, but Reggie's encounter was still too fresh in her mind. They walked out of school. It felt warm despite all the snow. Clouds covered the sky, threatening to dump even more snow on the ground.

"Did you take the bus?" Bree wanted to think of something else besides what happened. She looked up at the clouds, seeing the darkness overhead.

"No, I drove."

Bree frowned. "With a cast? Is that legal?"

"You sounded scared. I wanted to make sure you were okay. Besides, I treat it better than they do in physical therapy." Josh put his arm around her as they headed for his car. "What happened today?"

The conversation couldn't be avoided, so she plowed ahead. "You know the new kid?"

Josh stopped walking and slowly turned to her. "Yes."

Before she knew it, Bree repeated everything Reggie told her, even the insecurities she never told her mom. It made her shake and tremble all over again. Josh listened, his mouth dropping the more she talked.

"You should know by now your mother would never give you up."

"I know." Bree tried to rub the goosebumps away. "But how did Reggie know I'm a mistake?"

"You are not a mistake. Your mom loves you. Whatever that silly boy tried to do, don't let him scare you. Your mom would give her life for you, and so would I." Bree felt the tears come. She bit her lip to keep them from falling, but it didn't work.

"Come here." Josh opened his arms. "Everything's going to be okay."

The hug felt safe and warm, exactly what Bree needed to feel at that moment. He held her close, and she felt the fear disperse. She didn't want to let go in case the fear came back. Tears spilled from her eyes.

"Today we'll relax and do whatever we want. What do you think?" Josh said.

"Sounds perfect." Bree glanced at his casted arm again, excitement bubbling inside her. "Maybe I should drive?"

Josh gave a sheepish grin as he dug in his pockets for the car keys. "Let's see. Casted uncle, barely sixteen-year-old niece. Options are not pretty."

"Did I ever tell you that you're my favorite uncle?"

A laugh burst out of him and to her surprise, he tossed her the keys. "Smooth Bree. Smooth."

CHAPTER 15

D R. Webb opened the folded piece of paper and nodded her approval. "Good. You're eating more. Your sleeping isn't great, but still better than it was."

"Yeah." I stayed true to my promise to Jim of making sure to eat before I studied his brother's manuscript. "I do a lot of narrating at night, and have a hard time pulling away."

"And the antidepressants?"

"I think they're working."

"Excellent." She pulled her notebook toward her. "Do you have any concerns?"

I leaned back in the comfortable chair. "Tons."

"Well, what are you worried about the most?" she asked.

I closed my eyes. "The Rogue is freaking my characters out. Jim says it will get worse. I'm not ready for this."

The smile from Dr. Webb was strangely comforting. "You know the majority of the infiltrations are success stories, right?"

"I know the numbers, but I bet Jim wishes the percentage was better."

Dr. Webb's smile turned sad. "You're right. But I believe in you, Junior. I believe you'll make it through."

I didn't say anything. In my heart, I hoped Dr. Webb was right.

The next two days blurred together. I'm sure Devin wondered why I took a break from narrating, but I didn't care. My whole attention, besides the therapy trip, was in Kyle's manuscript. His story broke my heart. It started out humorous with amazing potential. At page four, when the Rogue introduced new characters, everything humorous went out the window. The pattern was similar to my own. The Rogue came in slowly and used dark threats to make the main character uncomfortable.

My heart sank as I realized the next thing the Rogue planned in my story, if the pattern stayed, was to kidnap the main character. I would either disappear like Kyle and Lydia or fight it and get away like so many others. Jim authorized two guards to stand by my door, with a possibility of more if needed.

Toward the end of Kyle's book, the voice of the writing got sloppy and sluggish, reflective of the drinking habit Jim mentioned. His character died in a way which made me almost throw up. The story ended abruptly with his death, and it broke my heart. Reading the lethargic narration brought a heavy weight to my heart. This story broke Kyle as much as it did his characters.

§ § §

"Good discussion, everyone." Allen collected his students' essays as they began gathering their things. "I'll see you next week." He answered a few questions while he erased the white board of a complex diagram before he left the classroom and headed up the stairs to his office.

The stack of books landed on his desk as Allen sat in his chair, rubbing his temples. It was a long day, but classes were over. The essays needed to be corrected, but he could relax for a moment. He looked out his window, and even though he didn't see her, he automatically thought of Sadie. The other day, after pepping himself up, he called to ask if she wanted to go on another date and was delighted when she agreed. Maybe he'd meet Bree under better circumstances.

A half-hour into correcting essays, he heard a knock at his door. "Come in." Allen circled a sentence and jotted a note in the side.

The door opened, but he didn't hear footsteps. Curious, Allen turned to see Riley leaning against the door frame, his arms folded with an envelope in his gloved hand.

"Good afternoon," Riley said as he strolled into Allen's office, keeping an eye on the window.

With a tap of his red pen, Allen tried to focus on the essays. "Do you need something?"

"I'm waiting for Sadie to go back to her office." Riley stretched and sat down in the empty seat. "You have a better view."

"She has back to back classes."

"Of course *you* would know." There was a second of silence before Riley pulled the chair closer to the window, sat down, and began tapping the note against his other hand.

"You have no business in my office." It was a struggle to keep the anger out of his voice.

"A simple colleague to colleague chat."

"I'm not helping you stalk Sadie."

When Riley kicked his feet up, resting them on Allen's desk, Allen resisted the strong urge to push them off. "How was your date with her last week? I never got to ask," Riley said.

"Fine." Allen refused to give any more details and continued to ignore Riley. He turned the page of the essay and busied himself with correcting.

"You know, I met her a few hours ago. It was unfortunate. My pencil stuck out of my book, and we ran into each other, quite literally. It split her skin a bit. Drew blood. But I think she's all right."

The conversation made Allen slowly raise his head, giving Riley a curious look. "Why are you telling me this?"

There was no answer, simply a smirk from Riley. Allen struggled to focus on the essays. He knew it wasn't fair for students if he didn't have a clear mind while grading, but he needed the busy work. Out of the corner of his eye, he saw Riley sit up straighter. "Ah, there she is."

Instinctively, Allen glanced up from his work, watching Sadie follow the sidewalk until she disappeared into the building. Her hood was lowered, so all Allen saw was her dark hair against her red coat. Riley continued to tap the note against his pointer finger as he stared at the building.

Sadie might be in her office for another hour, and Riley wasn't moving. "Is there anything else you need my office for?" Allen hoped Riley heard the sarcasm in his voice.

"No, no, I'm about—" Riley's cell phone went off. He checked the text. "Yep, I'm done. I wanted to give you this." The note Riley played with the entire time was placed in Allen's hands.

Puzzlement filled Allen's mind as he opened the unsealed envelope and pulled out the note card. It was plastered with cutout magazine letters that spelled out a simple message.

Riley, if you want to see Sadie again, exchange one million dollars for her.

The puzzlement deepened into confusion. "What's this?" Allen asked.

"It's a ransom note." For some reason Riley faked hurt and innocence.

"I found it in my office just now. Someone kidnapped Sadie." Riley took back the note as Allen stared at him dumbfounded.

"We just saw her."

"I don't know how you did it, either." Nothing Riley said or did made sense. Riley pulled out a handkerchief. A warning bell inside Allen was going off, but he couldn't understand it enough to act. Riley grabbed Allen's water bottle and dabbed the handkerchief with it before running it across the gum of the letter.

"What are you talking about?" Confusion turned into alarm. "Sadie's fine. I didn't do anything to her."

"All I know is when the police check her office, she'll be gone, and when I give them this note, they will find fingerprints on it." Riley sealed the envelope. "Your fingerprints."

Allen's face turned white. Time stood still as a million questions exploded in his mind. Was this some sort of horrible joke? Why was Riley setting him up to get arrested? Riley didn't like him, but kidnapping? And for what?

Adrenaline coursed through his veins. He tried to snatch the envelope back from Riley, but Riley laughed and held it just out of reach. The desire to see Sadie, to make sure it was simply a sick joke, filled his soul. He flew down the stairs and out of the English building, forgetting his coat. The ice and snow slowed him down, but he kept running past confused students as he threw open the doors of the math building.

"Sadie." The board by the main office listed all the teachers and their office number. His hands trembled as he desperately looked for her name. "Three-oh-four. Room three-oh-four."

Maybe the elevator would have been faster, but his adrenaline demanded he move. Instead, he took the stairs three at a time, ran down the hall, and threw open her office door. The chaos he saw made his breath catch in his throat. Papers were scattered everywhere, and blood was on the edge of the desk. The computer screen was cracked, the chair tipped over, a vase was broken, and little rocks were scattered everywhere. This was a nightmare. Why? Why would Riley do this?

He heard Riley making a scolding sound. "Returning to the scene of the crime?" Riley pulled off his gloves and stuck them in his coat pocket. "Interesting."

Grabbing Riley by the front of his shirt, Allen pinned him against the wall in less than a second. "Where is she!"

Despite the situation, Riley snickered. The anger surged inside Allen, but he resisted punching him in the face. "Keep it up, Allen." Riley's voice sounded hoarse. "You'll make yourself look guilty."

"You know perfectly well I didn't kidnap her!"

Riley threw Allen off him with a strength he wouldn't expect. If Allen hadn't grabbed the edge of Sadie's desk, he would have fallen over.

"For now, it's my words against yours. However, when the police read the emails from Sadie which say how scared she is of you, my words will carry a lot more weight. It might be more convincing when they find some of Sadie's blood in your apartment. She thought you were nice, but something happened on the date last week. What was it? Oh, yes. Your temper. You punched a drunk because he asked for change. They will find the drunk, of course, and he will give the full account."

The calmness in Riley's demeanor added the fuel to Allen's fear. He tried hard to keep in control. "We've done nothing to you! Why are you doing this? Bring her back!" Allen demanded.

"You better run," Riley said. "The police will start looking for you soon."

Allen stared at Riley angry and flabbergasted. "I don't even know you, yet you're willing to get me arrested for a crime you committed? Why do you hate me so much?"

Riley's smile seemed too calm for the situation. "I'm taking orders."

"Orders from *whom*?"

The door opened and Riley went into his act. "Call the police! He kidnapped Sadie and tried to hurt me when I confronted him about it!" Riley pointed at Allen.

"What's going on!" one of the math professors demanded.

"Call the police! He kidnapped Sadie!" Riley yelled again.

Panic rose inside Allen's chest as he tried to think of some way to get around this, but the evidence mounted against him. Allen's prints were on her desk, and he suspected his would be the only ones they found on the ransom note. The emails. The blood. What more did Riley have up his sleeve? Allen turned around and ran.

He sprinted down the hall, flew down the stairs, and found himself out into the open, frigid air.

§ § §

Twenty miles away, after returning with Josh from the ice cream shop back to her house, Bree's cell phone went off. She assumed it was her mom, asking why she called, but it was Holly's mother. Holly didn't arrive to her next class, and no one had seen her since the incident in the hall. Calling Bree was her last chance. Maybe Holly was with her? Bree dropped the last of her banana split.

CHAPTER 16

A S SOON AS the device stopped, I tore the headset off and threw it against the computer. It missed the screen by inches and hit the wall. My hands trembled as I covered my mouth, backing away from the computer until I couldn't go any farther. Panic robbed me of logical thought. The Rogue didn't do this in Kyle's manuscript. He kidnapped main characters, not side characters for ransom.

My phone went off. I crawled to my desk, ruffled through papers, and picked up the phone. Jim was calling.

"Junior," he said when I picked up. "Are you okay?"

"He's got them!" My voice trembled. "He'll use them to get my main characters and then kill them! What do I do!"

"Stay where you are. I'm coming." I heard something fall, clattering to the ground, and a door open and close. "Stay on the line. I'm getting Devin, and we're coming over." The longer I stayed in my office, the more I hyperventilated.

"Devin!" Jim said. "Call one of the guards around Junior's apartment. Make sure they're aware of what's going on."

"What *is* going on?" Devin asked. I heard more scuffling as Jim filled Devin in. Devin grabbed whatever he needed and followed Jim.

"Junior, you still there?" Jim asked.

"Yes." My voice sounded awful. Devin talked into his phone, snapping orders at the guards positioned around my apartment.

"We'll be there in two minutes," Jim said. Tears ran down my face as I stumbled toward the kitchen. I opened the cupboard under the sink and climbed inside to hide.

"Everything's going to be okay, Junior." Jim's voice sounded panicky.

"He's got Sadie and Holly." I moaned, hugging my knees. "I don't know what to do."

I heard them shut the car door. Jim heard me sob. It was pointless to hide. If the Rogue came, he'd find me because of how loud I cried. I kept mumbling how he had them and I didn't know what to do. Jim repeatedly told me to stay calm and for Devin to drive faster.

This would destroy Bree. As far as she was concerned, Allen would be at fault, and she wouldn't trust him. The mistrust would break apart Sadie and Allen's relationship, if they ever found each other again. The Rogue hit my story hard. Getting Bree to trust Allen at this point would be almost impossible.

Jim and Devin threw open my apartment door. I abandoned my hiding place and ran to them, throwing my arms around Jim, sobbing into his perfect suit coat. Jim placed his arms around my shoulders. Somehow I knew if he let go, every ounce of my stability would slip away.

§ § §

Devin, Jim, and the two guards searched through the house until every corner had been checked. Jim took the opportunity to hide Kyle's manuscript in his briefcase. Dr. Webb came over to let me talk through my troubles and did her best to calm my fears. Most of my fears were tied to my characters, and she didn't know much of my story. I heard her talk with Jim and Devin, their voices too quiet to overhear. She left close to midnight.

I don't know how long the day lasted. Exhaustion consumed me, but I couldn't sleep. Somewhere around three or four in the morning, Jim knocked on my bedroom door. I didn't answer. Instead, I continued to stare out the window at a single lamppost cutting through the darkness. The single sliver of light had all my attention, because I couldn't bring myself to focus on anything else. Jim poked his head inside before walking into my room. His suit coat and vest were off, and his tie was loose.

He placed a glass in my hands, and I felt the warmth before I realized it was milk. "I knew you weren't asleep," Jim said.

"This actually helps people?"

Jim shrugged. "It helps me."

The idea of warm milk never appealed to me, but I was willing to try almost anything—short of someone whacking me in the back of the head—to shut my brain off.

"Why aren't you and Devin asleep?" I asked.

"Vince requested a Guardian be present at all times. For these first couple of days, Devin and I will both stay here, then it will switch out between the Guardians for a while. You need to rest for a week or two. Devin and I will form a strategy to help those in your story."

I tasted the milk before allowing myself a long drink. "You don't know my characters like I do."

"Eventually the three of us will work together, but right now you need rest."

"What about your other work?"

"Vince made this top priority. Devin's given his predictions of where the Rogue might go next to Grace, and she'll pick up the search."

I nodded, draining the last of the warm milk. Jim took the glass back. My attention reverted briefly to the lamppost again. The light of the city drove some of the darkness away, but it still seemed unusually dark.

"Rest, Junior. Let us worry about everything for a while."

There were tears in my eyes when I looked at him. I thought I cried them all out, but some still lingered. "Why is he doing this to me?"

Jim put his hand on my shoulder. He looked like he wanted to say something, but nothing came out. Instead, he patted my shoulder and brought his hand to his side. "Guards are around the apartment. Devin and I will sleep in the front room and start planning. Get some sleep. You're safe." Jim gave a lame smile. Verbal comfort clearly wasn't his forte.

As Jim left my room, I remembered Kyle and Lydia. It didn't help my anxiety. I turned to my bed, which reminded me how much I needed to sleep. The milk seemed to do the trick. My eyelids felt heavy, and the exhaustion overtook me.

§ § §

After a week of rest, solid meals made by Grace inside me, and plans created by myself and two of the best narrators I knew, I felt ready to narrate again.

"Remember the notes." Jim handed me a notebook full of his, Devin's, and my own scribblings. "Use Josh. He's your best help. Make sure Josh tells her multiple times about how good Allen is."

"Make sure Bree is confident she can trust Josh, or else it will fall right on its face," Devin added. "Don't be afraid to pause the narration a lot if you need to get your thoughts in order."

"Thanks guys." I glanced through the notes.

Jim watched me. "There is no shame in narrating a quick scene and then letting it rest for another couple weeks." My nerves were jumbled, but after lots of rest and eating, I felt eager to get back to narrating.

"I'm heading back to headquarters. The guards and Devin will stay here. I trust these men and women with my life," Jim said.

"Thanks Jim." I hugged the notebook. "I assume you'll track the story at your office?"

"Yes. Any time it's in motion, we'll both be watching."

"Got special permission from Vince. It'd be nice if you don't narrate too late at night." Devin flashed a smile.

Jim left and I walked into my office. I sat down and stared at my narration device before taking a deep breath, and then I placed the headset over my ears.

§§§

Bree noticed how Josh kept glancing at her to make sure she was okay. She put on a good face for him, but she knew he saw through her fake smiles. The kidnappings happened two days ago, and they had still heard nothing. Bree stayed home with Josh, away from the craze. It was almost eleven at night, but she didn't want to go to bed. She hugged her knees and stared at the newspaper in front of her, the kidnapping still on the front page.

"Bree. Are you okay?"

"Why did he kidnap my mom?" Her eyes were red, and her cheeks tear stained. "She trusted him. She liked him. Why do men always hurt her?"

Josh sat down across the table from her. "Allen would not kidnap her."

Bree hugged her knees tighter, her fingers brushing against the table. "What if he kidnapped Holly, too? Maybe it's why they can't find her or Reggie." She felt so exhausted with everything going on in her life. Her best friend and mom getting kidnapped served as the mold-covered cherry on top.

"You're making an unfair accusation, Bree. Allen didn't know Holly or Reggie. Hey." Josh gave her a small smile. "I know these past few days have been hard, and I'm proud of how you've held up. Stay strong. Something will come of it."

"I want my mom back safe."

He ruffled her hair with his casted hand. "I know, kid. Believe me, Allen did not do this to her."

"Everything points to him, Josh."

"Not everything."

Bree frowned. "But the evidence. He's guilty!"

Josh shook his head. "He is a model citizen, with the worst thing on his record being a speeding ticket. A person like him doesn't wake up one day and decide to kidnap a person. Not in the way the news describes. They are struggling to find dirt on Allen. He didn't do this."

Bree's frown deepened. She believed Josh in so many things. It seemed weird and unnatural not to believe him in this. As much as Bree didn't want to admit it, Holly was right when she called Bree out on her mistrust of men. It was deeply seeded, as was her trust in Josh. An internal struggle began. "Then why is Allen running?"

Josh scratched his cast. A couple of weeks and the cast would be off, or so Bree heard. "Maybe because people have already made up their minds about him, and no one will believe him." Josh watched her carefully before glancing at his watch. "I think it's time for you to be in bed. I promised a friend I'd meet up with someone. I'll be gone for a few hours. Will you be okay?"

Bree gave him a weird look but nodded. Where was Josh going at eleven at night? She didn't think she'd ever understand the bachelor mindset. "Be safe, Josh. Please."

"I will."

§ § §

The sky got lighter. Allen hoped the sun would warm him up when it finally decided to rise. He was in and out of a restless sleep in a wooded area of a park. It was now day three since the kidnapping, and he ran as far as possible. He didn't dare stop. It felt so surreal.

He felt clammy and hadn't had a good night's sleep since it happened. The adrenaline was gone, replaced with grogginess. There were too many questions he needed answered and not enough mental capacity to begin to understand. Why did Riley want to ruin his life? It couldn't possibly be because he liked Sadie, too. Riley had to know Sadie would never find this level of extremism attractive. The thought of Riley trying to get with Sadie filled him with a rage that drove away the grogginess for a moment. As soon as he stopped thinking about it, the exhaustion returned tenfold.

Riley had to have a different motive. What would cause a perfect stranger to decide to frame him for kidnapping? No logical reason came to him, other than Riley being legitimately crazy. But if he was crazy, how did the university clear him to teach?

A hand covered Allen's mouth, which made his eyes snap open. Someone had snuck up on him without his knowledge, and it terrified him. He saw Josh and his heart sank. Of course Josh would be looking for him.

Josh put a finger to his lips and looked around the park. Who Josh was looking for was a mystery to Allen. It was too early and too cold for any sane person to be out. "I'm not going to turn you in." Josh turned back to Allen. "I know you didn't kidnap Sadie."

Allen stared at Josh in disbelief. This had to be a trick. There was no way Josh believed he was innocent. Josh took his hand away from Allen's mouth.

"I'm taking you back to Sadie's house." Josh extended his hand to help Allen up. "I don't know what's going to happen, but there's safety in numbers."

The grogginess took its toll as Allen stared at the extended hand. Did Josh have an ulterior motive? "Her place is crawling with policemen, all looking for me." Maybe it was Josh's plan. He'd lull Allen back with a false sense of security so he wouldn't struggle.

"I know Riley had something to do with this," Josh said.

"You know Riley?"

"No time for questions. Come back to the house."

Allen didn't know what made him follow. His brain must have been groggy from the running, the lack of sleep, and lack of heat. Whether Josh turned him in or was true to his word, Allen was sick of running. Either way, he would hopefully get a meal.

§ § §

"Knock, knock," said a familiar voice.

I stopped the device and turned around to see Grace walk in with my lunch. She set the tray on my desk next to the device. "Lunch already?" I asked.

"Sure is! How are things going?" she asked.

"Josh convinced Allen to go with him. I'm worried about how Bree will react, but Josh can be the mediator between Allen and Bree."

"Sounds excellent." Grace handed me a fork. "Take a break, enjoy your lunch, and don't stress."

"Thank you, Grace. You're amazing."

She hummed as she headed out of the room. I ate the salad, which tasted delicious. Anything she made was wonderful. I glanced at the screen. Allen needed to be with Josh and Bree. Most importantly, my co-main characters needed Josh's protection. He was gifted to help them from anything the Rogue threw at them.

I scanned through my notes again as I ate. This next part would be complicated. Somehow, Bree needed to trust Allen, even though her instinct was to distrust guys, especially guys dating Sadie. If Bree saw how Josh trusted Allen, maybe it could work. It needed to work. I scarfed down the last of the salad and turned back to the device.

CHAPTER 17

BREE YAWNED, SAT up, and stretched. Sunlight peeked through her curtains. It was another day of not going to school. No one blamed her, not when her mom and best friend were missing.

It was a pleasant discovery to find she slept at all. She didn't hear Josh come back from whatever he was doing, but she knew he was back because she heard the shower going. After getting dressed, she walked out of her room and into the kitchen. Josh hummed while he cooked. Overly well-done bacon wafted through the house.

Josh moved some darkening hash browns around with the spatula. "Good morning, Bree. Sleep well?"

She moved a blanket on the couch before she sat down. "Well enough." She yawned, rubbing her head. The shower shut off, which made her blink.

"Wait." Bree stood and finally noticed three plates on the table. Josh set down a huge pan of burnt eggs along with a plate of blackened bacon and hash browns. "Who else is here?"

There was no smile on Josh's face. "Promise me you'll listen to him."

It was the first time in her life that Bree gave her uncle a dark glare. "Are you telling me you brought my mother's *kidnapper* into this house?" Bree stiffened. "I'm calling the police." She reached for her cell phone in her pocket.

In an instant, Josh was next to her and grabbed her wrist. "He didn't kidnap your mom. Hear him out first."

Bree returned to giving her uncle another dark look. "I don't need my phone. I only need to scream and they'll hear."

There was some curiosity mingled with fear in Josh's eyes. "Would you?"

In return, Bree pressed her lips together and scowled at her uncle. "Why are you doing this?"

"He didn't kidnap her. More importantly, he's the key to getting her back. I trust him."

The words tumbled out before Bree could stop them. "Well, I don't."

Bree had never seen Josh look so serious. "But do you trust me?"

They heard footsteps and turned to see Allen appearing in the kitchen. No one said anything as Josh let go of Bree's wrist. Bree observed Allen. He was clean-shaven, and his hair was still wet from the shower. There was something in his eyes Bree was trying to understand. Josh glanced out the window to make sure no one was near.

"Why did you kidnap my mom?" Bree demanded.

"Bree!" Josh's voice was a mixture of love and correction. "Hear the man out first."

It dawned on her what the look in Allen's eyes was. He was afraid of her—afraid she wouldn't believe him. "A man named Riley set everything up. He kidnapped her somehow and blamed it all on me."

Bree physically turned away from Allen and looked at Josh. "Do you know who Riley is?"

"Yes. He is someone I wish would disappear. Let's eat. Allen is starving."

It was a struggle for Bree not to look at Allen with disgust as he sat down and started piling his plate with food. Why would Josh trust this man?

It took a while for her feet to obey and move to the table. Josh sat next to Allen, and she sat next to Josh, which also meant she was across from Allen. She grabbed the spatula and put some eggs, bacon, and hash browns on her plate. "How do you know Riley?" Bree asked Josh without looking at him.

"I don't know who Riley is, but I know about his boss. He's dangerous."

A choking noise took Bree's attention to Allen. Allen stared at Josh incredulously. "You *know* the person Riley takes orders from? Who is he? What's his name?"

Josh studied his plate carefully. "Heard of him, but never met him. Eat, Allen. You haven't eaten in a while." Allen must not have gotten a good meal since he was on the run, because he gave Josh a short glare before again inhaling his food.

Food was the farthest thing on Bree's mind. Instead, she folded her arms, watching Allen eat, trying to find something about him to hate. Josh cleared his throat, and Bree glanced at him. He motioned to her food, and Bree rolled her eyes as she gathered eggs onto her fork. "What about Holly?" Bree asked Josh. "Did this Riley person take her, too?"

Again, Josh didn't look at her. "I think Reggie might have something to do with it."

"Reggie?" Sure, he was creepy, but kidnapping? "But he's sixteen."

"It's to throw you off. He was never good at teenagers. Always made them too adult-like." Josh put a forkful of hash browns into his mouth.

What was *that* supposed to mean? Even Allen slowed down his eating to give him a questioning look. The silence made Josh glance up and notice the looks he was getting, and he stopped chewing his food. He exaggerated a slow swallow as though to stall and gather his thoughts. "Never mind."

"You're not answering a lot of questions," Bree said.

Josh prepared his next forkful. "Do you trust me?"

Why did he keep bringing that up? It had been a long couple of days. She cried, screamed, and threw tantrums. Josh stood by her side, dried her tears, and gave words of encouragement and hope. There wasn't a better uncle in the world right now, even though she wanted a better situation. If Josh decided to trust Allen, then so would she. If he decided not to answer questions, she would stop asking.

"If I can't trust you, the world will fall apart." She put a forkful of eggs in her mouth. She didn't know Riley. She knew Reggie, who scared her enough.

After piling more food on his plate, Allen finally started to slow down. Bree had a sick feeling in her stomach. Sure she trusted Josh, but did she have to like Allen?

There must have been a look on her face, because Allen didn't eat as fast. For three minutes, the sole sound was the scraping of forks on plates, primarily from Josh and Allen. Bree continued to sit and use her fork to push her food around.

Josh broke the silence with another clear of his throat. "Eat your breakfast, Bree." Bree glanced at her uncle, then quietly picked up some hash browns and ate them.

With a careful hand as though he was handling fancy china, Allen placed his fork down. "What's the plan after this? I appreciate your hospitality, but I can't stay here forever. Even if people listen to my story, they will have a difficult time believing it."

The question didn't seem to faze Josh. "I believe you. Being Sadie's brother, my support carries a lot of weight." Allen looked at Bree. Bree looked at him, broke away, and ate another forkful of eggs, staring at one of the pictures hanging on the wall of her and her mom. Josh patted her arm. "Say what's on your mind, Bree."

She felt uncomfortable as she skewered the blackened bacon. It crumbled beneath the prongs. "I agree Allen will have a hard time finding people to believe him."

Allen slowed down his chewing until he stopped all together. A weak smile fluttered across Josh's face before he turned to Allen. "She does have a point. What motive does Riley have for framing you?"

It was as though Josh wasn't there. Allen turned his full attention to Bree. "I truly do not know. I wish I knew so I could bring Sadie back." Allen kept his gaze on Bree. "His motives don't make sense."

This man seemed genuine, despite Bree wanting to mistrust him. If Allen was trying to lie, he would make up a motive for Riley to cover his tracks, but he sounded honest in his lack of understanding. It seemed like he cared for her mom. Her mind flickered back to the look she witnessed in his eyes on their date when he watched her mom go into the kitchen. More importantly, she remembered the panic she felt because she knew he loved her.

"If we want to figure out his motives, we need to know who Riley works for." Allen turned his attention to Josh. "Who is he?"

The question made Josh squirm in his chair. Before Allen pressed him further, someone knocked at the front door. Silence hit the table. Five minutes ago, Bree was ready to hand Allen over to the police. Now she wasn't so sure. She needed more time, more questions answered.

"What do we do?" Bree whispered.

The chair almost toppled as Josh stood up. "Allen, hide. Bree, stay silent and stick close." Bree nodded as Allen ducked behind the kitchen cabinets. As they approached the door, Josh gave Bree a quiet side hug before he opened it. A policeman stood there, and all of Bree's energy went to stifling a gasp.

"Good morning." The policeman stuck out his hand. "Josh, I believe?"

The fingers in Josh's good hand curled into a fist. Bree noticed the patch sewn onto the policeman's sleeve had the initials RN on it. Her gut told her these were not normal policemen. "You have no jurisdiction here." Josh's voice was dark.

The policeman whistled, a smirk on his face. "You get straight to the point, don't you?"

"I know what you are. You're not even a policeman. You're *his*. Get out."

"He asked me to bring Bree in for questioning. If you struggle, you're coming too."

Josh's eyes narrowed. "Over my dead body. Take your other so called 'police' buddies hiding in the bushes and get off this property."

"Incredible." The policeman shook his head, smiling. "They warned me about her, but I didn't think she'd be this good."

"Josh?" Bree asked.

"Stay behind me." Josh didn't take his eyes off the policeman. "This is my last warning. Get off the property, or I'll call the real police."

The fake policeman laughed. Josh's glare deepened. The man stepped closer to the door, and Josh stayed his ground. "In the time it takes the real police to get here, we will already have the three of you and be long gone. You will hand Bree over for questioning. Allen, who is hiding in your kitchen, will also come with us. Give them to us, and we'll be on our way."

Though Bree didn't understand what was happening, she still felt the terror of the moment. Josh's knuckles were white as he gripped the doorknob. "I don't care what kind of pretend authority you have, I'm not playing along."

"I know." The policeman took out a gun. "Over your dead body."

"Josh!" Bree screamed. Josh slammed the door against the man's arm. He howled and dropped the gun. Josh picked it up, shut and bolted the door, grabbed Bree's arm, and pulled her to the kitchen.

"What's going on? What's the plan?" Allen was on his hands and knees on the floor and looked paler than before.

"Listen closely." Josh crouched down near Allen, and Bree did the same. Josh inspected the gun briefly before turning back to the other two. "They want to kidnap you two, and it cannot happen. Understand?"

"You know who these men are," Allen said. "Do they have Sadie?"

"Yes."

"Then let's bargain with them."

"The only bargaining chip they will be satisfied with is your or Bree's dead body." Bree felt her insides turn to ice. No one ever talked about her death. Josh couldn't possibly mean that.

"You don't know for sure. They might be reasonable," Allen said.

"No, they won't. There has to be another way." Josh thought for a moment. "You two sneak out of here. I'll distract them."

"No!" Allen hissed as Josh made a break for the back door. With wide eyes, Bree watched as Josh ran into the backyard, trailing policemen. They watched him head for the streets. Allen turned to Bree. "Your uncle is insane."

"I don't know what's gotten into him," Bree said.

"Stay with me." Allen took her hand. "Do exactly what I do." They snuck out of the kitchen, and Allen peered out the front window. Josh sprinted down the sidewalk, and a throng of policemen followed him.

"Count of three," Allen whispered. "We'll run the other way."

Bree nodded. She closed her eyes and tightened her fingers over Allen's hand. Allen counted to three, and they flew out the front door. At first Bree was afraid she wouldn't keep up, but adrenaline pushed her through. They heard someone shout behind them, and then multiple guns went off. Instinctively, Bree and Allen both ducked. Josh wailed in pain.

"Josh!" Bree turned and felt Allen tighten his grip on her hand. "They shot him! They shot Josh!" She wanted to run to Josh even though she knew it was unsafe.

"Bree, wait."

"Don't move, Allen," someone yelled in front of them. "Or we will shoot." Allen and Bree spun around. Two policemen stood there with two other people. One of them was Reggie.

"You!" Bree said. His smirk made Bree edge closer to Allen. The policemen took out guns and pointed them at Bree and Allen. She whimpered as Allen stood between her and the guns.

"Hello, Riley." Allen sounded cold while looking at the man not dressed in a police uniform. "What happened to Josh," Allen demanded.

"He'll live," Riley said.

"What did you do with my mom and Holly?" Bree's voice was small but determined.

Both Riley and Reggie smirked. Bree felt tears sting her eyes. So it was them. Even with everything going on, it felt good to know Josh was right and Allen could be trusted. Two more policemen joined the group, dragging an injured Josh behind them. Bree wanted to go to him but stayed by Allen's side.

"Come join our other captives," Reggie said.

Bree didn't have a choice when she felt a gun at her back. A van drove up, and the fake policemen forced Bree, Allen, and Josh into the back of it.

§ § §

Grace found me in the corner of my office, sobbing. She tried to talk to me, but I couldn't. After a few more tries, she gave up trying to talk. Instead, she knelt and wrapped her arms around me. My tears soaked her shirt. She assured me she didn't mind.

Chapter 18

I F I COULD choose one point in time to do over again, it would be the day I applied for a narration device. I wanted to appear to my past self, show her the notches I added to my belt, let her see the dark circles under my eyes, and make her listen to my story. Maybe she'd at least re-think about being so eager to narrate.

The first couple of days after Bree and Allen's kidnapping, I stayed in bed all day. Toward the end of the second day, I started to get a cold. Jim and Devin again camped at my apartment, going through more plans and strategies. I didn't know what good it would do. It didn't work last time.

I battled a black depression. Jim, Devin, and even Dr. Webb gave me their lecture about taking care of myself. I ate some toast to shut them up. Even Vince arrived for a few minutes before leaving again. Just so I wouldn't hear a lecture from him, I pretended to be asleep.

Grace was more kind about it. While I ate and only while I ate, she read some of my favorite poems of hers, and they would ease the hurt in my soul. Sometimes if I wasn't feeling like poetry, she would tell me funny stories about her kids and grandkids. I wanted Grace to be there all the time, but her other job was to track down the Rogue, and I didn't want to stop her.

The third day, despite feeling sick, I forced myself to fight the depression and get dressed. I needed a change of scenery.

"Junior." Jim knocked on the door before opening it. He saw me leaning against the end of my bed heading toward the door.

"Sorry." I gave him a weak grin. "I wanted to get out of bed today."

"Junior…" He lost his train of thought. I must have looked awful—skinny, gaunt, and depressed. Jim tried to say something, but whenever he looked at my face, he kept forgetting what he wanted to say.

"I'm okay." I tried to get him and myself to believe it. My normal voice sounded no louder than a hoarse whisper. Devin joined Jim and tried to smile when he saw me, but he was also surprised to see me up. "Any news on the Rogue?" I hadn't thought of the Rogue in a while. My characters, on the other hand, always stayed in the front of my mind.

"Don't worry about it. You're sick and need your rest. Devin and I are going to cook some lunch."

I rubbed my head. "I'm sick of food."

Jim scolded me with his gaze. "Junior, you—" Devin started to say.

"I know, you've told me a thousand times." Jim narrowed his eyes. He acted as though I had some secret plot hatching in my brain. I was just grumpy and irritable.

"Jim will make some sandwiches. You've done a great job getting out of bed, but maybe consider resting longer."

Too exhausted to show any emotion in my face, I pretended to head back to bed. When I heard the door close, I stopped, turned around, and walked over to the door. I opened it enough to check Devin and Jim's positions. Both were out of sight, most likely in the kitchen. My feet pushed me forward as I fought off the gray dots beginning to cover my vision. I crossed the hall and entered my office, refusing to look at the computer screens. I fought down a cough so Jim and Devin wouldn't hear.

Last night I had an idea. If I ended up kidnapped, another narrator would eventually be in my same predicament. I brought out a fresh sheet of paper and began writing what happened to me since the Rogue decided to stick his characters in my story. Another narrator could learn from my mistakes, and they'd be able to beat the Rogue. It was like commentary, but sadder. I tried not to think about the poor soul reading the notes, because then they'd be in for an awful time, but at least they'd be more prepared.

Devin walked down the hall and headed for my bedroom when he noticed me in the office. "Drop the pen."

I finished the sentence and looked up. "What?"

"Drop it now."

The pen clattered onto the desk. Devin walked in, took out one of his own pens from his pocket, and forced me out of my office by pen point. I rolled my eyes as he led me to the table. Devin walked fast, and I struggled to keep ahead of him, the gray dots coming back. I was glad when I reached the table for its support.

"What were you doing?" Jim asked me, his voice stern.

"Nothing, I—"

"She was in her office, writing something," Devin interrupted.

"It's an idea I've—"

Devin pushed the pen farther in my back. "Sit." Obediently, I sat in the chair as Jim placed a sandwich on a plate and slid it in front of me.

"Eat." Jim's voice conveyed I had no choice.

I missed Grace. She cooked better and didn't treat me like a criminal. I paused long enough to sneeze before I picked up the sandwich. Peanut butter and honey. Jim sat across from me and took a bite of his sandwich, watching me close.

"What were you working on?" Jim asked.

"I was writing notes for any other narrators who might ends up in my situation."

"Don't give up on your characters." Devin bit his sandwich and began to chew. I let out a loud sneeze that shook my body.

"I haven't." I picked my sandwich apart. "It's me I've given up on." My mind toyed with the possibility of using Josh's illegal power, but I couldn't risk it. There were too many factors, and I didn't feel comfortable using it while all the Guardians watched my story.

I popped a torn piece of sandwich in my mouth. The grains of the bread and the sickly-sweet honey mixed with the too-thick peanut butter coated my dry mouth. It made me cough. Jim and Devin watched, concern playing across their faces. I picked up my glass of water and took a drink to try to wash out my mouth, but it didn't cut it. The sticky taste remained. I needed milk but wasn't sure I had any.

Jim put his sandwich back on his plate. "We'll find a way to get them out."

"And what if we don't?" My desire to eat any more of my sandwich was gone, but I knew they wouldn't let me go until I finished it.

Jim gave me a good glare. "Every narrator worth their salt knows there's always a way out, and if there isn't, they create one."

I picked up another piece of the sandwich but stopped when an idea began stirring my creative juices. Jim almost took another bite when he noticed my trance-like state. "Junior?"

Devin looked up.

"Genius. Absolutely genius," I said.

Confusion filled Jim's eyes. "Sorry?"

"Deus ex Machina." The piece of sandwich dropped from my hand. "God in the machine."

"Junior." Jim pushed his plate to one side. "Wait a minute—"

I bit my lip in thought. "If it gets Bree and Allen out of the Rogue's hands, it's worth it. I could help the plot along and make it how I want it."

"You are too exhausted to narrate right now," Devin said.

"Besides, you can't implement anything new until the Guardians agree on it." Of course Jim would remind us of the law.

"Guys, please." I pushed my chair back and jumped to my feet. The rust from staying in bed for two days disappeared. "These are my characters, and they're in danger."

With the reflexes of a healthy, not depressed individual, Jim stood and pinned my hand to the table. "And right now they are safe, frozen in time. You can't face the Rogue like this."

Devin stood up. "Please Junior. Wait a couple more weeks."

Jim didn't let go of my hand, and I was getting annoyed, but the look on his face stopped me. He wasn't angry; he was genuinely concerned. Still holding my wrist, he came around the table.

"Think of your characters, Junior. They deserve the best, and you cannot give them the best right now."

The words rang true, and I hated it. I stared at Jim, my eyes filling with tears. "They're in trouble."

"And we will save them. Later. Please rest. If not for me, if not for Devin or Grace or Vince, do it for your characters' sake."

My tears surprised me as they slipped down my cheeks. Jim pulled me in for a hug, and I let the tears come. I didn't have the energy to sob. Jim was right. I couldn't narrate like this. What my characters needed was for me to get better. Though I needed to give them my best, a small part of me was afraid my best still wouldn't cut it. "I'm scared, Jim."

"I know. I am too." Jim helped me back to bed, and I pulled the covers over my head so I wouldn't have to see his face.

Coughs brought me out of my sleep more than I'd like. Sometimes I saw Grace sitting in the corner of my room, working. Sometimes she and Jim were whispering to each other. Other times it was just Jim.

I woke up in my dark room. It must have been well into the night. I rubbed my head, feeling exhausted despite waking up. By the light of the streetlamp, I saw Jim on a chair in the corner of my room, asleep in an uncomfortable position. He used his suit coat as a blanket. A book was on the floor, looking as though it had fallen there. His vest, tie, and socks were draped on another chair with his shoes placed beneath it.

Homemade chicken noodle soup sat on my nightstand, some medicine was to the side of it, and there was a glass of orange juice. I took the pills and began eating the soup. It was room temperature, but delicious. Did they try to wake me? If they did, I must have been out of it.

Jim stirred and opened his eyes. "Junior?"

"Sorry, I didn't mean to wake you."

His uncomfortable position probably woke him more than anything. He stood up and in two strides came to the side of my bed. "How do you feel?"

"You don't have to stay here." I ate another spoonful. "I'm fine."

Jim looked out the window. "Yes, I do."

At first, I wondered if Vince ordered the Guardians to be in my physical presence 24/7. The guards outside were doing a fine job. Then I remembered Jim's experience with his girlfriend. Jim grabbed the chair holding his other clothes and pulled it closer to my bed. He sank into it, placing his elbows on his knees and tucking his hands under his chin.

"Vince held a conference. We agreed your idea of Deus ex Machina is smart, but we also agreed it's more important for you to get feeling better. We don't want you working on your story or anything to do with narration for a week or two."

My head buzzed with ideas and a fever, both fighting for dominance. I ate another spoonful and tried to smile at Jim. The idea of Deus ex Machina made sense to me, but I wasn't sure how to implement it. If it failed, how much worse would my characters find themselves? Then again, what choice did I have? "Okay."

Jim let a ghost of a smile cross his lips. "Things will be alright, Junior. Devin and I will work hard with this new idea in mind." Jim stopped when he saw tears in my eyes. "Junior?"

"It's cat and mouse. He knows what to do to destroy my characters. I don't know how to help them."

His big brother instincts kicked in. Jim took my hand and patted it like I was his little sister who admitted a fear of darkness. I turned away and wished more than anything he could dispel the fear with a simple motion like switching on the light.

"Why haven't you caught him yet?" Guilt pinched my soul when I heard how angry I sounded.

"We're trying. I'm sorry."

CHAPTER 19

I SAT IN front of the two computers. Jim and Devin refused to let me in the office until they agreed I was ready, which was a few days longer than I wanted. The experience of the past couple of weeks taught me to listen to Jim and the other Guardians. It shocked Jim a few times when I obeyed without getting snarky.

The notes on how to use Deus ex Machina rested in front of me. My fingers ran over the headset as I stared at the frozen screen. Allen, Bree, and Josh were being dragged to the back of a van. If this didn't work I was out of ideas, and I was terrified where my characters would end up.

Jim walked in with some toast and jam on a small plate and a glass of orange juice. He placed it next to me. "Devin left with Grace on a lead, so I'll be here while you're narrating."

"Okay." I situated the headset over my ears.

"Don't do anything stupid."

A smile flickered across my face at his attempt to make things light. He walked out of the office. I took a deep breath, and then slowly let it out.

"Resume."

§ § §

They pushed Bree, Josh, and Allen into the back of the van. The door closed and the fake policemen locked it. Josh winced, leaned against one of the walls, and held his left shoulder as he slid into a sitting position.

"Josh?" Bree moved past Allen to get to him.

"I'm fine. It's a graze." Josh covered the wound with his hand so she couldn't examine it any closer. He looked pale.

"What do they want with us?" Josh squirmed under Allen's gaze.

The van sped off as Bree focused on Josh. "Do these people have Mom and Holly?"

"Yes." Josh looked down. "They'll most likely exchange Allen for your mom and you for Holly."

"Why?"

Josh smiled. "Don't worry. We'll find a way to save all of you."

She didn't want to push it. The van continued to drive down the road. The drivers didn't see the broken glass ahead of them. Josh placed his feet against the wall. "I suggest you brace yourselves."

"What?" Allen looked around the van. "Why?"

"A hunch." No sooner had Josh put his good arm around Bree than the van came to a crashing stop. She would have slammed against the van wall if it weren't for him.

Bree gasped, holding tight to Josh. "What was that?"

Allen got up and brushed himself off. "Don't know." The impact made the two guards in the front of the van unconscious. Josh led Bree toward the back of the van.

"Josh?" Bree asked.

"We've got an escape. We're using it."

Bree panicked. "What about the guards?"

"They've been knocked out."

Allen glanced in the direction of the driver's seat. "How do you know?"

"Trust me."

The lock jiggled loose in the crash, and with a small push from Josh, the door swung open. He led them to an abandoned yet recent model car on the side of the road that happened to have the keys inside and a full tank of gas.

"What about Mom and Holly?"

With his free hand, Josh brushed off some dirt. "I don't know where they are, but we'll find them on our own terms." Allen headed toward the driver's side. "Allen, I'm driving," Josh said.

"But your shoulder. Your cast."

Josh waved his concerns away. "I'll be fine. Adrenaline turns it numb. I can hardly feel it."

It was so strange, Bree felt like Allen's skeptical look was warranted. "You sound ridiculous. Let me drive."

"I'll explain everything later, but these first few minutes are critical, and I need to drive. Get in the car."

Bree didn't hesitate and climbed in the back. Allen took a second longer before getting into the passenger side. Though Bree had no idea how Josh knew, he didn't hesitate as he grabbed the keys on the floor of the driver's side before getting behind the wheel.

"Who owns this, anyway?" Allen asked.

There was no answer as Josh fiddled with the rearview mirror. "Everyone buckle up. I don't know what's out there." They obeyed. Josh started up the car, pulled out, and sped in the opposite direction.

"You know a lot more than you want to admit," Allen said.

Josh kept his gaze on the road. "I will admit I'm not allowed to answer questions."

The agitation came out in Allen's voice. "When will you be allowed?"

With his good hand, Josh tapped the wheel. "I hope never. I'm not in charge of when I'm allowed to talk about these things."

Bree leaned over closer to the driver's seat, staring out the window. "Why do they want us?"

"It's nothing you've done. It's who you are," Josh said.

"You're not—" Allen stopped when three cars appeared out of nowhere and headed for them. With a jerk of the wheel, Josh spun the car around and stepped on the gas. Bree heard a gunshot and screamed as glass showered her head.

"Bree!" Josh shouted.

"I'm fine." Bree shook glass off her.

"Stay down," Allen said.

Because she didn't want to get shot, Allen's order wasn't difficult to follow. Three more cars came to block them. Josh narrowed his eyes, swerving the car every which way, barely nicking them all before speeding off. Bree stared at Josh, her jaw slack.

"Are you a professional driver?" Allen sounded impressed, though scared.

"Right now I am."

More shots came from behind. Bree ducked farther, covering her head. The car spun and turned, making her stomach flip. Josh slammed the brakes, and Bree peeked over the seat to see hundreds of cars with no chance of escape. People got out of their cars with guns and headed toward Allen, Josh, and Bree.

"What do we do now?" Bree asked.

"Wait," Josh said.

Allen squirmed in his seat and opened his mouth to ask a question, but the ground began to shake.

Despite the guns coming ever closer, Bree sat up more to see. "What's happening?"

Before Josh gave a non-answer, the ground cracked around them. Her jaw fell open. Men screamed in shock as cars fell through the cracks and men were trapped or dead in deep canyons.

Bree couldn't look away. She wanted to, but the bizarre scene kept her attention. The earth didn't crack by their car. Before long the deep canyons were full of men and cars. Josh threw his foot on the gas and the car lurched forward. Bree shrieked, and Allen swore loudly as he grabbed Josh's seat, but they didn't fall into the earth. She watched in amazement as a path closed for them in the direction they needed to go. Bree noticed Allen's white knuckles on Josh's seat. They sailed free of the cracked earth and continued on their way.

"Did you do this?" Allen asked.

"I have no idea where they're hiding Sadie and Holly." Josh got back on the road. "But we'll find them."

"Would you please answer just one of my questions!"

Riley sauntered onto the road and stopped in the middle. Josh slammed on the brakes. The car didn't slow down enough. Josh swerved, but hitting Riley was inevitable unless the man moved, and he was rooted to the spot, sneering at them. Bree grimaced and closed her eyes. Even if he helped steal her mom and best friend, she didn't want to see him get hit.

As disgusted as she felt, though, Bree cracked an eye open. She saw Riley bring his fist down against the hood of the car right before it hit him. The car sailed over Riley, and Bree covered her face as it landed on its top.

The car settled. The seat belt kept her in place, but it tore at her skin as gravity took hold. Blood ran into her eyes. Her fingers brushed the roof of the car and at times touched the asphalt. The last thing she saw was Riley's feet walking toward the car.

§ § §

I stopped the narration, took off the headset, and let it fall onto the table. I grabbed the book entitled *Narration Law* and threw it against the wall. It made a nice sized dent. Tears stung my eyes. Jim opened the door and looked concerned.

"It didn't work!" My voice was sharp and angry. "I tried everything, but he still got the upper hand and used it against me!"

Jim frowned, tucking the small screen with my story in his pocket. "I'm sorry." He leaned against the wall and rubbed his head. "We should have known. If you're allowed to use Deus ex Machina, he'd find a way to use it, too."

"Well, he shouldn't! It's my story."

"I know, but if you can bend the laws in your story, he can tack on to the power."

I sat down, feeling adrenaline and hate running through my veins. "It's not fair! Why can't he leave my characters alone?"

Jim was about to reply when he noticed the dent in the wall. "Junior? Did you—" His phone went off. He paused to give me a chastising look before pulling his phone out.

"Devin?" He studied the dent further. "What's going on?" I heard Devin tell Jim something, and his face brightened. "I'll tell her. Thank you." He turned off his phone. "Devin thinks he and his group found the Rogue's hideout."

"What!" My rage melted into joy. "Really?"

"They saw sights of him and some of his guards enter a house, and they're surrounding it now. He needs you to keep narrating to distract him so they can catch him off guard."

The weight of the world lifted off my shoulders. The horrible nightmare could finally come to an end. "How long will it take for them to catch the Rogue?" I asked.

"It can't be long now."

For the first time in a month, I grinned. "I'll keep narrating." I picked up the headset from where I dropped it and stuffed it over my ears. The darkness of the screen signified Bree's unconsciousness. Yes, I was playing in the Rogue's field now, but we had something up our sleeve.

"Resume."

CHAPTER 20

BREE HEARD HER name close to her ear. Taking a deep breath, she opened her eyes, and her mom came into focus, leaning over her with a smile.

"Mom!" Bree shot up and wrapped her arms around her mom's neck.

"Hey, sweetie." Her mom hugged her close. "Are you okay? Did they hurt you?" She broke away and her fingers brushed over a cut on Bree's chin Bree didn't know was there.

"Car crash." Bree winced. The crash itself was weird, she remembered. "Mom? Are you okay?"

"I'm fine. I'm so glad to see you."

The room they were in was small with no windows and had a solid steel door. Holly was a few paces away from her mom, looking shaken. Josh sat on the floor, his hand firmly against the gun wound to stop the blood flow, paler than ever. Allen was a few feet away from her and her mom, watching them, a nasty cut across his eyebrow. Her mom helped Bree to her feet, and she didn't realize how sore she was. Bree gave her mom another hug.

Looking embarrassed, Holly walked over. "Bree." Holly wrung her hands and didn't keep eye contact. "I'm sorry. You...you were right. About him."

It was enough. Bree gave her friend a hug and turned serious. "Did he do anything to you?"

Shaking her head, Holly said, "No. Except the whole kidnapping thing."

"Are we friends, then? All this stuff between us?" Bree asked.

"Forgiven." Holly nodded. "Bridge under the water." Bree froze, and then started to giggle which made Holly frown. "Is that phrase wrong, too?"

Bree nodded. She got her best friend back. Yes, they still had things to talk out, but Bree was willing to forgive.

"Josh?" Allen asked.

"I'm fine." Josh bunched up his shirt to try to give some more cloth to block the blood.

With a glare aimed at Josh, Allen folded his arms. "You know what's going on."

It didn't take Josh long to realize everyone had their attention on him. "I'm sorry, but what I know must remain a secret for as long as possible. If you knew everything, the integrity of the—of the world would collapse."

With a gasp, Bree's mom stepped forward, exchanging a shocked look with Allen. "That's almost word for word what the drunk said," Allen said.

Still Josh refused to look at any one person. "Makes sense. The same laws apply to him as they do to her."

"Who is she?" Allen sounded frustrated.

Josh just about stood up but thought better of it and stayed on the floor. "Look, I know we're frazzled, but—"

"We've all been kidnapped." Her mom took a step closer to Allen. "You know something and haven't told us? It isn't like you to keep secrets."

"What happened to those cars? Why could we drive past with no trouble?" Bree asked.

"Stop, everyone." Josh's voice cut across their questions. Bree noticed he looked tired as he checked his wound. "This wasn't supposed to happen. This is bigger than anyone could have predicted. I'm sorry, but I've got to keep things secret as long as possible."

"Can you tell me what Reggie wants with me and Holly?" Bree asked.

"He won't, but I'll enlighten you," a new voice said. They turned as Riley walked into the room, flanked by half a dozen men. Reggie elbowed his way into the room.

Holly looked pissed. "You lied to me." She tried to head toward Reggie, but Bree and her mom stopped her. If Holly had her way, she might do something stupid, like try to hurt Reggie, with six grown men holding guns in the immediate vicinity.

"We never wanted you. We wanted Bree the whole time," Reggie said.

"Me?" Bree felt surprised. "Why me?"

Riley looked at Josh and smirked. "Were you going to tell them?"

"Of course not. Her name can never be mentioned, or else this world will collapse," Josh said.

"Of course, never her name," Riley said with a shrug.

"But we can say she's the narrator." Reggie smirked. "The narrator of this story we've gained control over."

The information was so strange, Bree wasn't sure she heard right. "A narrator?"

"Yes." Reggie looked beside himself. "The narrator of *your* story, Bree. It's the only reason we bothered with a boring teenager like you."

The insult didn't register for Bree because of the absurdity of what he said. Maybe Reggie was more unstable than she thought. She tried to laugh it off, but when she saw Josh's face, she stopped. This boy wasn't trustworthy, but Josh had an apologetic look. Josh got her to trust Allen when all evidence supported him being a kidnapper. If he was right about Allen, could he be right about this, too? It made all her insides seize up for a couple seconds.

She gave herself the option of believing him to make sense of it all, and to her horror it did make sense. Everything Josh did must have been guided by this narrator. Having Josh always there when Reggie was giving her a hard time seemed unbelievable. A few times, yes, but every time? What did this all mean, though? If they were in a story, then who were Riley and Reggie? Were they the designated villains? Did the narrator put them there? Millions of questions bombarded her. Instead of asking them, Bree stepped into her mom's open and protective arms.

There was a gleam in Reggie's eyes that Bree didn't like. "Takes a while to get used to. Honestly, why anyone would want to focus on your life is beyond me. Boys hate you, and all your friends leave you in less than a month."

"Don't talk to my daughter like that." Her mom tightened her hold on Bree, but Bree felt Reggie's words sink in with icy clarity. She hugged herself, trying to get some warmth back inside her.

"You're all crazy." Allen glanced from Josh to Reggie to Riley.

"How else did I know about your wife and child?" Riley asked. Some of the color drained from Allen's face. Bree didn't know he had a wife or child.

"You must have read their obituary, done your research." Allen sounded unsure and caught off guard. "There's a logical explanation."

Riley's laugh made Bree feel the ice inside her spread throughout the rest of her body. "You let every woman walk past you, because you're too scared to have your heart ripped apart again. Not because of anything they might do, but because of the threat of mortality. You wanted this to work between you and Sadie, because you hoped the massive hole in your heart would be filled by her and her daughter despite your fears. Despite all this, the danger is real. If she refused you, it would destroy you. If they died, it would drive you insane."

"Shut up." Allen backed away from Riley. Riley chuckled and Bree felt her stomach twist. This was exactly what Reggie did to her, the uncanny ability to know her insecurities. Her mom let her go, taking a step toward Allen.

"You know what scares you the most?" Riley walked right up to him. "What scares you is I'm right. There is a narrator. Your wife died from complications of childbirth, but the doctors didn't understand why it happened. It's bothered you for a long time. Why, with our medical and technological advances did it happen? Now you know." Riley pointed toward the ceiling. "*She* simply decided to kill her and your daughter."

"She's not like that!" Josh said. Allen's frightened eyes flickered over to his direction, then back to Riley.

"The purpose she found in killing your wife and child is for pure entertainment. She doesn't care. Everything bad you've experienced is because she hopes it'll make her a more renowned narrator."

The frightened look in Allen's eyes quickly shifted to anger. Bree watched a tear fall down his cheek as his chest heaved. She'd never seen a man cry.

Josh stepped forward, ready to punch Riley, but two of the guards held him back. "He's a liar, Allen. Don't believe anything he says!"

"Anything I say?" Riley turned to him. "But I'm right, Josh. There is a narrator. You kept the knowledge from Allen to protect him from figuring out his deepest sorrow is purely for other people's entertainment." Her mom tried to put a hand on Allen's arm, but he jerked away and took a few steps, his back toward everyone. His frame trembled in rage, and his fist hit the wall.

Josh struggled in the guard's grip. "No! I kept it secret because this kind of knowledge is dangerous!" Another guard joined in trying to contain Josh. "She is a good, kind woman. Riley doesn't know what he's talking about!"

"Maybe in her world, but when she's a narrator, all bets are off. Why else did she kill Allen's wife and child? Why did she allow a man to get Sadie pregnant then leave her to bear everything alone?" Riley asked.

Josh looked stumped. "She had her reasons."

"Then what are they?" Riley asked.

"I don't know! But I know she is kind and concerned for all her characters! She's sacrificed everything for us!"

"She makes mistakes because she's too focused on you all." The scowl on Riley's face sickened Bree.

"Leave us alone. We've done nothing to you," Bree said.

"It's not your fault." Riley turned back to Bree, and she wished she hadn't brought attention to herself. "The narrator wishes to focus on you and Allen, but you especially, Bree. And therefore we must destroy you."

Bree wanted to throw up. What did he mean?

"Never." Bree hadn't heard that tone in her mom's voice before. Holly stood next to Bree, her arm looped through hers as her mom stood in front of them. Even Allen turned, watching Riley closely. Bree reached out with her free arm and held her mom's arm in case they tried to pull her away.

"Touching," Riley said.

"Why her?" Allen asked.

"Destroying Bree means my narrator will be in control of this story *and* your narrator. We can do whatever we want." Riley laughed. "This story will become ours to make your lives as miserable as possible."

Josh scoffed. "My narrator is protected. It's *him* who should worry."

Riley was beside himself with glee. The smile on Josh's face fell, his eyes widening. "What have you done?"

"We've done nothing. Yet." Riley's gaze turned upward. "But the status quo is about to change."

§ § §

The air felt thinner when I stopped the narration. I slid the headset off. If Riley told the truth, the Rogue was seconds away from kidnapping me. My breathing was rapid and deafening in the silence I found myself in. I looked around my office, taking in everything. Being immersed in my story for so long, I didn't realize how dark it had become. Where was Jim? Why was it so quiet?

My hand trembled as I grasped my phone. I had Jim on speed dial and punched the number. I didn't dare close my eyes, not even to blink, as I put the phone to my ear. It began ringing. A second later, I heard Jim's cell phone go off near the front door. The longer it rang, the paler I became. He must be hurt. Or worse. I couldn't hear any of the guards talking or whispering at the door.

Trying to keep my breathing normal, I ended the call. With my phone no longer ringing, silence settled over the apartment. Fear heightened my senses. My breath created sound reaching every inch of the apartment.

I tried to keep my panic at a minimum as I searched for Devin's number. He called a few times during this whole ordeal. When a number looked promising, I called it, willing Devin to answer. I tapped my fingers against my arm, feeling more anxious as time went on.

"This is Devin's office, leave a message aft—"

My heart rate spiked. I started to dial the police when the phone was knocked from my hand. Screaming, I turned and saw someone dressed entirely in black with a black mask over their face. Instinct told me to run, but I was sitting down. The intruder got ready to punch me, so I pushed against the floor. My rolling office chair carried me safely away from the intruder's punch. My hands fumbled for something on my desk and I picked up a thick, hardback dictionary. I threw it with all my might. To my utter surprise, it hit its mark and the intruder crumpled. It almost made me feel sorry for the intruder.

I picked up the dictionary again, holding it like a baseball bat as I dashed out of my office. My mind scrambled a plan together. As soon as I got out of my apartment, I'd run for it. I didn't know where, but my panic demanded I leave now.

Another intruder in black charged toward me. In surprise, I shrieked and chucked my dictionary at the sprinting intruder. He dodged the book. I bolted for the door, but someone appeared from the corner and tackled me. My screams filled the silence before I broke free and got to my feet. Someone threw me against the wall. I barely kept my balance as I grabbed the knob, but one of the intruders seized my shoulder.

"No! Leave me alone!"

One held a rag to my mouth and nose. A simple inhale of the strange chemicals and I knew I was in trouble. I fought the darkness, but it didn't take long before it covered my vision.

CHAPTER 21

SOMEONE GENTLY SLAPPED my face. I wanted to grab the hand so they'd stop, but my own hands didn't obey. Memories came back, and I felt myself coming around. I tried blinking to make my vision reappear. The clearer my vision became, the clearer my recollection returned of what happened before the blackout. It didn't take long to remember how much trouble I was in.

The intruders brought me back to my office, but more importantly, I saw Professor Andrews kneeling in front of me, smiling. I wanted to yell but couldn't. Someone gagged me while I was unconscious, as well as tied me firmly to my office chair. I struggled, but the rope held me. A guard held the chair in place so I wouldn't scoot it around. Professor Andrews watched me struggle.

"Calm down, Junior."

Hearing his voice after so many years made me yearn for the mentor in him. I didn't want him to be the Rogue. It surprised me when I felt a tear roll down my cheek.

He was a tall man. His curly, dark brown hair had more gray to it than I remembered. His dark eyes looked almost black. Four men in black crammed themselves into my office, holding guns. None of them had the black masks on their faces, though I didn't recognize any of them. I looked at the screen with my characters, frozen in time. More tears formed in my eyes. I had lost control of my story. Every worst-case scenario of my characters' deaths came to me. It was only moments away now.

Professor Andrews stood up, folded his arms, and smiled. "I'm impressed, Junior. You almost escaped." His voice sounded kind, but the look in his eyes told a different story. He leaned against my desk. "I know you have questions, but I cannot risk you yelling for help. No one is supposed to know I'm here. If you promise not to scream, I'll untie the gag."

I thought and then allowed myself to nod. Professor Andrews gave me a scrutinizing look, and then reached over and untied my gag. All four men pointed their guns at me.

"Why did you enter my story?" My voice was low and angry.

Professor Andrews folded the cloth before placing it on my desk. "To put you and the Guardians through a series of tests."

Maybe I was more injured in the struggle than I thought. "Tests?"

"Yes." His smile grew. "Tests to see how you treat rules, and whether or not you're good enough for the team. I guess they're more like tryouts than tests," Professor Andrews corrected.

I tried to pick up his facial clues, because he couldn't be suggesting what I thought I heard. "I'm sorry." My anger began to rise. "This whole thing, the hell you put me through, was to see if—"

"You wanted to join my group." Professor Andrews finished for me.

My rage reached a danger point. "I told you two years ago I'd never join the Rogue, and it hasn't changed now! Not even when I found out the Rogue was you!"

Professor Andrews shook his head. "The difference is now you've seen the hold Vince has. It's a joke. As soon as the Guardians introduced more laws, narration dropped. We need a new leader."

"Like you?" I tried to strain the anger out of my voice, but it didn't work. "With your radical ideas?"

"Hear me out."

"Those are my characters! I put my whole heart and soul into them to save them from you! What makes you think I'd ever—"

He stuffed the gag back in my mouth and tied the cloth around my head. I glared at him, not letting the gag deter me. I continued to tell him how stupid an idea this was. He couldn't seriously think I'd join him after what he did.

"I didn't want to do that, but I need you to listen without interrupting." He straightened and folded his arms. The emotions on his face were impossible to read. "To tell you the truth, doing what I did to your characters wasn't my idea. It's an ugly thing, but majority rules, as they say."

My chest heaved and the blood in my heart began to boil. I didn't know if I could trust what he said.

"Some people think I went away in a huff after the Chairman elections and this is my revenge, but it's not. This happened way before Vince. Rules destroy our way of life. No one has the right to tell anyone else what to do, especially when it involves creativity. This device is an accidental miracle, and we aren't using it to its full potential."

I looked at the ground so he wouldn't see my expression. Yes, I didn't like how Vince treated my story, but it wasn't to the point where I wanted to force him from Chairmanship. The devices were too powerful to use them however we wanted.

"I wanted to show how Vince controls you. He didn't trust your judgment as the narrator. Devin told me how angry you got at him."

My head jerked up, staring at Professor Andrews.

"Yes, Devin." He snickered. "He's my inside man. Rather handy, actually. It's one of the many things the Guardians got wrong. Devin didn't beat me—he joined me. Anyone who doesn't join me is taken away."

Devin deceived us all! No one in the Guardians suspected him. This changed everything. All those "success" stories! There were way more Rogue supporters than the Guardians or I originally thought. I had to find a way to escape and warn Jim and the others. We still had a fighting chance if I could escape.

"Devin saw how angry you got at Vince. You told him I was the best professor you ever had. I'm honored." He placed a hand on his heart, mocking me. I winced. It sounded much worse when he said it.

"The way you counterattacked my men in your story was genius." Professor Andrews turned and looked at my narration device. I stole a glance at my characters. They had no idea how much trouble was coming.

"Josh is a masterpiece." He touched Josh's face on the screen. "One Vince wanted to get rid of, right?"

I barely listened. My mind reeled as I tried to understand everything. Devin helped Professor Andrews all along. They wanted to recruit me.

"It happened to me with a different Chairman. My last manuscript was never published. I had a character the Guardians didn't approve of. They asked multiple times, then threatened, but she was my best creation. The story would have crumbled without her. In the end, they refused to publish it. They're cowards, all of them, scared of exploring the narration device. If you join me, when we overthrow Vince, you don't need to get rid of Josh. Your imagination and creativity would never be limited again." He reached over and untied my gag. "What do you think?"

Yes, Vince acted ridiculously strict. Yes, he drove me crazy. Yes, many times I wanted to slap some sense into him. But what Professor Andrews suggested was borderline insanity.

"I created Josh because you started messing up my story. He wouldn't be there if it wasn't for you."

"But no character should be kicked out of the story. You should be able to have whatever character you want in there. There is no reason to have strict laws on creativity. It inspires the exact opposite of creativity."

"It's not creativity the Guardians are limiting. It's the narration device. Yes, it was a miraculous discovery. And dangerous. Narrators are given unthinkable powers which could destroy us."

With a shake of his head, Professor Andrews chuckled. "Everyone uses that story of the five scientists to scare us. It's insulting. Four people die, and instead of honoring them by pushing on in the name of progress, we slink back into the corner and are at a standstill. It's disgusting."

I couldn't look at him. "You don't see the damage this has already done to you."

Professor Andrews scoffed. "Made me stronger. I thought the laws were important too, but the more I researched them, the more I realized they keep us back."

"Then tell me this. Is it true you are tied to the unsolved murders a few years ago? Is it true a few people figured out you were the Rogue, and you killed them to silence them?"

At first, Professor Andrews did nothing, then the smallest hint of a smile crossed his lips. It made my heart sink as another tear came to my eyes. "I could never follow a murderer."

"What you claim is a different conversation for us to have."

"No! It's the same conversation. You don't think any laws are important. You think you're justified in murder. Murder!" I trembled in the chair, feeling sick to my stomach. "I don't support what you've become."

The smile on Professor Andrew's face grew. "For claiming to be a law-abiding narrator, you broke a lot of them. Having a character able to hear your voice? None of my other characters *ever* had the conversations they had." He pointed to the text part of the device. "No one else admitted to the existence of the narrator. Vince will not let you go without a hearing now, even if I do set you free. He'll be furious."

My eyes traveled to the device. Professor Andrews was right. Vince would call it an abuse of power. I remembered my conversation with Vince where I told him I didn't care if the manuscript would be published later. My manuscript needed to stop the Rogue. I still believed that. Somehow I needed to give Vince a message and warn him about Devin.

"Why would people join you after you ruffed up their characters? Why would they think it was a good idea?"

"Your story was different. The more you fought, the more I fought back. There's a reason Devin didn't let you read his manuscript. He had an open mind as to why they were there instead of trying to kick them out. So technically, it isn't my fault your characters are in this situation. You shouldn't have fought me so hard."

I almost bit a hole in my cheek to keep the anger at bay. "What makes you think I'd agree to people entering other stories?" I almost screamed. "To change other narrator's plots? To harm other people's characters because it fits with their creative desires?"

Professor Andrews gave a knowing smile, making me nervous. I tried hard not to let it play across my face. "Devin had such high hopes for you, but I knew this is how you'd react. Maybe with your disappearance, it will break Jim and he'll resign from the Guardians. He was our only threat of the three."

He never answered my question. Did he know chaos would ensue if he let narrators do whatever? Was he expecting it? I wanted to push him for an answer, but my throat went dry as he headed to my narration device. He had a dark look about him.

"No." I felt numb as I remembered Kyle's manuscript and the cries from his main character. "Please, leave her alone."

"I will give you one last chance, Junior." He turned to me, his eyes blacker than I'd ever seen them. "You don't have to murder your main character. Instead, be our informant. You will claim to write a sequel, and one of my followers will narrate this story once a month while someone monitors you to make sure you don't spill anything you're not supposed to. If you do well, my follower will stick to whatever outline you give him. If you don't, he won't. If you keep disobeying, I will have my follower "forget" to narrate that month. This is your last option."

It was a hostage situation. My mind raced, wondering how many of the "successful" stories ended up like this. How many people followed him because they didn't want their characters doomed to limbo?

It was tempting. I gave it two seconds of thought before I knew I couldn't agree. Professor Andrews would still be in control of my characters. Death was bad, but threatening them with limbo was worse. I would not be threatened into compliance.

Professor Andrews saw the look on my face. I didn't have to say anything. He reached into his bag and pulled out a microphone. "I thought so."

At that moment, he was no longer my mentor. He was the Rogue. I spent so long separating them, trying to remember the good he did and hoping there was redemption for him, but I couldn't. The Rogue and Professor Andrews were the same person.

"Not Bree!" Panic took over. "She's sixteen!" One of the guards threatened to hit me, but the Rogue shook his head.

"Bree's your main character, Junior." He plugged in the microphone next to the headset, and then put the headset on me so I could hear every sound my characters made. "No one is exempt."

Tears warmed my cheeks as they fell. The microphone on the headset didn't work while the Rogue had his own plugged in.

"Resume." My device unfroze. "Riley took Bree away and began to torture her in front of her mother."

My characters started moving, and I struggled against the rope until I felt my wrists burning. I watched, horrified, as Riley turned to look at Bree, a cruel smirk on his face. She paled. The Rogue continued to narrate. More of the Rogue's characters spilled into the room. There were two men for each of my characters. Riley dragged Bree away. Sadie screamed. Bree struggled against her captors.

"No!" I shouted. "Please, no!"

The Rogue stopped the narration. "Join my team, and I'll let her go."

More tears spilled out of my eyes. I couldn't join him. He was wrong. I resolved never to join his side, no matter what, but I also loved my characters so much I would do anything to protect them.

My shoulders shook as a sob traveled through me. "I can't join you." My voice sounded small, childlike. The Rogue's face remained cold.

"Resume. Kill her." Reggie held Bree pinned, and Riley got himself ready. The Rogue faced me. "She's only a character in a story. She's not real."

"You unfeeling monster!" My voice was dark, and I wanted nothing more than to break free and punch him until every bone in his face broke. My mentor was dead. Bree was real to me! I wanted to scream some more, but something stopped me. Riley hit Bree, and Bree yelled out in pain.

I threw myself against the ropes. "Please!" I begged one more time.

"You know my conditions, Junior. I will only stop if you agree to them." He continued to watch Riley torture my sixteen-year-old character with a sick satisfaction on his face. It made me want to throw up.

Sadie dissolved into tears. I saw her future clear in my mind. This would destroy her. To watch her daughter killed in front of her; she would be inconsolable after this. Allen would not be able to help her, and the hole would deepen in his own heart. When she and Bree met up again after the story, they would try to help each other, but Sadie would never forgive herself for failing her.

Josh screamed at Riley to stop, but one of the men hit the wound in his shoulder. Josh's loyalty was on overdrive as he tried to save Bree. More of the guards came to help the other guards holding Josh back. He tried again to break free, but they kept hitting his shoulder, and Josh cried out in pain. Ignoring the almost unbearable pain, Josh struggled to help. This time the guards whacked his head with the back of a gun, and he crumpled to the ground, unconscious.

The guards pushed Holly into a corner, and she turned away so she wouldn't see. Riley began to tighten his fingers over Bree's throat. She began to struggle for air. Bree couldn't die. My hope rested in Allen. He would do everything in his power to make sure Riley wasn't successful.

Bree struggled to loosen Riley's grip, but it was impossible. Allen struggled with the two guards holding him back. Something in him snapped. Something about hearing Bree choking for air made him go into frenzy mode. He couldn't save his own wife and daughter, but he was determined to save Bree.

He thrashed about until one of his hands came free. Allen elbowed one of the guards in the face and punched the other. He sprinted over to Riley and Reggie. He pushed Reggie out of the way and tore Bree out of Riley's grip. Bree gasped for air, stumbling until she fell to her knees.

"What—" Riley began to say. Allen cut him off by giving him a firm punch to the face.

The Rogue chuckled. "He's got spirit. I'm impressed." I swallowed, fixated on the screen. I couldn't do anything but hope they could make it on their own.

Allen knelt, taking Bree's arm. "Are you okay?"

Bree nodded, massaging her throat. He helped her to her feet.

"Change focus to Allen," the Rogue said into the microphone. "Kill him and wait to see how Sadie reacts."

The guards seized Allen and dragged him away. He resisted, and Bree clutched his arm, bellowing at the others to leave him alone. A guard placed his gun against Sadie's head, demanding cooperation. Allen instantly complied. One of the guards pushed Bree over toward Sadie, who clasped her arms around her.

The guards drew their guns, pointing at them to keep them from saving Allen. It also kept Allen from acting out. Holly joined them, and Sadie hugged the two girls. More guards tackled Allen, pinning him against the wall. Josh remained on the ground, unconscious, as Holly and Bree both wept in Sadie's protective embrace.

I wanted to throw up. Allen's death would destroy Sadie. This was Sadie's chance to have a good man in her life. Watching Allen die would be detrimental toward the relationship between Bree and Sadie. Sadie would struggle to recover, and Bree would not be able to comfort her. Bree would never understand why their mother-daughter relationship wasn't good enough. Bree and Sadie would fight, and they'd grow distant.

Riley walked over to Allen and started punching him. Bree and Holly covered their faces in Sadie's shoulders.

"Don't watch, girls," was Sadie's quiet plea. Bree whimpered, covering her ears.

"Eventually you'll see the Guardians are wrong," The Rogue's voice was emotionless. "Even if it takes killing your own characters to see it."

My stomach twisted itself into knots. Ashamed, I turned away from Allen's beating. I closed my eyes, hoping it would make everything hurt less, but it didn't. Chaos still entered through my ears. I heard Allen screaming in pain. Sadie, Bree, and Holly were sobbing. Trouble surrounded them, and I sat powerless in my chair.

My mind spun through hundreds of ideas to save Allen. I needed the microphone. Having use of the microphone, I could activate Josh's dormant power. I peeked at Josh, still lying unconscious on the ground. Even if he used his power, would it be enough? It could heal the physical damage, but what about the psychological damage? Allen's screams would forever haunt their nightmares. They'd haunt mine.

Closing my eyes helped me know Allen's thoughts, and I hated it. He felt confused. He took the beating because he knew if he received it, Bree wouldn't. It didn't stop the frustration growing inside him. He chalked this up as another torture I allowed.

As soon as he heard of me, he went through all the dreadful things in his life and realized someone could have stopped the pain but didn't. Me, his narrator, looked on and did nothing. His mind lingered on the slow healing process after the deaths of his little family. I did not save them. He assumed I saw him shed tears at their funeral, watched his mental breakdown as he tore apart his house, breaking every frame and overturning every table, desk, and chair. He believed I watched with a grin, because his actions made the story more dramatic. He believed his pain meant nothing to me. He believed while he was in his darkest hour, I turned my back on him to plan for more.

I began to sob.

He struggled with my reality. They told him I existed, but he refused to believe. It sounded outlandish. If he did believe, the anger he tried so hard to dispel would be concentrated on me. It would flare up again and consume him. He had to live his life as if I didn't exist, or else he wouldn't live.

My tears turned violent.

Allen, I thought. *Please understand I care about my characters. I want you to be happy. I'd let you live in paradise if I could, but I have to follow rules, too.*

It was useless. He'd never know my thoughts. When the Rogue gave me control I could activate Josh's power, and Josh could attempt to explain why. It might not work, but I had to try. Knowing of my existence would make Allen miserable if I didn't help him to understand.

"Hold him," Riley said.

I opened my eyes as Riley took a gun from one of the guards. Allen was beaten and bruised. He stared at the gun as though willing it to go off and end everything. I closed my eyes and turned away again, giving a whimper. The gun went off three times. Sadie screamed in shock. Bree and Holly, their faces still hidden, gasped.

Peeking at the screen, I saw Allen tumble to the ground. He landed on his back with three shots to his chest. His soul swirled out of his mouth until it hovered a couple of inches above his body. The ghostly figure of Allen waited, eyes closed, for me to accept his death. This time I couldn't look away.

"Stop." The picture froze. The Rogue unplugged his microphone and turned to me. "You know what to do." His voice was cold and dark. Allen was as good as dead, and now I had to do the one thing reserved for the creator of the story.

But I wouldn't. My mind went through Josh's secret power. It had to work. I needed it to be powerful enough to bring Allen back from the dead and help him understand my existence. This was going to break a lot of laws, and it was dangerous, but if it saved Allen's life, then I didn't have a choice. The Rogue looked at me, his eyes black and harsh. I took a deep breath and let it out before I stared at the screen.

"Resume." I glared at the Rogue to let him know he didn't win. "Josh, now is the time."

On the screen, Josh's eyes snapped open.

CHAPTER 22

B REE COVERED HER eyes, afraid of the silence and what it meant. She didn't want to look. She hardly knew him, but she would have died if it wasn't for Allen.

An explosion momentarily deafened her. She gasped and looked up from her mom's shoulders. The guards around Josh had fallen to the ground, and the wall behind him was blown away. Josh stood up as the gun wound stitched itself back together. He glared at the men beside Allen. Even the scar on his head from the crash weeks ago disappeared. With a flick of his wrist, the cast on his arm burst apart. He flexed his now healed hand. Bree blinked, wondering if trauma caused vivid hallucinations.

"Get away from Allen." Josh took a step closer.

"He's dead. There's nothing you can do to bring him back," Riley said.

Josh raised his hand, and to Bree's amazement Riley lifted into the air. He flicked his hand, and Riley flew into the wall and crumpled to the ground. Josh turned and saw the guards pointing their guns at him.

"Shoot him!" Reggie sounded insane with anger.

The guards didn't hesitate as they pulled the trigger. Bree screamed, thinking she would lose her uncle, too. Josh held out his hands, and the bullets simply disappeared. With a snap of his fingers all the guards, including Reggie, collapsed. Bree stared transfixed at Josh.

"Josh?" Her mom was also amazed. "How—"

"No time." Josh turned to Allen's body on the ground.

§ § §

"Stop the device," the Rogue demanded. I didn't comply. Josh needed to heal Allen, and then I needed to make the power dormant again.

"Junior, stop it."

A guard hauled Jim inside my office and threw him on the ground.

Jim groaned as he landed. The drugs must have started wearing off. He got up on his hands and knees, rubbing his head.

"I'll say it once more, Junior." The Rogue nodded toward a guard who pointed his gun at Jim. "Turn off the device."

I winced. I needed to know Josh could heal Allen, and then I needed to take the powers away and end the story. The philosophical discussion of my existence would have to be in the sequel when the Rogue was captured and couldn't get into my story. With the small power Josh had before, I didn't fear it corrupting him, but this much power would unquestionably corrupt him. It was only a matter of time. If I took it away before he realized how much power he had, everyone would be safe.

Jim looked at the gun, not a single emotion on his face. I saw Josh kneel next to Allen right as the gun cocked.

"Stop," I whispered. The device froze, and tears came to my eye. I loved my characters, but I couldn't let Jim die. One guard ripped the headset off my head as two more grabbed Jim and hoisted him up.

"What were you going to prove?" the Rogue asked.

I began breathing deeply, not sure how to answer him. What I did was doom my characters. I traded their lives, all of them, for Jim's. Tears began to flow more steadily. Jim raised his head, looking fully awake now. The Rogue's eyes were dark. His hands tightened into fists and released.

"You've made it worse for yourself." He didn't need to tell me. I already knew. The Rogue would kidnap me, and my story would still be in his hands. The Rogue would either narrate it and end my story with my characters dead or miserable, or he'd abandon it and destroy them all. I was so focused on saving Allen I didn't think about the consequences. Why does this always happen!

He nodded to one of the guards who began to untie me from the chair. Jim watched me closely, looking concerned. Revelation struck me, and I turned to Jim. "Devin works for the Rogue. All the success stories are really narrators who agreed to work for him."

If I couldn't save my characters, I could save the Guardians.

Jim's mouth dropped open, his eyes wide with horror. I realized Devin probably helped kidnap his brother and girlfriend. The guard hit me on the back of the head and I cried out in pain, landing on a knee.

"Leave her alone!" Jim glared at the Rogue.

The Rogue ignored Jim and turned to me. "Ah, Junior. Always the hero." He leaned back, tapping his fingers on his arm, trying to think. He glanced at his watch and frowned before he turned to Jim. "A small step back, but it's proved profitable. Half the Guardians will now follow my instructions."

"What makes you think I'd ever…" The realization hit Jim the moment the Rogue's twisted sneer crossed his face. Jim paled and pain filled his face. "Free Lydia and Kyle." Jim was quiet. "Let them go, and…and you have a deal." My heart tore in half. This wasn't how it was supposed to go. Jim learning about Devin meant things would get better, not worse.

The Rogue laughed. "It's not a business deal, it's a threat. You will do what I say, or I will kill one of them."

My knees buckled in fear. Jim's look was menacing, his eyes filled with tears. I realized I never saw Jim cry before now.

"I don't trust you," Jim said.

The Rogue smirked. "Fine. Don't trust me. Tell Vince what happened here tonight, but I know where your feisty little redhead is. How much do you want her unharmed?"

Jim thrashed against the guards' grip. "How dare you! You are breaking the law!"

I closed my eyes as the Rogue laughed. The biggest insult Jim could give to someone was they were breaking the law? If I wasn't so terrified, I would have laughed, too. I would miss him.

"I'm not breaking the law if half the people making them are under my control."

"I will see you behind bars."

"The cost will be the life of someone you hold dear. Is it worth it?"

Jim was fuming. Tears raced down his cheeks, and I felt my own fall. I failed. I was so close, but I realized how stupid it was. Not only did I hand over the destruction of my story, but also the destruction of the Guardians. I memorized the carpet, too ashamed to meet anyone's eyes.

The Rogue walked over to the guard holding Jim. "Tie them both up and knock Jim out so he won't follow us. Send word to Devin. Have him give Jim basic instructions."

"No, please." It was pointless for me to argue. I felt nauseated. The guards holding me tied my hands behind my back. Jim turned to me.

"Junior—" he started to say. Again, he struggled to find words to comfort me. Before he said anything more, the guard covered Jim's mouth with a cloth. The Rogue grabbed my arm and dragged me out of my office as Jim fell to the floor. I didn't struggle. I'd lost, and in losing made a bigger mess than anyone could imagine.

A limo waited in the parking lot. It had to be midnight, and everything was still and quiet except for my pounding heart. The Rogue pushed me into the limo and got in behind me, followed by a guard.

The Rogue talked to the guard in the driver's seat and the one holding me, giving them instructions. Tears continued to run down my face as I tried not to have a breakdown. The Rogue won, but I wouldn't give him the satisfaction. The door closed and the Rogue left for a different vehicle.

The trip was, to my surprise, short. The guard yanked me out of the limo and hauled me across the lawn. I caught a glimpse of a mansion with tons of lights on before going to a smaller house on the yard. Inside, the guard led me down the stairs to the basement. He opened the metal door with a key. I saw two people, one I recognized as Lydia. They were talking quietly on the couch. I expected them to be asleep, but they turned when I was thrown inside. The metal door slammed shut.

Lydia got up and walked over to me. "He got you too, huh?" She untied my hands. As soon as they were free, I covered my face and began to sob.

CHAPTER 23

I DESPERATELY NEEDED sleep, but it didn't come. My mind kept me up, taunting me with my mistake. I was so convinced I could save Allen I didn't think about the towering consequences of what would happen if I didn't save him in time. A tiny voice told me it would have been better for Allen to die, but I kept shutting it up.

The hatred I felt toward the Rogue, for the choices he forced me to make, kept me up, too. Imagining the different ways I'd make him suffer if I had the chance kept me too entertained. It also scared me, realizing how entertained I was by imagining him suffering.

Lydia got up a while ago. I pretended to still be asleep. The basement was unfinished; the floor was hard cement. Lydia and I slept in the bedroom. It was sort of finished. Walls separated it from the main room, but not much else. Lydia had a cot set up. She offered it to me last night, but I declined. I remained on the ground, shivering, trying not to cry too loud.

The main metal door opened, and I heard the sounds of a scuffle. Lydia gasped. "You hurt him!"

Jumping to my feet, I left the bedroom to see what was happening. Kyle was on the ground panting as he held his ankle. Lydia and the other guy knelt next to Kyle. A guard placed a tray with breakfast on a small card table. He was about to leave when Lydia stepped forward.

"Ricky, we have a new girl here. We need another cot and blankets. And we need bandages for Kyle's foot."

The guard scoffed. "Kyle's an idiot for trying to escape. It's his own fault for getting hurt."

"It's against the law to kidnap someone, so it's your fault I keep trying to escape," Kyle said.

Ricky kicked him in the stomach, and Kyle gave a strangled groan. "I should have thought about twisting your ankle ages ago. If I catch you out again, I'll start breaking bones."

161

"You won't catch me again. I'll be gone, and you'll be in prison."

Ricky kicked him again. Lydia pushed Ricky and stood between him and Kyle. "Stop it! The cot. I don't want her sleeping on the floor again."

"You'll get your cot if you all behave." He glared at Kyle before he left and slammed the metal door. Lydia and the other man got on both sides of Kyle and helped him get up.

"Thanks Lydia, Drake."

"When did they hurt your foot?" Lydia asked.

"Before they sent me to solitary." Kyle said. I waited, not sure what to do. They helped turn him, and Kyle saw me for the first time. "Oh, hi."

"Like I said, we have a new girl."

A weird sensation came over me of feeling so awkward I didn't know what to do with my hands. "Can I help with anything?"

"Bring over the tray. We can have breakfast on the couch," Drake said.

I carried the tray as they helped Kyle to the couch. He plopped down, wincing in pain. Lydia lifted his pant leg and inspected his ankle. It was then I realized none of them had shoes. I set the tray down on the other couch since there wasn't a table to put it on. Kyle and Lydia looked like their picture, except more worn from their year of capture. Lydia didn't have any makeup on, and Kyle looked thinner. However, the mischievousness was still in his eyes. Drake had dark brown hair and blue eyes. He seemed more broken than Kyle or Lydia. I didn't know how long he'd been here.

Kyle shifted to a more comfortable position. "I think it's a sprain."

"It's bad, whatever it is," Lydia said. "It's swollen a lot. It might be smart to get on Ricky's good side so he'll give us some bandages and an ice pack."

"Can't do it, Lydia. I see Ricky's face and it fills me with the desire to mouth off. So, new girl, you must have come last night," Kyle said.

I nodded. The memories were still too fresh in my mind. It was barely a day ago, but so much happened since then it felt like it lasted a decade. "You can call me Junior." I sat down on the couch, kind of close to them.

"Is Jim still in the Guardians," Lydia said.

Lydia gave a sigh of relief as I nodded. "I was worried he'd resign after I got kidnapped. Is he all right?" Lydia asked.

"As good as can be expected. He's worried about you two."

Kyle turned away, looking at one of the windows, which I realized was bricked in. I finally had a good look at the unfinished basement. Lydia's and my bedroom was off in a corner. Judging by the cots in one of the unfinished sections on the other side, I figured the men slept there. The bathroom was finished with tile. It was on the opposite corner of the bedroom and had a working shower and toilet. The rest of the room seemed empty. Nothing on the walls—no books, no boxes. It felt cold for some reason. We sat on a couch by a small TV in the corner. Another couch stood adjacent to the one we sat in.

"Breakfast," Drake said. He passed out four oranges to each of us, pieces of toast, and apple juice in a box.

"Would it hurt Ricky to give us some jam?" Kyle mumbled as he munched on a piece of dry toast.

I looked at the breakfast, not feeling hungry at all.

§ § §

Josh knelt and examined Allen. I didn't know what he expected to see. Allen was dead. Holly crept forward, but I still kept my distance. With a startled look, Josh turned to look at me. I stared back, confused at his look. "Bree?"

"What?" He blinked a couple of times and looked frightened. "Josh, what is it?" I asked.

"Ask me later."

He turned back to Allen. I took a step closer, covered my mouth, and swallowed the bile creeping up my throat. Mom cried softly as she knelt and touched Allen's hand. My heart ached for her. Those goons had no right to murder Allen. I shook, trying not to freak out; I had witnessed a murder. Allen's eyes were open and sightless. He had bruises, cuts, broken bones, and three bullets to the chest. I took steady breaths to control the nausea.

Josh swept a hand over Allen's body, centimeters from touching his flesh. At first, I didn't know what he was doing, but then I saw bruises and small cuts disappear on Allen's body. Some of the blood soaking the floor snuck back through his open wounds. I couldn't turn away. How did Josh do this?

After touching Allen's nose for a second, the once broken bones fused back to place. Was Josh bringing Allen back from the dead? Was it possible? I didn't dare hope, realizing my mouth was hanging open. He ran a finger over

Allen's shirt, and it fell away as if he cut it open with scissors. His ribs didn't look right. Before I knew it, Josh healed those, putting them back into place with a touch of his fingers. At times Josh placed his palm flat over his abdomen to heal some organs I'm sure were damaged.

My mom always acted strong for me even at times I knew she wasn't. This time I saw her pain. Tears streamed down her face as she watched Josh anxiously, a glimmer of hope coming through.

We all watched as Josh placed two fingers on the edge of a bullet wound. A few seconds later, the bullet came out of the wound, and Josh tossed it aside. Placing his palm flat against the wound made a lot of blood return to Allen's body. When Josh took his hand away, the wound was gone. He did the same with the two other bullet holes. He flicked his wrist and the shirt, moving on its own, came back and wove itself together around his torso.

The anticipation was there. Allen's body was now completely healed, but he still didn't move. Josh furrowed his brow as Mom leaned down and pressed her ear against Allen's chest. She came up, looking crestfallen. "His heart's still not beating."

"The soul is still separated." Josh tapped his finger against the floor in thought before he touched Allen's head and heart. Josh closed his eyes and looked like he was meditating. The rest of us didn't dare breathe.

There was a pause, and then Allen gasped like someone drowning finally breaking the surface and finding a sky full of air at his disposal. His hands trembled as he felt his chest, expecting to feel the wounds. My jaw went slack. I witnessed someone coming back from the dead. Mom helped him sit up and hugged him tightly. She cried quietly in his chest.

Allen wrapped an arm around her. "I'm all right." He sounded as surprised as anyone by this knowledge. "I'm okay."

I stared at Josh, frightened. "He was dead, and you brought him back."

Looking nervous, Josh gave a nod. He took a step toward me and touched my nose. At first, I wondered why, but then I remembered it was still bleeding. The dull pain stopped. After he brushed a finger over the cut on my chin and ran his hand over my neck, I felt almost normal. He stepped aside, and I couldn't help but touch my neck.

"We've got to get out of here." Josh glanced out the hole in the wall and then at all the unconscious bodies. "Riley knows where you live, Sadie. Is there any other place we can go?"

"My apartment is in the city." Allen struggled to get up. Mom put his arm around her shoulder to help him balance. "It's not big, but it's something."

"That'll work. I need somewhere to think," Josh said.

"How did you bring me back?" Allen asked.

"As a last resort, the narrator gave me powers to use in this realm. Because she hasn't taken them away already, she's in trouble, and things will get worse."

Holly frowned. "Why didn't she give you this before?"

Without looking at us, he started walking toward the hole in the wall. "Because it comes at a price."

"What price?" Mom asked.

Josh hesitated. "At the very least, when they are taken away, it will drive me insane."

I gasped, tears coming to my eyes. Allen asked the question I was thinking. "And at the worst?"

There was a pause before Josh turned to look at us for the first time. "Everyone dies painful deaths."

Mom and Allen exchanged looks while I stared at Josh. One of the guards stirred. Josh brushed his hand in the guard's direction, and the guard fell back into unconsciousness. Allen watched with surprise, but also a hint of fear. I didn't know what to think. How would Josh go insane from this?

Shouting came from the other side of the door. "Come on." Josh turned and headed toward the hole. "We've got to go."

We left through the hole. Josh jogged to one of the cars with a piece of the building on top of it. He brushed his hand over it and the building piece crumbled into dust. I watched the car fix itself and turn on without Josh doing anything. I nodded, impressed. I was about to tell Josh, but saw him touch a finger to his forehead and shake his head as though dispelling some thought. A group of guards left the building and started shooting. Josh created a force field to protect us.

"Sadie, help Allen in."

Mom went in the back with Allen and Holly, and I sat in the passenger seat. Josh looked around before climbing in the driver's side.

"Are you okay?" I asked.

"I will be when we get to Allen's apartment," Josh said.

§ § §

I hardly talked. Ricky came down at lunchtime to give us food and a cot with some more blankets. Lydia asked if they could at least have something to ease Kyle's pain, and again he scoffed. Drake set up the cot in the bedroom, and Ricky told me to give up my shoes. I did, confused, until Lydia told me Kyle used his shoes as a weapon once. When Ricky brought dinner, Drake turned on the news, and we sat on the couch watching it while eating.

"There you are," Drake said.

My face filled the screen as a reporter talked about how I was the fourth missing narrator since the Rogue started infiltrating stories. Lack of sleep took its toll, and I sat back against the couch exhausted. Lydia watched me carefully. I pushed around my food, my character's situation in the front of my mind.

"There's Jim!" Kyle said. Lydia whipped around and looked.

The camera shot was of a press meeting. The Guardians were all there, including Devin. It sparked my dull senses with hatred. Devin leaned over and whispered something in Jim's ears. Jim closed his eyes and nodded. It looked like it cost him his soul to do so.

Drake glared at Devin. "It bugs me. I know he's a mole and I can't tell anyone."

Kyle swallowed his potatoes. "We'll get out, Drake. And when we do, we'll tell everyone what kind of person Devin is."

"Jim already knows." My voice was quiet, but all three of them turned to look at me. I stared at the TV instead of meeting their eyes. "Before I got captured…" I didn't want to go into detail about my stupid mistake. "I managed to tell him about Devin, but the Rogue was there. He told Jim if he doesn't do what the Rogue wants or spills his secret, the Rogue will kill us."

They continued to stare. I turned to meet their gaze. Drake looked uncomfortable. Kyle frowned, and Lydia had her mouth slightly open.

Kyle was the first to recover. "But if Jim follows the Rogue's orders, then—"

I nodded. "Half the Guardians are secretly with the Rogue."

"This is worse than I thought." Kyle turned back to the TV. "We've got to get out of here."

"How?" Drake shook his head. "I hate to be pessimistic, but you've tried to escape ever since you got here, and we're not any closer. The more ways we try, the more they restrict us." Drake lifted his foot and wiggled his toes. I couldn't help but look at Kyle's foot. It was badly swollen.

"We can't stop trying when all the narrators in the world are in trouble," Kyle said.

"We've got to think of something we haven't before. The Rogue can't win," Lydia said.

I stared at my food, trying to fight the heavy weight pressing against my soul.

CHAPTER 24

THE RIDE TO Allen's apartment was strange. I watched cars chase us from the side mirror. When they tried to shoot, Josh put up a force field and forced the car off the road. When one car was forced off the road, three more took up the chase. Sweat lined Josh's forehead as he kept looking in the rearview mirror. I glanced behind me every so often to see Mom and Allen cuddling. Allen went to sleep at one point. I didn't know anything about being brought back from the dead, but it must be exhausting.

Snow began to fall, and I tried to watch it to calm my nerves. It was a few more miles before we got into the city. Another car drove off the road. Usually car chases were intense, but Josh made it so we were winning.

"Bree, do you sense anything different about yourself?" Josh asked.

I gave him a strange look. "Should I?"

"Maybe."

I tried to think but shook my head. "No, not really. Why?"

He tapped the steering wheel. Allen and Mom were alert and listening with Holly watching. The wind picked up and blew the flakes around. "There were times when I heard *her* doing the narration. I knew she was around and in control. I can't hear her voice anymore. I hear you."

"Josh, what are you saying?" Mom asked.

Josh bit his lip, glancing at the rearview mirror as he put up another force field around the car to block the bullets. "Someone had to start the narration. Every single time it's been her, but not lately. I hear you. Something happened to her. If she were there, she'd take away my powers. She should have taken them away as soon as I healed Allen. I don't know what's going on."

"Why can you hear me?" I asked.

"You're one of the main characters. The things I'm hearing are not coming from Allen," Josh said.

"Wait." Allen frowned. "I was one of the main characters?"

"Yes. You and Bree were co-main characters."

169

From the unsettled look on Allen's face, it seemed like this information bothered him. We passed a tree blowing in wind stronger than I ever remembered. The wind didn't bother the car at all. "So, I'm narrating?"

"It's through your point of view, yes."

"I don't want it."

"Our narrator isn't the one who turned on the device, so someone went to plan B. They don't want me to hear their thoughts, and the next best option is first person narration."

Fear punched my stomach. I didn't know the first things about narration. What was I supposed to do? Another thought hit me.

"Does this mean you hear everything I think about?" I felt my face go red. Some things I wanted to keep to myself. Though I cared about Josh, I didn't want him knowing some things about me. My mind instantly went to my embarrassing crush on the cowboy bus driver before quickly stifling it.

A weak smile flickered across Josh's face I didn't know how to interpret. "Don't worry. I don't hear everything."

We entered the city where the wind and snow continued to blow. The cars stopped following us. I frowned as small trees were almost bent in half because of the wind.

"What do we do?" Holly asked.

"Little. I shouldn't use my power much. We might have to wait it out and hope our narrator comes back."

"What if she doesn't?" Allen asked.

Josh didn't say anything for quite a while. "Let's hope she does." So much relied on a hope for some mysterious person who controlled our existence to be there without us knowing why she went missing in the first place.

"Can't you do anything with your powers to bring her back?" Holly asked.

"My powers work in this world. I can't use them in her world."

I checked behind me to look at Allen and Mom when I saw the blackest clouds I'd ever seen in the back window. "Josh?"

He didn't take his eyes off the road. "I know."

"Snow clouds don't get this black, do they?"

"No." At this point, everyone in the back seat turned to see the clouds. The cars following us were long gone now.

"It's just a storm, right?" Holly asked.

"Let's err on the side of caution," Josh said.

I turned and saw some poor soul stuck outside with their dog. The man looked freezing, about ready to head back to his house. One second he stood there, pulling his dog toward the direction of the house, and the next second he and his dog blipped out of existence.

I gasped. Josh's head snapped over in the direction I was looking.

"Bree? What's wrong?" Mom asked.

"That man! He disappeared!"

Everyone turned to Josh for an explanation. He looked as surprised as everyone. The driver of a bus on the other side of the lane disappeared, and the bus careened toward us with no one to steer.

I screamed and braced myself for the impact before Josh threw a powerful force field over the car. The bus smacked into it and flipped itself over on our car. Josh pushed his hand up, and the top of the car popped off. We all watched transfixed as he flew through the roof and pushed the bus off the force field as if he was moving a newspaper. I tore my eyes away from Josh and watched as hundreds of cars began to go every which way as their drivers disappeared. Snow mixed with ice began to pelt our vehicle. Josh flew back through the hole and fixed it up.

"Everyone disappeared. There's not a single soul on the bus."

Holly stared at him, infatuated. I covered my eyes and groaned. This was not a good time for her to get a crush, and on my uncle no less. Josh watched the cars as they ran off roads and into houses and streetlamps.

"Everyone's disappearing," I said.

Josh frowned. He continued to drive, cars magically moving out of the way as the snow and sleet continued to batter the car. This was no normal storm. "We'll get to Allen's apartment, and then we'll talk," Josh said.

§ § §

Once again I curled up and pretended to be asleep. I was too busy beating myself up about the stupid decision I made which got my characters and the Guardians in trouble. An hour later, I still wasn't asleep. From the sound of Lydia's breathing, I knew she was.

For the past twenty minutes I heard the TV on low; most likely Kyle was watching it. I finally rolled off the cot and got up. Sleep wasn't coming, so I might as well join him. I opened the door and saw Kyle on the couch.

His eyes were closed, pain evident on his face. His eyes opened, and when he saw me he tried to sit up.

He reached for the remote. "Is the TV keeping you up?"

"No, it's fine."

He still grabbed the remote and turned the TV off. Trying to keep the pain a secret from me, he almost moved his leg, but I held up a hand.

"No, stop. I'll sit here." I sat on the other couch.

"Can't sleep?" he asked. I shook my head. "I couldn't the first couple of days either."

I looked around. Drake snored softly from his cot. Kyle must have had the TV on to keep his mind off the pain. The pain returned to his face, and he struggled not to let me see it. Maybe I could help distract him.

"What was it like, growing up with Jim?" I asked.

The corners of Kyle's mouth twitched up. "Ugh, nightmare."

That surprised me. "Really?"

"Yes. Typical older brother who never did anything wrong. Can you imagine following his straight A report card in high school? College was no different. Then he landed a position as a Guardian not long after graduation. Youngest ever, I might add, with rumors of Chairmanship in his future. Disgusting. Honestly, I only got into college because Jim was my brother."

His words sounded harsh, but I sensed complete adoration hidden beneath them. "You have talent, too," I interjected.

He paused and looked at me. "How'd you read my stuff?"

Heat crept up my cheeks. "I asked Jim if I could get an idea of what the Rogue did in other stories."

"Sorry, not my best work." He looked embarrassed as he stared at the opposite wall.

"I know how it is." I wanted to comfort him. "The Rogue makes you do awful things to your story." I paused as I recalled my current situation.

Kyle nodded, studying me. "It's hard to see your work ruined."

There were tears in my eyes as I looked at him. The truth was so much worse. I didn't kill a character, I destroyed all of them and their chances for happiness. Who knows how many times the Rogue's minions turned the device on to start the narration? How long was Josh forced to use his unlimited power? Or will they even narrate it?

"What about Lydia?" The subject needed to change before I sobbed in front of a guy with a badly sprained ankle. "How'd they meet?" I tried to focus on him instead of thinking about my characters.

"They met at the library, of all places. They hated each other at first, both trying to outsmart the other. And believe me, Lydia is someone hard to outsmart, even for Jim. After they both got over their stubbornness, they realized how much they loved each other. They've been grossly lovey-dovey ever since."

I allowed myself to smile. It felt good to do so. Kyle shifted around to a new position. "What about you, Kyle?" I asked. "I've asked about Jim and Lydia. What about you?"

Kyle placed a hand on his leg. "Not much to tell about me."

"Oh come on. There's got to be something." I watched the sliver of sadness stretch across the mischievous eyes, and it made me curious.

"Oh, same old, same old. Followed my brother's footsteps and graduated in narration. Then I got a narration device and started narrating a story. Though the Rogue bit was unexpected."

He used humor to mask something, but I didn't want to push it. Clearly he didn't want to talk about himself. I tried to find a new subject when I saw his foot. "Why'd they hurt it?"

"I tried to escape again. Got as far as the grounds the other night before they captured me. Ricky made sure I couldn't run anymore before sticking me in solitary."

"Solitary...confinement?"

"Sort of. They have a room up there without any windows they keep us in if we do something they don't like. Usually for 24 hours. It's not truly solitary; whenever I need the bathroom, I knock on the door, and they escort me to one down the hall. They also come in to give me food. It's more separating me from the others. Sometimes I'd go to the bathroom a lot to spite them."

I laughed and brought my knees to my chest, hugging them tightly.

"It's sad, though. Across the hall from the bathroom is one of the devices the Rogue uses to narrate his characters into other's stories."

My heart dropped into my stomach as I stared at him. "What?"

"Yeah, can you believe it? I don't know how many bases he has, but he has one at all of them."

I released my legs, and my feet hit the floor. My mind shook off the pity party and became alert and alive. My mind instantly went to hope, though I still didn't want to tell Kyle about what happened to me.

"Did you ever try to get to the narration device to send a message to the Guardians?"

"Once. The Rogue tinkered with it so it will only respond to him or one of the guards. Not to me."

My mind exploded with ideas. "The Rogue's tinkered device would have to let the narrator on it though, right?" Kyle glanced at me, doubt playing across his face.

There was still hope I could save my characters. If I got to the device, I could read what happened and then reverse it somehow. My first act would be to get rid of Josh's power. The longer Josh used his power, the more it corrupted him, and a corrupted person did a lot of damage. After I took it away, I could see if any of my characters needed help. I became aware I didn't talk for a whole minute and noticed Kyle watching me.

"Junior, I was thinking about it for a while after. There's no way to get a note to the Guardians. Devin or Jim will find it and hide it. It's not possible." Kyle spoke quietly, afraid to remind me of a tender subject.

He saw me sad and depressed. He'd never seen me when I had an idea I couldn't let go. My mind tried to decide what to do. If Kyle got to the narration device once, then so could I. With hope flooding my system, the depression left.

"I don't care. I need to try."

I didn't want to tell Kyle about my true predicament. Someone must be narrating it to force Josh to get corrupted. And if they were ignoring my story, then I needed to get to it more than ever.

Kyle frowned. "Well, I guess so. Who am I to stop someone's crazy escape plan?"

§ § §

Allen tried the light, though we all knew it was hopeless. The entire city had no lights, which also meant no heat. Josh walked over and flipped it on, and light filled the room. He then walked over to the thermometer and tapped it. Heat began to blow through the apartment. I shivered. Walking from the car to the apartment everyone got soaked. Josh went from person to person. A simple touch made them look like they'd been inside for hours. When he touched me, I felt the much-needed physical warmth.

I glanced around Allen's apartment. It was a small, two-bedroom place. A couch, a coffee table, and a desk sat in the living room. There was a table next to a rather small kitchen. From the living room, a small hall led to three other doors. Behind the doors were a bathroom, his bedroom, and the final room looked like an office full of bookcases. Other than books, Allen didn't have a lot of things.

"Are my parents going to be okay?" Holly asked.

Josh looked out the window, acting as if he hadn't heard Holly's question. He closed his eyes, taking a breath.

"Josh? Can you pick up my parents?" She shifted from one foot to the other, watching him anxiously.

There was a sadness in his eyes when he turned to us that made my knees shake. "I'm sorry, Holly. They aren't there."

I walked over to my best friend to be a comfort if needed. She was shocked. "They disappeared?" she asked, and Josh nodded.

"Then bring them back." Holly's voice was sharp and demanding.

"Holly, I—"

"You brought Allen back from the dead. Bring my parents back."

Josh looked surprised, then his eyebrows furrowed. "That's not how my powers work. Whatever made the filler characters disappear is something out of my control. It's something *he* did."

"Make it work! My parents aren't filler characters! Bring them back!"

"Holly..." I reached out to comfort her, but she batted my arm away.

Josh folded his arms, and his jaw began to twitch. The beginnings of anger entered his eyes. He closed his eyes again, touching his forehead to dispel whatever thought made him angry.

"Holly." Mom stepped forward. "Josh is doing the best he can."

"I want my parents back! Why is Allen's life more important? What's the point of having powers if you can't control anything! You can't bring back the narrator! You can't bring back my parents! You can't even stop this storm!"

Josh straightened to his full height, and there was something in him I'd never seen before. Something I didn't like.

"I could stop this storm, but I won't. Allen is a co-main character, so his life is important. More than yours, more than mine. If you want to see your parents again, you better hope the narrator takes control. And you better hope this world is in a state to be fixed when she does!"

My heart pounded in my chest. Josh was so cold and heartless. Holly's mouth shut as she trembled in fright. Mom inched closer to me, and Allen looked ready to protect us if needed. Josh looked at Mom and winced. He touched his forehead again.

"Excuse me." Josh crossed the living room and entered the bathroom, where he slammed the door.

No one moved. I didn't dare breathe. Mom hugged me. "Are you okay?"

I tried to nod, but I didn't feel okay.

Allen walked over to us. "Maybe it would be smart not to get him mad. He does, after all, have a lot of power."

I shivered. Josh wouldn't...he'd never hurt us. Would he?

CHAPTER 25

MY HEART POUNDED in my chest as Ricky opened the door for breakfast. I was anxious for this to work. Kyle stood up and leaned against Drake to keep his balance. I remained behind Ricky, barely out of sight.

"Ricky, my friend, how are you?" Kyle asked. "I need you over here for a second."

Ricky groaned, but didn't move. "What is it this time?"

"Check my foot, would you? It's giving me a little pain."

The glare Ricky gave him was dark as he moved into the basement prison. "I see the problem. It's supposed to give you a lot of pain."

I made a break for it, made it up the stairs, and almost to the front door when a guard tackled me to the ground. Ricky came up the stairs, a hint of annoyance in his eyes. "You, new girl. What's your name?"

One of the guards helped me to my feet. "Junior."

The grip used to seize my arm betrayed his calm demeanor. "You're new here, so let me give you some advice. No one escapes here. Remember Kyle's foot? I suggest you don't give me any trouble."

He started leading me toward what I thought was the direction of solitary confinement. My mind went over the next part of our plan, but I began to panic when Ricky turned and dragged me down the stairs to the basement again. He opened the door and threw me in. I tried to catch my balance, but I fell to my knees.

"Next time I catch you, I'm putting you in solitary confinement." He closed the door, and I almost kicked it in frustration when I remembered my shoes were off.

"Junior, what were you thinking?" Drake asked.

I folded my arms and marched to the couch. "I can't sit here, Drake. Kyle had his turn, now it's mine."

My heart dropped in disappointment. Every day wasted was another day my story got deeper in danger. I needed to be in solitary confinement already, trying to figure out a way to get out and help my characters. Kyle gave me some ideas on how to escape solitary, but I couldn't repeat what he did. They anticipated everything Kyle tried. In the end, it would be up to me to think of something.

Kyle sat on the couch. He gave me a charming smile as though he knew I was disappointed. "It's okay, Junior." Then he whispered quietly enough the other two couldn't hear, "Next time."

§ § §

"I don't have much food." Allen opened the cupboards, frowning. "I'm not much of a cook."

Mom walked over to the kitchen. "You've got bread."

"Bread and fruit." Allen pulled out a can of fruit. "It's a start."

The door of the bathroom opened and Josh emerged. He caught the tail end of the conversation, snapped his fingers, and the tabled groaned under the weight of a feast fit for the holidays. My mouth watered.

He turned sad eyes toward Holly. "If I knew how to save your parents, they would be here. I'm sorry I got mad. I shouldn't have acted the way I did."

After taking a few steps away from Josh, she nodded. Allen looked hesitant as well, but I wanted to believe the worst was behind us. We knew not to get Josh angry.

Mom walked over and gave Josh a hug. "Thank you for dinner."

"Let's eat."

Since I hadn't eaten anything since breakfast that morning, I was famished and dug into the feast. The storm raged outside, but we were safe because we had Josh. Or at least a happy Josh.

"I'm sorry for yelling at you." Holly's voice seemed a few octaves higher than usual. I looked up and noticed she had barely touched her food.

Josh, who sat across from her, wouldn't look at her. "You are grieving. I forgive you."

Slowly, Allen placed his unused fork on his plate. "These powers, what can you do?"

For the first time, I noticed everyone else did not share in my comfort. I was worried about the storm outside, but Allen, Holly, and even Mom looked like they ate with one eye on the food and one eye on Josh. Even Josh gave the impression he was distracted with something.

"I don't know." Josh tried to smile. "I don't want to know. I was supposed to get them in a life or death situation, which it was. But now I'm stuck with them, and I have to control how I use them."

"What do you mean?" I asked.

Josh still didn't look at anyone as he tapped a finger on the table. "The narrator created me because I could handle things outside her original outline. I have to make sure I don't mess anything up."

"Can't you put it back on track?" Mom asked.

"If the bad narrator is in control he can send more of his minions, and I can't control him. The more power I use, the more dangerous it is."

"Why is it dangerous?" I asked. It was the thing everyone else seemed to understand.

Josh continued to push around his food. "The more I use them, the more I understand what I can do. I could have anything in the world, but I shouldn't because it's not what the narrator wanted." Josh looked at Allen. "You needed to come back, but what's stopping me from bringing back others who the narrator already deemed needed to die?"

Allen shifted in his seat and turned his focus back on his full plate of food.

"What's stopping me from having my own agenda?" Josh looked out the window. His voice was far away. "I could force people to love who I wanted them to love, to kill who I wanted to have killed." He looked at Mom. "Make those who hurt anyone I care for suffer in an irreversible way." Mom dropped her gaze. "It scares me."

There was silence.

"I believe the narrator will gain power back, though," Josh said.

We all ate, and though it was the best food I ever tasted, an uneasy feeling settled around the table.

§ § §

After dinner, I sat on the couch trying to fight boredom. Allen and Mom talked quietly at the table, and Holly was asleep next to me on the couch. Josh wandered over and sat on the floor. He leaned against the front of the couch.

"There's room. Do you want me to move?" I asked.

"No. Stay there." It made me feel bad that Josh sat on the floor. Josh watched Mom and Allen chatting, looking pleased.

"Bree, there's something I want you to know." He turned his body so he could look at me without hurting his neck. I kept eye contact so he knew I was listening. "I'd rather die than hurt you."

I cocked my head to one side. "Do you think it will come to that?"

"You trust me so much. You're amazing." He looked up at the ceiling. "I haven't begun to tap into my powers. The farther I go, the more they corrupt me. I don't want it. I could do bad things, and I refuse."

"I believe you, Josh."

His smile was weak. "Thank you. I will stay true to my word, and true to your trust." He got up and joined the conversation with Allen and Mom. I watched for a moment before looking back at Holly. She was in an uncomfortable position, but it seemed to work for her.

Josh worried about the powers. I believed him when he said they were corrupting, but I felt safe. The narrator chose the right person to give them to. I didn't trust anyone else with them. Not even Mom.

Mom walked over to me, leaving Allen and Josh to talk at the table. The corners of her mouth flipped up, and I could almost believe she meant it. "You okay, Bree?"

I nodded. "I hope the narrator gets control back. Josh is doing great, but I want things normal again."

Mom squeezed my hand. "She'll come. Everything will be fine." Her voice caught at the end. I knew she felt scared, but like so many other times, she stayed strong for me.

I hugged her tightly. The past couple of days turned everything I thought I knew upside down. My mind still tried to wrap around the idea of being in a story. It was strange, but it was my life, and for the next little while, I needed to survive it.

§§§

Ricky came in with lunch, seeming a lot angrier. I didn't know why.

"Well, aren't you in a happy mood," Kyle said.

"No sarcasm from you, Kyle. I would break your leg right now and not even care."

"What happened to ruin your day? Oh, did someone kidnap you and make it so you didn't see your family for over a year?" Kyle asked.

"Shut up!" Ricky slammed the food down and stormed out.

"Is he usually like this?" I asked.

"No, but it's not like we haven't seen it before." Lydia shrugged.

Everyone ate in silence. Getting kidnapped was boring. No one said anything to each other. We tried to entertain ourselves. We gauged time by Ricky coming with breakfast, lunch, and dinner. I hated it. No wonder Kyle wanted to leave. The boredom itself was too much.

I needed conversation. "Drake, when did you get kidnapped?"

Drake glanced up from his food. "Six months before Kyle got here."

"How did you survive the boredom?" I said.

Drake smiled. "The Rogue ordered someone to talk to me every day. They didn't want me revealing what I knew, but they also didn't want me to go insane."

Part of me wanted to know what Drake was like before being kidnapped. He must have been brave. The Rogue gave him the option of either joining him or holding his characters hostage to force him to join him, but Drake refused to be on the Rogue's side in any way. Instead he killed his main character to save his other characters from being in the Rogue's reach. Did Drake ever wonder, in the moment he refused to side with the Rogue, if he was going to die?

My frown deepened. There had to be some reason the Rogue held us prisoner. Part of me hoped he still had his humanity not to kill us. "What does he plan to do with us, anyway?" I asked the group.

Lydia shrugged. "Who knows."

Kyle placed his plate to one side. "Probably leave us here until we're too late to stop anything."

We finished our lunch. It was the first time I noticed the gloom and the pessimism hanging heavy in the air. Kyle kept trying to put on a brave and painless face for the rest of us.

"Kyle, what do you need?" Lydia gathered his dishes and put them with her own before putting them by the door for Ricky.

"Don't worry about me."

I held the metal fork in my hand and glanced at the bricks. It would never work. I couldn't scrape my way to freedom, but if it looked like

I had tried maybe they'd put me in confinement. I stood up, walked over to the bricks, and began scraping.

"Junior, what are you doing?" Drake's tone of voice made me feel like a toddler.

"I've got to find a way out." I continued to scrape the mortar.

"You know it's impossible, right?" Drake asked.

"I haven't been here long enough."

"It's not—"

He stopped talking. I continued to scrape hard. Maybe if I made a mark on the brick they'd notice and ask questions. A few more seconds of silence went by before I realized the room was eerily quiet. I turned and saw Ricky had come in. His arms were folded, and he glared at me as though I was responsible for every bad thing in his life.

Another way to go to solitary is if I unknowingly got caught trying to escape. Ricky bounded over to me and grabbed my wrist. He squeezed until I let out a gasp of pain as he pried the fork out of my hand.

"Plastic utensils from now on! How much more will it take before you realize escape is impossible?"

"I'm going to get out of here!" To my surprise, Ricky hit me with the back of his hand. Hard. I threw my hands out in front of me to catch myself and landed on the concrete.

Kyle tried to stand up. "Junior!" Ricky gathered the rest of the dishes and left without another word.

Lydia helped me up and inspected my face. "Are you all right?"

"Fine."

She brushed her hand over my cheek, and I gasped as it stung. It brought tears to my eyes. I felt more disappointed Ricky didn't place me into solitary confinement. What more did I need to do? I was running out of ideas, and I needed to save my characters.

§ § §

I vaguely remember Josh carrying me to Allen's bed. I protested, saying the couch was fine, but Josh told me to hush and keep sleeping. Josh brought in Holly as well. She woke up long enough to shift her weight to a more comfortable position before she went back to sleep. Josh pulled the covers over me.

182

"I will keep you safe," he whispered.

Not long after I closed my eyes, I felt my mother stroking my hair. It reminded me of my younger years. She'd stroke my hair and somehow everything felt safer. It was more comforting than light in the darkness. For this moment in time, I felt safe and was ready to enter a deep sleep.

"Are they asleep?" Allen asked from the doorway.

"Yes," Mom said.

My heart quickened, but I still pretended to be asleep. I used this tactic a lot in bad times. Mom never told me what bothered her, and I always resorted to eavesdropping to understand how she felt.

Mom crept out of the room, and I thought they left. I cracked an eye open and saw them in the doorway. "Both of them were exhausted. These past couple days took a toll on them."

"Are you going to be okay?" Allen asked.

"I'm nervous for her." Mom ran a hand through her hair. "I'm glad she's sleeping, though. She needs it." My eyes got used to the darkness, so I saw them well enough. Enough to see the frown on Mom's face.

"You didn't answer my question."

It was a long moment before Mom turned her attention to Allen. "I'm scared. I don't like waiting. Josh is quietly suffering, which hurts because I want to help him. There are still people searching for us, wanting us dead, and the extent of Josh's plan is to wait and see. To hope someone who I didn't know existed until today will take control of...this again."

"Do you believe she'll come back?" Allen asked.

"I have to believe, for her sake." Mom looked at me. I shut my eyes so she couldn't catch me. "I don't want her to die." They were quiet for some time. "Do you believe she'll take control?" Mom asked.

I opened my eyes again. Allen put his hands in his pockets and leaned against the door frame. I didn't see his face since his back was to me, but by the way he stood with his shoulders slouched, he had something heavy on his mind.

"I've tried to see things positively, but things look bleak, and I don't like waiting. We don't even know what's going on in her world." Allen took my mom's hand. Mom nodded and glanced at me again. They were far enough away that I kept my eyes slightly open, and they didn't notice. "I'm sure it will work out somehow." He didn't believe what he said. I heard it in his voice.

"I don't want her to die." Mom was crying, and it broke my heart. "I don't want this to be the end."

"I don't either." It seemed Allen wanted to believe the narrator would take control, but life conditioned him to imagine the worst.

Mom reached out and brushed her fingers over his chest. She must have been thinking back to when he was dead on the floor. It shook her up. He should have died. Allen wrapped his fingers around Mom's hand, keeping it on his chest. She wiped her eyes dry.

"You're still here, and by all accounts, you shouldn't be. We're all still here because of Josh's power. If the narrator can come back, we'll survive. If she doesn't, we won't stand a chance. But I won't live my remaining moments depressed about something I can't change."

Allen leaned over, about to kiss her. He hesitated, as though not sure he was allowed to. Mom grabbed his shoulders and kissed him a lot harder than he probably expected. It took him half a second to match her intensity.

I wasn't happy.

I liked Allen. Through all the life-threatening situations we've been in, he'd shown his true colors, and I'd been impressed. But part of me died inside. Something about the way they kissed each other revealed they were desperate. They didn't know if the other would die, and this attraction they felt needed to be expressed before it was too late. Both still had a sliver of doubt they might not make it.

And then there was the fact my mom was kissing a man, *really* kissing him, and she had no idea I was awake a few feet away. It was awkward. I closed my eyes to give them privacy, but I still heard their heavy breathing as they moved away from the doorway. It didn't sound like they planned on stopping soon. Ugh, I might put this down as the most awkward thing I'd ever overheard my mom say or do. I did *not* want to overhear anything worse.

I never thought mom would get into another relationship. She was a strong, independent woman who raised me well. We were fine by ourselves.

Then again, there might not be a lot of time left for a relationship.

CHAPTER 26

I WAITED UNTIL Lydia was asleep. The way she looked at Kyle's foot and my new bruise made me think she wouldn't be on board with our plan. My characters didn't have time for people who doubted. The blanket I was given was old and falling apart, which gave me an idea.

As soon as I heard Lydia's heavy breathing, I slipped out of my cot with my blanket and crept into the main area. Kyle was awake with his arms folded, staring into space. He focused when he saw me and smiled.

"Hey, Junior."

I returned his smile and sat down on the couch next to him. "I had an idea. This might help." With a little struggle, I tore a strip off the blanket. I wrapped his ankle with the strip as he watched. We were quiet for a few moments while I worked.

Kyle broke the silence. "I've been thinking."

The tone in his voice made me hesitate. This was one of those sentences boyfriends or girlfriends use right before they're about to break up. I frowned, pausing long enough to glance up at Kyle before returning to his foot.

"I don't like you getting hurt," he said.

My frown deepened. So it wasn't only Lydia I needed to be afraid of. "I'm still going to try to escape."

"I didn't think Ricky would hit a woman."

I touched my cheek, feeling the bruise. "We've got a small window where we can escape, and we can't dawdle because I got a bruise. It's not like I broke a foot or something. No offense." Kyle glanced at his foot as I finished wrapping it and tied the ends together. If anything, it should have made Kyle want to escape even more. "I appreciate the gentleman in you who doesn't want to put me in danger, but I assumed this would happen."

Kyle still looked hesitant. "We can't even be sure your story is still there." Kyle turned away. "Your main character is dead, and you ended your story. Even if we could get a note in, Vince or Grace won't see it. It's not worth getting hurt over."

I didn't move. My pride got in the way. I didn't want Kyle to know about my mistake.

Kyle misinterpreted my silence. "I'm sorry for bringing it up."

"She's not dead," I found myself saying. If he knew how dire the situation was, he'd understand. I explained everything to him, even though it hurt my pride. He listened, his mouth shut as my face went redder and redder. "So they're either in trouble of limbo, or Josh will murder them all," I said.

I buried my head in my hands so I wouldn't have to look at him. It hurt to admit my mistake. It was such an idiot move. If it wasn't for the hope I could save them, I'd still be depressed.

Kyle didn't say anything, and curiosity made me peek at him through my fingers. He met my eyes, his face hard to read. "It's not about escaping, is it? It's about saving your characters."

I lowered my hands. "Your foot looks bad, Kyle. Of course I want to escape. Escape doesn't seem likely, but I'm willing to try. However, this is a chance to save my characters, and I'm going to take it."

Kyle frowned. "You're obsessed."

"It's my first story. Some of these characters have been with me since junior high."

There was a touch of compassion I was happy to see in his eyes. "If I wasn't a narrator, I'd say you were crazy. But I understand. Can we try not to get you more hurt, though?"

I gave a lame smile. "I might not be able to keep that promise."

The bedroom door opened and Lydia peeked into the room, looking tired. "Hey, what's going on?"

"We're thinking up plans to help Junior save her characters." My face instantly flushed red again.

"Oh?" Lydia sat on the couch by Kyle. Kyle turned to look at me and noticed my beet red face, which of course made it more red.

"It's too embarrassing." I touched my cheeks. "It was a stupid idea, and I endangered them all."

Kyle gave me a look that I couldn't interpret. "Stupid or not, it's our situation, and you have an opportunity to save them." He explained my mistake so I didn't have to. Lydia listened.

"So it's not escape, just solitary?"

"Correct," Kyle said.

Lydia nodded. "I'll distract Ricky so you can escape the same way by running up the stairs."

"Will it work?"

"Ricky doesn't have a high opinion of women. He'll probably expect you to do something like try the same escape route. And judging by his actions last time you tried to escape," her eyes flickered to the bruise on my face with a small frown, "he's irritated enough with you and will stick you in solitary."

"He doesn't let us get close to the door, though," I said.

"I have a way to get him deeper into the basement."

"You do?" Kyle asked.

A smirk crept across Lydia's face.

§ § §

"Bree." Josh's voice was urgent. "Bree, Holly, wake up. Come into the living room. There might be a situation."

I rubbed the sleep from my eyes. It felt like I had barely closed them, and suddenly it was early morning. We got out of bed and followed Josh. Mom was looking out the window.

"What's going on?" Holly asked.

Her question was answered. People surrounded the apartment building outside—hundreds of them, all with guns, all shooting at us. The force field Josh put around the apartment shivered constantly with rebounding bullets.

Allen came out of his office, worried. "At least five hundred."

"Josh? Can you do anything about this?" Mom asked.

Josh brushed some sweat from his face. "We've got to leave. We've got to make it to a better-fortified place. Fewer windows, stronger building."

"Leave?" Allen made it a point to look out the window and then back at Josh. "How?"

"And where do we find this better fortified place?" Mom asked.

With his hands covering his eyes, Josh looked either deep in thought or in denial. He dropped his hands and looked up. "The house two blocks down. It's a single level house. I'll go to make it more fortified." Before we could stop him, Josh ran right through the wall. We scrambled to the window and watched as he flew away, a protective bubble around him to ward off the gunfire. Holly pressed her face against the glass, trying to see where Josh went.

"Did you sleep well, Bree?" Mom asked.

I gasped and jumped back. "Oh, mom. Hi. Hi, mom. Mother."

Mom stared at me alarmed. "Bree, are you okay? Josh will be back. He'll be fine."

How was I supposed to pretend like I hadn't seen Mom making out with Allen? "Yeah, I know." I winced. The smart thing would have been to go along with it so she'd stop asking me. I sat on the couch, rubbing my head so I wouldn't see my mom. She sat next to me, clearly concerned.

"Bree, honey—"

"I'll be fine."

Josh came back, which ended any additional conversation mom and I might have. I was glad, though Josh looked more exhausted than before. "Alright." Josh ran a trembling hand through his hair to keep it out of his sweaty face. "Let's go."

"Are you okay?" I asked.

"Yes."

"How are we going to get there?" Holly asked.

"I'll create a force field, and we'll walk." Josh nodded. It seemed like even nodding exhausted him.

I watched him. Was that it? We didn't question him; it was clear he was tired. I don't know what happened when he fortified the house, but it must have drained him. We gathered close as Josh created a more visible force field around us.

"Don't leave the force field," Josh said. We walked down the stairs. The gunfire was muted in the bubble, but still quite loud. More sweat rolled down Josh's forehead.

Outside, the people pointed their guns toward us and shot. It was deafening. Holly plugged her ears. Men tried to get us, but as soon as they hit the force field they were shot back. Mom dug her fingers into my shoulder and gripped Allen's hand. Holly had a good hold on my arm. Between my mom and Holly, it was getting difficult to feel the tips of my fingers.

The trek was nerve-wracking and slow. Josh tried to make a path by knocking people out, but then we had to walk over bodies so he stopped. We continued to walk through the throng as men and women were thrown back from the force field. Why did they even try? Couldn't they tell it was hopeless? Then I realized the more they swarmed, the slower we moved, and Josh got more uncomfortable.

Josh began to tremble. "Change of plans."

"What?" Allen asked. The force field solidified and lifted in the air. The people went back to shooting.

"I'm landing right beside the house." Josh sounded like he was in the middle of running a marathon. "Get in as fast as possible. I'll hold them off."

"But what—"

"Do what I say!" Josh snapped, cutting me off. I winced. Josh was not in a good state. He looked physically and mentally exhausted. A tear rolled out of his eye. "I'm sorry, Bree."

I swallowed. "I know."

Josh had a determined look in his eye as more tears coursed down his cheeks. He landed by the house. He fortified the house well, making it out of bulletproof material. There were no windows anymore. Holly, Mom, and Allen ran to the front door. I ran too, but hesitated at the front steps and turned.

It was hundreds against Josh. He stood, facing them. The crowd began shooting. Josh created the bubble around himself. They kept coming, and I saw Josh's frame tremble the more he kept the force field going.

"Bree come on, hurry," Mom said.

The men closest to Josh tried to punch him. With one touch from Josh they were unconscious. I turned to go up the stairs and was about in the house when Josh let out a yell. A nearly invisible wave travel through the group. All of them toppled over and lay motionless on the grass. Josh collapsed on his hands and knees, panting. I looked at the men and women and realized they weren't unconscious. They were dead.

Instead of entering the house, I ran toward Josh.

"Bree, no!" Allen tried to grab me, but I slipped out of his reach.

I needed to know Josh was okay. Josh grasped his head in his hands and spoke in a low murmur. I knelt next to him and put a hand on his shoulder. He kept breathing heavily, his eyes closed, groaning from whatever he saw in his head. When he finally opened his eyes and looked at me, I saw deep sadness. I realized what would happen next. He said so himself—he'd rather die than hurt me.

"Josh, no." My grip tightened on his shoulder. "Don't go, please!"

He reached out with a hand and stroked my cheek. At first, I thought it was a gesture of affection, and maybe it was, but then a vision came into my head. A vision of the future. Everything burned. Our bodies lay crumpled on the ground as Josh flew above us. Power and greed consumed him. He wasn't the Josh I knew. I felt his emotions. The power he felt was incredible. He could have anything he wanted, anything at all. It was something he desired almost more than anything. The thing keeping him from murdering us was the look I gave him. The absolute trust, the love, and the knowledge he would never betray me.

"I have to go." The vision wasn't predicting the distant future. It would come true in less than half a day if Josh didn't do something.

"Josh." A tear fell down my cheek. "Please, we'll find another way."

The sorrowful look on his face said it wasn't up to me to decide. Josh gave a violent shiver and stopped. He smiled as though telling me everything was all right. Before I knew it, he fell into the snow and stopped breathing.

"No! Josh!" To save us from the future, Josh killed himself.

Allen appeared at my side. "We have to go."

I grabbed Josh's shoulders and shook him. "Josh! Come back!"

"We have to go now." Allen was urgent. I looked up and saw a new group coming down the street toward us.

Everything inside me felt numb as Allen helped me to my feet. We ran into the house, and he closed the door and locked it. The metal lock clicked into place, and we were plunged into darkness. I crumpled to the ground and sobbed.

§ § §

I waited again for Ricky. He didn't let me by the door anymore. I sat on the couch, arms folded, obedient and docile. The door opened, and Ricky strolled in with breakfast. Lydia didn't give Ricky any time before she started.

"Ricky, I need your help."

He gave her a terrified look. "Is it…"

"Yep. My period started last night. I'm out of tampons, so I need—"

As he placed the tray down in its designated spot, Ricky groaned. "I don't want to hear it."

Lydia looked surprised. "But I need them. I'll leak through, and then you'll have to buy me new clothes. Also, you might want to look at this stain in the bathroom so we can be allowed to use cleaning chemicals."

Ricky covered his ears. Kyle tried his hardest not to laugh. "Fine!" Ricky looked sickened. "Women are disgusting."

"And your attitude about women is disgusting. Now come on."

As they passed me to head to the bathroom, Lydia winked at me. I smiled back. When Ricky was in the bathroom, I bolted for the open door. Ricky's shout of annoyance gave me the energy to clear the stairs and head toward the front door. Once again another guard caught me.

"You're starting to be a real thorn in my side," Ricky said. He grabbed my arm, and instead of turning toward the basement, he headed down a different hall and threw me in a room with no windows. "Twenty-four hours, stupid girl. And looks like you missed breakfast."

He slammed the door, and I grinned at the empty room.

§ § §

I never sobbed so much in my life. Josh, my best friend and uncle, was dead.

Allen kept a lookout. Josh's fortified house was done well. He didn't leave us any weapons, though. For two days we stayed in the house. Those two days did not change my feelings. I felt as distraught the second day as I did the first hour. Mom held me tight, but I knew she felt worse. Josh helped Mom when her life got bleak.

The gunfire continued to batter the house. I was surprised we lasted this long without Josh. I stayed on the couch, a blanket over me. Mom tried to get me to eat, but I had no appetite. Instead, she stroked my hair. It didn't comfort me. Holly sat silently on the opposite couch. Allen paced the floor with his arms folded.

At about eleven o'clock in the evening, the gunfire stopped. We waited, watching each other, but nothing happened. The silence terrified me more than the constant gunfire.

Soon Holly went to sleep. I tried. Every time I closed my eyes, I saw Josh die in front of me. That or the vision of him being consumed with power played before my eyes to keep me awake. I didn't want to fall asleep and have the vision play out in a nightmare. Eventually Allen noticed me still awake.

"Did you wake up?"

"You have to be asleep in order to wake up." I rubbed my head and pushed the blanket farther off. Mom had stopped stroking my hair and was asleep on the other side of the couch. I put the blanket over her. The light from the digital clock showed it was three in the morning. Allen walked over and sat next to me on the couch. I moved a bit farther so we wouldn't be too close.

"Hungry?" He had two cans of peaches in hand. I shook my head.

"Yeah, me neither." He opened one of the cans and handed it to me with a fork. He opened another can for himself. I went through the motions of scooping out a peach and eating it, but my grief must have deadened my taste buds.

"Do you want to talk about anything?" he asked.

I watched him pick up a peach and eat it. Of anyone, he was the most familiar with death, but I wasn't ready to talk about it. I wanted to forget this nightmarish situation we were in and talk about something semi-normal.

"So, you like my Mom a lot?" I heard a splash. Allen accidentally dropped one of the peaches back into the juice. He cleared his throat before glancing at me.

"Um, yes. I do. Why do you ask?" It was clear he didn't expect to talk about his feelings for my mom. I shrugged. I tried not to remember them making out, though it was better than seeing Josh die over and over in my mind.

"She is an amazing woman." Allen looked over at her, and I saw happiness flickering in his eyes. "Do you...I mean..."

"It's fine." This was the normal conversation I craved. "You're good for her."

Allen chewed for quite a while before swallowing. "You and your mother are both so self-sacrificing."

"What do you mean?"

"What do *you* think? She is your mother after all. I don't want to barge into your life if you don't want me there."

A warmth I didn't expect filled my heart as a smile crept across my face. It was a comfort to know Allen acknowledged how hard this was for me. "I'm warming up to the idea." I paused to eat another peach. "Give it time, and

I'll like the idea. It might be awhile before I love it." I stopped to think. "If we have the time."

Allen watched me. "Yeah. Hopefully. Because dating your mom, getting to know you a bit better, it sounds like a great plan for the future."

I nodded. It surprised me. There were many things about Allen that caught me off guard. It was all new and scary, but maybe it would be okay.

We ate again in silence. I couldn't get over how strange my heart felt. All my life I built up anger toward my father for what he did to my mom, to me, and the anger must have spilled over to most men my mother's age. I never recognized it until I sat next to Allen, both of us eating peaches. I felt comfortable next to Allen. Peace moved in and began to clean up the mess that anger left in my soul.

I moved a peach around and refused to look him in the eye. "I never thanked you for saving my life a few days ago. So, thank you."

Allen grinned into his peach can. "Any time, Bree."

I felt his sincerity. My mom chose a good man. "I didn't know you had a wife and child."

Allen didn't look up, focused on his own food. "Yeah. It's been about five years now." He was being careful. It still hurt.

"Boy or girl?"

"Celia." His voice caught. I looked up at him. There were tears in his eyes. "We were going to name her Celia." He stared at the can, trying to compose himself. He set it down on the coffee table, and I noticed his hand shake. I was at a loss as to how to comfort him.

"My wife, Naomi, she was a lovely woman. I miss her. But my daughter? She's why it's taking so long to come to peace with the situation. Celia is a stranger to me; a stranger that I loved instantly, deeply, and was forced to say goodbye to before I got to know her. I'll never see her grow up. Her death broke me. Broke me in a way I..." Allen rubbed his forehead with his palm. "I don't know how to put the pieces back together. I don't think I ever will. It's been five years, and it still hurts like hell."

I watched Allen, unsure what to do. I felt my own tears burn in my eyes. Compassion flooded my system for him. Here was a man who had a daughter he wanted to keep more than anything and couldn't. It seemed a strange concept for me to understand. Some men don't abandon their families.

"I'm sorry."

He tried to smile. He opened his mouth to say something, but men started beating the walls. I jumped, the peach juice sloshing around. Josh had fortified the wall very well, but it still frightened me. Especially after hours of silence. Mom and Holly woke up with a start. Allen jumped to his feet and helped me up.

"Stay with your mother," he said.

He had a hand on my shoulder and nudged me toward Mom. She leaned over and kissed my forehead. I felt her tear fall on my cheek. "I'm never leaving you Bree. Never."

I looped my arm in Holly's arm when she appeared next to me. "Stay with me," I said.

Holly nodded, fear making her mute.

"Take the girls and go into the kitchen," Allen said.

Mom took us by the arms and led us away from the pounding. I trembled, thinking this was it. Holly had tears in her eyes, and I hugged her tight. The pounding spread until it was all around the house. As they continued, I felt a strange peace. Whatever the outcome, either my death or the narrator's return, this wouldn't last forever. This constant fear of not knowing what to expect, of simply wondering when it would all end, it couldn't be long now.

The building started to shake. "What's happening?" Mom asked.

Allen pressed his ear against the wall, then shook his head and started walking toward the kitchen. "I think—"

I heard an explosion. Chunks of wall and ceiling came toward me and I screamed.

194

Chapter 27

I SAT AT the door, not sure how much time passed. Earlier when I went to the bathroom, I studied everything in hopes of finding something to help me. There wasn't much. While being escorted back, I noticed the room opposite the bathroom. The door was ajar. I wasn't positive the room had the narration device, but Kyle said it did and I trusted him.

Back in the room, I searched for anything I could use. I already tried the knob, but a bolt on the other side kept it closed. There was a cot with no blankets or pillow. Even the light was a bare bulb.

My back hit the wall and I stared at the door, trying to think of a plan. There were four guards total, one for every person kidnapped. One guard at the front door, one at the back, one was new, and then Ricky.

As I stared at the door, a plan fell into my head. I stood up, thinking through everything. Like a scene in a story, I played the escape plan over in my mind until I knew it backwards and forwards.

§ § §

I coughed, feeling dirt and debris lodged in my throat. Boards and bricks kept me from seeing the sky. My head throbbed, and my ears rang as I pushed away the debris. The snow fell on the coat I borrowed from Josh, and I looked up at the sky. It was too quiet.

"Sadie?" I called out. "Holly?" No answer. "Bree? Are you there?" The silence was turning into my enemy. I struggled to my feet, my legs made of wood. A dull pain in my left leg made me limp.

"Sadie!" Panic rose in my voice.

Again, silence. I treaded carefully over the remains of the house, wiping the blood from my forehead. Fear gave me added strength. I moved bricks and rubble where I thought the kitchen would be. I moved a board and found them all lying crumpled under the rocks.

"No."

They didn't move. They looked...

My worst nightmare came back to haunt me. It wasn't my wife and child now, but I again saw my life, my hopeful and happy future, crumpled next to them. Pain tore my heart apart as I sank to my knees and sobbed.

"Hello, Allen," the last person I wanted to see said. "I thought you died."

My hands tightened into fists. I spun around, a chunk of brick in my hand. The brick and my anger were my weapons against Riley. It might have been enough if he didn't have hundreds of other men with him.

"I wish you would." My voice was cold and unwelcoming.

Riley chuckled. "Not going to happen. *He* promised this world to us as soon as we took control of *her* characters. The ones with small parts and no names were easy enough, but we had to hunt the rest of you down. Since we took out the substitute narrator, you are now the only main character left."

"Then kill me, since it's what you're here to do," I said.

Riley shook his head and pulled out a gun. He didn't point it at me, instead looking at it like it was an annoying bug. "Believe me, Allen, I wish I could kill you. I wish this bullet would make its mark and drop you dead, but it can't. Since *she's* not the one narrating, she can't accept any of your deaths. Sadie, Bree, and Holly are barely alive, like you were before Josh healed you."

"What does it matter? Shoot me."

A strange darkness filled Riley's eyes. "Those aren't my orders. I am to arrest you, throw you in prison, and watch you go crazy with grief. This situation, if *he* is correct, will break you."

Alone. Again. My stomach twisted in anger and hate for Riley. I didn't want this life. I glanced at Sadie, lying in the mess before I chucked my brick as hard as I could at Riley. It hit him in the forehead. He yelled in pain, which gave me much satisfaction.

Riley glared at me. "Death is what you want, but you're not getting it. Instead, you will live the rest of your life thinking about what you could have had, and how I took it from you."

A pain hotter than a bullet tore my chest apart as tears fell down my dirty cheeks.

§ § §

I was on my cot, staring at the ceiling. Dinner felt like a while ago. If I arrived at breakfast time, it meant I might have twelve hours left of my twenty-four. My mind came alive with images of Allen, Bree, Sadie, Josh, and Holly all in trouble with no one to help. Even the Guardians, too. The Rogue controlled half of them, and I couldn't let it continue. I needed to execute my plan.

"Excuse me!"

The guard opened the door and stuck his head inside. "What?"

"I've got to go to the bathroom, please." I tried to sound nice and pleasant about it.

He grumbled about how small a bladder some people had as he led me to the bathroom. Adrenaline coursed through me as I closed the door. Part of me felt nervous, because I didn't think I had the guts for my plan to succeed. A key element in making the plan work was causing pain to the guard, and I hated causing pain to others. I listened at the door and heard his feet shuffling. This guard stood between me and my story, and I didn't even know his name. Would knowing his name make a difference? If I knew his background, his family life, his social life? Would we be able to talk things out instead of fight over our ideas?

I strode to the sink and unscrewed the lid to the hand soap dispenser. Most of the soap I poured into the toilet to make it sound like I did some business. When I had a couple inches left in the bottle, I flushed the toilet to get rid of the evidence and filled the container with tap water until I had a good amount of soapy substance. I hid it in my pocket without the lid, making sure it didn't spill.

When I turned off the tap, I waited a moment before opening the door and smiling at the guard. "All done."

He grunted as he grabbed my arm and started to lead me to the room. As soon as he opened the door I struggled out of his grip. He tightened his grip on my wrist, glaring at me. I grabbed the soap with my free hand and threw it at his face. It wasn't enough to do true pain, but he let go of my wrist to cover his face as he let out a scream. I shoved him into the room, slammed the door, and locked him inside. He thrashed around more inside, and I had no time to lose.

"Escape! Escape! The prisoner has escaped!" The other guards probably rushed to the front door to wait for me. Instead, I ran for the device and shut the door. I grabbed one of the two chairs and put it under the doorknob.

"Where is she!" I heard Ricky yell.

The chair might hold for a while, but I needed to know what was going on in my story and how to fix it. I turned on the two screens and skimmed as fast as possible through the text, my heart sinking deeper and deeper. It wasn't the worst possible scenario, but it still made me slam my fists on the desk and swear. Josh was dead, and I knew he'd rather die than kill the others. But what did it mean for Sadie, Holly, and Bree who were in critical condition? Even if they went to a hospital, modern medicine couldn't fix them. They'd forever be in a coma until I accepted their death. They had no hope without Josh.

And what was worse, Allen was alone. This would break him. I didn't know how long he spent on his own, but he had some psychological damage more impossible to fix than the girls' situation. I massaged my head and tried to keep tears at bay.

Someone pounded on the door, and it made me jump.

"Get out of there, Junior!" Even though the door was closed, it felt like his voice boomed throughout the room. "Get out of there now!"

Did Ricky think that would work? I glanced at the screen. It was a new scene, ready for anyone to continue narrating. It was in a quiet cell; Allen was chained to the wall. The chain gave him enough room to curl himself in a ball, eyes closed, fingers tangled in his hair. I understood him. All alone, faced with an eternity of regret. It made my stomach churn. He despised me. Josh was so busy saving them he didn't have time to heal the heavy damage Allen went through by knowing of my existence.

"Go get an axe!" Ricky yelled.

I winced. The axe cut my narration time considerably. My mind raced through every possible idea. How was I going to save my characters before they axed down the door?

The more I thought, the more frustrated I became. I wanted to alert the Guardians, but knew it was impossible. My heart sank, remembering Kyle in pain. I'd have to fix my story and then worry about an escape plan later.

I went through my characters, trying to decide who would cause the least damage by remaining dead. It took a moment of contemplation before I shook my head. I would save all my characters, or I would do the merciful thing and cause an earthquake to kill Allen. All or none.

The door trembled beneath the thwacks of an axe. There was less time than I thought. With tears, I put on the headset. I had to kill them all. My heart ached until it broke in two.

In despair, I closed my eyes and rubbed my forehead. I yearned to tell Allen why I had to do all those things to him. More than anything, I wanted him to be at peace in his final moments. But I couldn't tell him. Not unless…

My eyes snapped open, and I gaped at the wall. Another idea filled my mind. Different, fabulous, and lawbreaking. One insane enough to alert all the Guardians to our position as well as let me save all my characters. At least, that was the best-case scenario.

A chunk of the door came free. This idea was everything I needed. The worst-case scenario didn't have time to flit across my thoughts. I sat in the other chair and brought the microphone down toward my mouth. Another portion of the door fell away, and I heard the chair clatter to the ground.

"Stop right there!" Ricky yelled.

"Code 0000. Junior enters her story."

Everything around me went black.

CHAPTER 28

I WOKE UP outside Allen's cell. Two guards were there, pointing guns at me. Part of me wanted to make a better entrance than waking up outside Allen's cell, but I didn't complain. I'd do anything for my characters, like breaking the number one law of narration. Breaking it also meant alerting the right authorities to my position. Everything would be right in the world where I came from, but I needed to correct things here before I left.

I stood up, and the guards cocked their guns. "Stop. Who are you?"

"Someone you don't want to mess with."

They started shooting. I was surprised at their stupidity. My mind forgot I had powers, so I never put up a force field. I glanced down, thinking I'd have to use some healing power, but the bullets ricocheted off me.

"How?" one of the guards asked.

"I'm not from this world. Your weapons can't harm me." The information came to me the moment I thought about it.

Instead of being scared, they continued shooting until a bullet ricocheted off me and hit one of the guards in the arm. He yelled out in pain. The guards ran, leaving the cell door free. I unlocked it with a thought and about walked inside when I paused. Meeting Allen terrified me. I wanted him to be happy, but also knew he despised me. Was he broken beyond repair? A small but powerful part of me didn't want to see him for fear I'd failed him. The larger, more hopeful part knew I couldn't let this go without trying.

I stepped inside. Light spilled into the room from the door behind me. I saw the dim outline of Allen on the ground. He shivered, the chains clinking as he tried to warm himself. He didn't notice the new light source or me. I waved my hands, and the room became a comfortable temperature. Balls of light blinked into existence. Allen paused and sat up, his eyes darting around before resting on me. I had started towards him but stopped the moment he saw me. His heart knew me instantly, but his head fought it. I interviewed Allen for six days. Yes, he forgot what I looked like, but he could never forget what it felt like to be in my presence once I was with him again. His mind wanted to reject what he felt. He couldn't believe the person who caused him so much pain was the same age as the students he taught.

"Are you...the narrator?"

My voice was quiet. "Yes, I am."

His eyes darkened. "Oh."

I understood his thoughts perfectly. Though I didn't have much time to read over his situation, I sifted through his memories of the past few days. I felt his bewilderment at finding himself alive after getting shot. His fear at realizing how dangerous Josh's power was. His deep love at being able to express his emotions for Sadie physically. His hurt at reliving and telling Bree about his daughter. His fatherly love for Bree. His agony at discovering his future gone. And now? He was furious with me. He knew if he got me angry enough I'd kill him, and a tear fell down my cheek as I realized how much he wanted to die.

"I got here as fast as I could."

"You're too late." His voice lowered the temperature in the room.

I rubbed my upper arm, keeping my gaze on him. "I can still bring Sadie, Bree, and Holly back."

"I meant Celia and Naomi." I knew who he meant. I gnawed on my bottom lip, trying to think of what to say. "All for the entertainment of others. You are heartless."

Tears came to my eyes despite my desire not to cry. I took a few more tentative steps before I sat on the ground across from him, not quite sure what to do. I loved Allen. He also had five years of pent-up anger rotting in his soul that he now directed at me.

He ached to know why I didn't save them. He couldn't have a good relationship with Sadie until he felt closure, but he also needed a good relationship with Sadie for him to feel closure. Before I knew it, I was crying. How was I going to help him? I kept rubbing my cheeks to dry the tears. Despite his frustrations, Allen felt surprised. He didn't expect the narrator to cry.

"We'd never understand, let alone create you, if we didn't feel like you."

Anger dissolved into confusion. "Then why did you kill them?"

I never in a million years thought I'd have to explain myself to my creations while they lived in the story itself. Ideally, I would explain after the story was done, when they were incorporated into the database and living in paradise.

Allen still held on to the anger. I placed my hands in my lap, the tears still pooling around my eyes.

"Stories are beautiful things," I said.

Allen froze, watching with wide eyes. I was quoting his beginning lecture for new literature students— a lecture I gave him during his interview.

"They take the chaos of the world and give it order. Some help open our eyes to the beauty of the world. Others help us live the lives of different people and cultures. And yes, some help us imagine different worlds which could never be, whether they be good or ill, in hopes our own society becomes better. Even tragedies help us discover something about ourselves."

I looked up at him with tears in my eyes. "The truly wonderful stories are those which help us face our own. To read others battle against all odds, be they conundrums or dragons or villains." I reached out and touched his hand. He stiffened under my touch but didn't move away as I added a line to his lecture. "Or great heartache and loss." Allen turned away, a tear rolling down his cheek. "They cleanse our soul."

Allen closed his eyes. "But it's so hard."

I nodded, refusing to turn away from him. "I know."

His frame trembled. "Did it have to be them?"

I squeezed his hand. "Yes."

"Why?" It was a simple question asked out of pure pain.

I waited until he turned to meet my gaze. "Please understand, I didn't come to the decision lightly. I put you through this because you needed to grow. In order to grow, I had to break you so you could rebuild yourself. I never left you alone while you put yourself together, Allen. Not once.

"I also knew, with time, you would change Sadie and Bree's lives. These two women have suffered quietly for long enough. Sadie is mentally exhausted from carrying her burdens alone. Bree has deep wounds in her soul she doesn't realize are there. You've already helped her begin to heal. She sees in you a father who loved his family, and she needs to know such men exist."

Surprise came over Allen, and he looked away. I closed my eyes and knew he needed one last stitch to the wound in his soul to keep it from opening again. I had to promise him something, and I had to word it carefully.

"I won't tell you much about what happens after your story, because I don't want you to pine for an afterlife and forget to live in this one. However, I will tell you one thing." I opened my eyes and met his, letting him see for himself that

I wasn't lying. "I didn't deny you the opportunity to raise your daughter, I only postponed it for a while." Allen froze, and his mind whirled and danced, daring to hope what I said was true.

"You will watch your daughter grow up in a place where anguish and pain don't exist. You will get to know her and love her. You still are, and forever will be, her father."

The pent-up dam of anger broke, and Allen sobbed. I put my arm around him and felt every tear he shed wash away the pain that weighed so heavily on his soul.

After a while, Allen dried his eyes. He still had many questions, some new ones, but he didn't know if he should ask. "Don't worry, Allen. I wouldn't give you this opportunity with Sadie if I didn't know you could handle it. I won't let them die as long as I have control of this story." Slowly he nodded. I touched the chains holding him back and they disappeared. "Come on, let's get the others."

I extended my hand. He hesitated before placing his hand in mine, and we became lighter than air. I created a hole in the ceiling, and we flew through it. Allen squirmed as we flew to the remains of the house in the city. We landed, and I pushed the debris away with my mind until Sadie, Holly, and Bree were on the ground, unconscious. Their souls hovered above their bodies.

Since I skimmed over how Josh did it, I knew what to do. Running my hand centimeters from their skin, I let the healing power sprinkle down and dissolve into their bodies. The small bruises and cuts healed themselves. My eyes saw into their bones and I began healing everything broken. I placed my hands over punctured organs. It took ten minutes to heal everyone. Allen watched on anxiously. I closed my eyes and touched their hearts and heads, allowing the soul to come back into the body. Bree was first. She gasped and her eyes popped open.

She looked at me, a little frightened. "You're her?"

I smiled as I moved to Holly, who also gasped and began to cough. Last, I healed Sadie. Like the others, she gasped and sat up quickly.

"Bree? Allen?" She looked around, seeing the debris piled up to the side, and for the first time seeing me.

Allen knelt next to Sadie. "Are you okay?"

She touched her head. "I think so."

It's all Allen wanted to hear. He grabbed her face and kissed her hard, not caring that Bree and Holly could see. I beamed and stood up, brushing myself off before walking over to the two teenagers and helped them to their feet. Bree had something on her mind, and when she saw I expected her question, she gave a sigh.

"Why am I the main character?" The question had formed the moment she learned of me. She felt embarrassed, looking everywhere but at me. I wanted to hug her but decided against it.

"I wanted someone like you to be my friend when I went to high school. In a way, I was a bit like Holly." I turned to Holly and gave her a nod.

With eyes wide, Holly felt both honored and shocked I knew so much about her life.

"I was bullied by the people I thought were my friends." I didn't expect it, but another tear rolled down my cheek. "I created you in my head to give me a friend. Someone loyal, who wouldn't make fun of me, or what I wore, or my name, or my hair. I know it sounds crazy, but it helped. You helped. You kept me happy until I found better friends, and you made me want to narrate. I wanted other people to love you like I do."

Bree looked surprised. "I don't remember."

"You were in my head. I created you with the ideas I had from school, not with those memories. Reggie may think you're nothing, but you mean the world to me."

"She's right. You're pretty amazing," Holly said, giving Bree a side hug.

The feeling between us shifted, and Bree looked at me, her eyes begging. "What about Josh? Can you bring him back, too?"

I frowned, looking over at Josh's body. "I'll bring him back so you can have a proper farewell. But he can't stay long."

Bree's countenance dropped, but she nodded. Josh's was a different death because he chose it. I swiped my hand again to put his powers back in a dormant state. It took a wave of my hand to bring his soul back. Josh sat up with a gasp, looking around before inspecting his hands. Bree ran over, dropped to her knees, and gave him a hug. He returned the hug and then looked up at me and winced.

"Are you supposed to be here?" Josh knew how much absolute power corrupts. What kept me from going insane was I didn't stop to realize how much power I had.

A group was on their way. I turned and saw the largest group I'd ever seen, being led by Reggie and Riley. I glared at them. These people were the reason my outline became obsolete. These people caused my characters more grief than they deserved. My bottled-up rage began to crack.

"Be careful." Josh knew what I wanted to do.

I turned to him. "Protect the others."

He nodded, got up, placed a hand on Bree's shoulder, and joined my other characters. I created a force field around them and ran at a super-fast speed toward the group to lead them away from my characters. Once again, they tried to shoot me and, once again, bullets ricocheted off. This time I willed the bullets to strike the guards. The more I killed, the more anger pulsed through me.

I closed my eyes and soared into the sky. The wind tore at my hair, and when I opened my eyes, I found myself fifty feet above the massive group. It was liberating. Nothing could stop me, not even gravity. It was something I wanted to explore, but the safety of my characters came first. I was invincible in every other way, except for my love for my characters.

The rubble and debris gave me an idea. I closed my eyes and stretched out my hands, willing what remained of the house to lift off the ground. Every nail, board, and glass turned into pure energy by the time it reached my hands. I opened my eyes, looking at a light brighter than the sun hovering between my fingers. My anger peeked, and I threw the energy ball to the ground. It burst in the middle of the group, and energy traveled through them, stopping all their hearts and dropping them dead.

As I landed on the ground, I willed the earth to crack open to its core, swallowing the dead bodies before closing again. I panted, feeling infuriated and fascinated. That was awesome! Again, I flew up in the sky. I felt the wind on my face as my body twirled and twisted into the air. It was beautiful.

Focus! I had to focus! My characters were still in trouble, and there was one last thing I needed to do.

With a cry of exertion, my whole body filled with light. It started slowly, and then grew until it pulsed out of me. Light came out in waves. Black clouds disappeared. The skies turned a clear blue, and the cool spring sun beat down on the snow. Buildings returned to normal. My side characters and nameless ones reappeared. The snow melted until patches were left. Light filled the whole earth, and I swiped my hands away to create an invisible force field over everything I created. If they weren't my characters, they weren't allowed inside.

This time when I flew to the ground, I stumbled to my knees. I looked at my hands, panting. Tears ran down my face as my body quivered. Something inside me snapped. I possessed overwhelming power. The thought of returning to a weaker body filled me with disgust.

A wicked smirk crossed my face. I could get used to living here. Something moved outside my vision. I got up, saw it was human, and grabbed his throat. My fingers tingled as I squeezed the life out of him.

"Josh!" Sadie screamed.

It took me a second to realize what I was doing. I was strangling Josh! Memories flooded into my mind of his creation. I remembered writing his name down on my palm and fleshing out his character. The interview played across my mind where Josh told me about his life, and I felt my love burning deep inside.

I gasped and let go of him. He stumbled, coughing. I turned to my characters. Bree cowered behind Sadie. Allen held Josh's arm to steady him, giving me a terrified look. They were all afraid of me. Josh motioned Allen back to the others. Allen stood in front of the girls protectively.

"I know how tempting it is." Josh coughed again. "You've done what you came here to do. It's time to go, before you kill us all."

My mind struggled with the truth, and I raised my hand to strike him for suggesting I go. Leave my powers? Never! In fact, I didn't need to strike him. Flames burst out of my hands. I had every intention of seeing the fear in Josh's eyes, but he did not cower back. The memories came back stronger of me creating him, but I wanted this power. With a thought, anything and everything could be mine.

Why couldn't I have both my characters and my power? My mind reeled, a vision of the future. Eventually I'd succumb. I already was. Josh would never relent to me staying here, and I'd get so angry I'd kill him and all my characters. I'd create a new world and make new characters who would worship the ground I walked on, no matter what I did.

I blinked, tears in my eyes, forcing my mind to see the truth. It was unavoidable. I would kill Josh, Allen, Sadie, Holly, and Bree if I stayed here. My hand holding the flames shook as I continued to look at Josh. He understood me so well because he was there. He saw what he could do with this power, and he was brave to give it up. He was the protector of his family, and he still stood true to his calling.

"Do the right thing," Josh said.

"I want this so bad." My frame trembled.

He was calm and steady. "It will kill us all."

The flames trembled in my hands. I noticed my other characters and remembered all their interviews, my eyes resting on Bree. She looked at me with fear, and it tore me apart. Of all the characters, I did not want her to be afraid of me. Allen moved to stand in front of her. He studied my face to make sure I wouldn't hurt Bree. It was only a half an hour ago I helped him want the future I created for him. I would destroy it if I stayed. Slowly, the flames extinguished, and I lowered my hands. Tears fell from my eyes. Josh was right. The price to keep my power was too high.

With a sob, I let the power slip from my fingers. Everything went dark around me.

CHAPTER 29

FEELING QUEASY DIDN'T begin to describe it. My head spun as though my mind was figuring out how to get back into my body. I resisted the urge to throw up and willed my brain to think straight. My first duty was to stop the device, but I couldn't talk. With a trembling hand, I raised the microphone to put it on a soft pause so I could gather the strength to stop it.

"Hello, Junior. Seems like you managed to come back. Not many do. I'm impressed."

I turned my head. My eyes still tried to focus, but I saw a blurry outline of the Rogue. His voice sounded far away, even though he was right next to me. Beads of sweat formed on my forehead. I opened my mouth to talk, but immediately closed it again so I wouldn't throw up.

"In the half an hour you were in there, alerting the Guardians, no one came but me." His image came into focus, and his voice sounded clearer. "Devin isn't the only one undercover. I've got a few everywhere. Most especially, I've got some in the police. They're giving Jim, Vince, and Grace a good fight. It might be chaotic, and they won't be here for a few more hours. Plenty of time for me to finish you."

Tears fell down my cheeks as I closed my eyes. The Rogue once again had me cornered. I had to run, but the thought of leaving the chair made me dizzy. The Rogue's eyes were black with hatred. I defeated him, but I now had the strength of a sloth.

"I salute you, Junior. You've done well. You destroyed most of what took me almost a decade to plot and plan, so you'll understand why I hate you most of all."

He grabbed my wrists in one hand. I didn't struggle. The narration device was on a soft pause. If he brought the microphone down again, the story would resume. I didn't know what would happen, but it couldn't be good.

"It was tempting, wasn't it?" He laughed, and it sickened me even more. Tears continued to run down my face. I lamely struggled to get a hand free, but as soon as I did my head throbbed.

"They don't teach you what happens when you enter your story, do they? No, they simply tell you not to. You've come from your created world, and your mind is deciding which world you belong in. It will stay confused until someone stops the device. If the device continues, piece by piece you will return to the story world. Maybe this time, the temptation will be too great, and you'll stay there." With his free hand, he reached for the microphone. I tried to tell him to stop, but I couldn't do it. It made me nauseous.

More tears fell down my face. My body tried to create adrenaline for me to fight. My limbs didn't respond. The microphone reached my mouth, and the story started up again. My characters unfroze. The Rogue covered my mouth so I couldn't speak, and he tightened his grip on my wrists. My head began to swirl all over again.

"You destroyed everything for me, so it's only fair I destroy everything for you."

I watched my story. Bree cried into Josh's shoulder as he held her protectively. Sadie and Allen held hands as they watched. Holly found her parents and embraced them.

I needed to figure out how to get out of here. I couldn't go back. Not this soon. My body began to shake as it went into shock. I struggled to get his hand away from my mouth so I could speak into the microphone. How was I going to survive this? Darkness began to flit around the corners of my vision, but I shook it away.

It felt like someone took my sloth strength and snapped it in half. My body relaxed more and more. The Rogue laughed, and I tried to use it as motivation to stay here. My fingers and toes turned numb. Somehow, I needed to speak into the microphone. My body went slack as I slid out of the chair. The Rogue kept his hand over my mouth as we both knelt on the ground.

"You're going to be sucked into your story by default." His voice close to my ear sounded maliciously gleeful. "And I'm going to watch every second of it."

Struggling was useless. I tried to speak anyway, but nothing escaped the Rogue's hand. My brain felt fuzzy. Logic flew out the window. One thing I knew for certain was I could not return. Maybe I could get back out again, but the Rogue would still be here, and he would keep sending me back until I destroyed everything.

"Close your eyes," I heard the Rogue whispered. To my horror, my eyes started to close, and I could have sworn I felt a cool, early spring sun on my face.

"Junior, hold on!" I heard Jim yell.

My eyes snapped open, and I returned to the room. I hoped I didn't imagine Jim's voice. I wanted to smile but didn't have the strength. My energy was focused on breathing because the air coming through my nose wasn't enough.

"Junior!" Jim entered the room.

My back was toward Jim, but the Rogue looked livid. He pushed me, and I toppled to the ground. I finally saw Jim, and he looked awful. He didn't have his vest, suit coat, or tie on. Some buttons were torn off his shirt. His hair was windswept, as though he ran the whole way here. Blood dribbled from a cut on his lip. Jim stopped when he saw the Rogue. He glanced down and saw my open eyes and gave a relieved smile.

Jim moved with authority into the room despite his beaten look. "Get away from her."

The Rogue growled. "This plan took years to execute. I won't leave without a casualty. She'll be gone any second now."

When Jim saw the headset over my ears, he winced. It took so much energy to keep my eyes open. I stared at the ceiling and wished the world would stop spinning. Jim tried to take another step in my direction, but the Rogue stepped in front of me and unsheathed a wicked knife.

The room spun faster and faster. I closed my eyes, felt the cool spring breeze, and gasped. I snapped my eyes open in fright. My eyes were the only thing on my body still moving. I clung to one idea—stop the device. Even though closing my eyes would be easy, even though I desired more than anything to feel powerful again, I believed in Jim and the Guardians.

Jim and the Rogue started to fight. I couldn't see much, but I heard a fist contact flesh. My vision blurred, but I refused to close my eyes.

Jim shouted in pain. "Fight it, Junior!"

I tried to tell the device to stop, but it came out as a groan. Everything

211

about my body felt heavy. My lips felt impossible to open. I blinked and felt power pulse through me for a millisecond before I came back to my clammy body.

Focus! I was a narrator. Words were my specialty. I needed to find a way for my weakened self to say 'stop.'

The S was easy enough. My mouth made the hissing sound. I stopped the hissing with a short T. The vowel, however, would be the hardest. My energy quickly siphoned out of me, and I needed to move my vocal cords to make the O. I tried, but my head throbbed with pain. I tried thinking it through. The O sounded like a gasp, and I could make one of those right now. Then I needed to cut it off with a quick P sound.

Jim fell to the ground and groaned. I hoped it wasn't from getting stabbed, but I couldn't see. The Rogue walked over to me, rubbing his jaw, triumph evident in his eyes. I didn't want to see his triumph, but if I closed my eyes, he would win. I fought by staring back.

"Stubborn narrator." His twisted sneer returned to his face. "But I've won."

I mustered the last of my strength. I stared right into his face and took a breath. "Sssst." He looked at me funny, not understanding what I did as I took another breath and began to gasp. "Aaaaahhp."

All my energy came back at once. I coughed, feeling bile creep up my throat. I threw the headphones off and crawled away from the Rogue, which burned through my energy.

"No." The Rogue tried to grab me. "NO!"

Panic rejuvenated my energy and turned into adrenaline as I backed away. The Rogue grabbed his knife and brought it down hard. I deflected the blow to my heart, but screamed as the knife cut deeply into my arm.

I gripped my arm as pain exploded throughout my numb body and blood gushed from my wound. The Rogue lifted the knife again, and this time I knew I couldn't block it. My heart seized up inside, and my mind raced through all the deceptively happy times with the Rogue, back when I knew him as Professor Andrews.

At the last second, Jim appeared and grabbed the Rogue's wrist. Oxygen flooded my system. For a second there I forgot how to breathe.

Jim's hands shook as he struggled against the Rogue. Blood poured down his cheek from a wound above his eyebrow. Jim gave a shout of exertion and pushed the Rogue back with all his might. The Rogue toppled over, and the knife flew to the corner of the room. I held my arm and gave a small gasp of pain. It bled a lot.

The sleeve on Jim's shirt was torn with a bad knife cut across his shoulder, but he was still standing. He moved in front of me and raised his fists. Vince and Grace ran into the room. They didn't look as bad but were still bruised and hurt from a struggle.

"Jim!" Vince looked at Jim, saw me holding my bleeding arm, and then glared at the Rogue. "You are coming with me."

"Never."

The Rogue lunged toward Vince, but he dodged the Rogue. He gave a powerful punch to the Rogue's head, and the Rogue buckled. He swung wildly and hit Vince in the stomach. Jim tackled the Rogue to the ground while he was distracted. Vince pulled out some handcuffs and put them on the Rogue's wrists.

Grace knelt beside me, looking concerned. She had a black eye and a good size goose egg on her head. "Junior, are you all right?"

I didn't have the strength to answer. Jim was there next to me, pale and trembling. "You brave, wonderful, amazing woman!"

"The other narrators. They're in the basement."

The talking at last made me vomit. My body shook as I released the contents of my stomach. I coughed and something red escaped my mouth and hit the floor.

Grace felt my forehead. "She needs a hospital. Now."

"Vince?" a different voice said. A policeman stood in the doorway.

"The other narrators are in the basement," Vince said.

"What about him?" The policeman nodded toward the Rogue.

"We'll take care of him," Vince said, the distrust evident in his voice. "Grace, go with the Chief." Grace nodded as she and the policeman left. Vince left, a firm hold on the Rogue.

Jim took a handkerchief out of his pocket and placed it over my arm. "Can you stand?"

"Maybe."

Jim helped me to my feet keeping the handkerchief pressed over my wound. My legs trembled as I took a step forward.

"The narration device. My story."

"We'll take care of it," Jim said. He continued to help me out the door and through the hallway.

Lydia met us at the end of the hall. "Jim!" She looked radiant.

Jim looked up and new strength filled him. "Lydia!" He let me go as Lydia ran into his arms and hugged him tightly. As he held her close, I thought I could see tears in his eyes.

Drake and the policeman helped Kyle up the stairs. My vision started blurring, and I tried to shake it off. My knees buckled, and my ears rang.

"Junior? Are you okay?" Kyle sounded far away.

The room began to fade. The last thing I remember was Jim scooping me up in his arms and telling me to hold on.

CHAPTER 30

I T WAS HARD to tell the difference between dreaming and being in my story.

I woke up but pretended to keep sleeping so no one at the hospital would bother me. The dream was so vivid, and I wanted it to last longer. It wasn't a normal flying dream. No, I experienced what it felt like to fly, and it was so real. Instead of flying in my story, though, I was flying over the world and correcting every wrong with a blink of an eye. In no time at all it was a perfect utopia. My imagination ran wild with everything I could do to make this world right. No more hunger, no more pain, no more sadness. I ached to be able to heal this world.

A knock came to the door, and I pretended to be asleep. Someone sat down beside my bed. "Junior, wake up."

It was Dr. Webb. I pretended to wake up and glanced at her. She didn't look at me and instead looked at her notes. "Tell me about your dream."

How she could possibly know. "Um…" I felt my face turn red.

The corners of Dr. Webb's mouth twitched up. "You have discovered for yourself why the device is the most dangerous thing on this planet. I've been trained to help narrators who wrote themselves into their stories." Again, I could have sworn she read my mind. "I know what to look for."

I shifted uncomfortably in the hospital bed. Dr. Webb nodded as though she understood. "I have to train you not to think about those things. You can't have those dreams, and you need to discipline yourself not to have those thoughts, either."

My lower lip stuck out. "Why not? It's not hurting anyone."

She tapped her pen against her notes. "How long after the dream did you think about it?"

After opening my mouth to give her a definite answer, I had to pause because I didn't have one. How long was I pretending to be asleep? It could have been ten minutes or an hour.

"Vince's notes say you were in your story for a good half an hour. That's a lot of exposure. A whole wing of this hospital is dedicated to patients stuck in their stories. They live in this reality in a coma while their minds live out everything they could ever dream. Good and bad. Many patients like you who re-enter reality still can't shake off the desires. The more you live in your head, the less you live in the real world. People waste away from imagining themselves with power again, and some find their way back to a device and enter a story. The Guardians created this law for a reason. It's dangerous what you did."

I stared at my hands so I wouldn't have to look at her. She was right, of course. A lot of therapy was in my future.

§ § §

The blank page in my notebook stared at me and I tried not to cry. I knew the next step in my story, and Jim expected my notes. There was a knock on the door.

"Come in." I placed the pen and notepad to one side, grateful for the distraction. Kyle maneuvered his way inside with crutches. He had a boot on his foot.

"Hello!" he said brightly.

I couldn't help but smile. "Hi, Kyle. So your foot is doing better?"

"Doctors examined it. Hairline fracture."

I winced. "I'm glad it wasn't worse."

He sat down in the chair by my bed. "I was practicing with my crutches and decided to come see you. I figured if I messed up bad, I'm already in a place where people know how to help me."

"How kind." I laughed. It felt good to do. Kyle looked like he had more to say, and didn't know how to say it.

"What you did was insane, but it worked," he said. "So, thanks. We'd still be trapped in the basement if it wasn't for you." He didn't look at me. My face flushed and I tried to relax. Before either one of us could say any more, there was another knock on my door.

"Come in," I said.

Jim and Lydia walked in. Lydia waved at Kyle. "I guess it would be hard to find her by herself, Jim. She's a popular person." She held Jim's hand, and he looked far more relaxed. Jim was still healing from the fight, most noticeably the stitches on his lower lip and forehead.

"The doctor says I can go home tonight." I grinned.

"Yeah." Jim frowned. It killed the happy mood. "It's why I came."

My grin disappeared. "What is it?"

Jim rubbed his upper arm. "It pains me to do this, Junior. Technically you didn't break any civil laws, but since you did break narration laws I have to put you under house arrest."

"What?" I thought I heard him wrong.

"We've got a hearing scheduled for you in a couple of days. It's after the Rogue and Devin's hearing."

I winced and looked down. It wasn't the fear of the hearing; it was seeing the Rogue again. He would have killed me if Jim didn't stop him.

"Hey, if your hearing is right after theirs, the stuff you did won't sound nearly as bad," Kyle said.

I appreciated him trying to cheer me up. For Jim, Kyle, and Lydia, everything was right in the world. For me, I had therapist meetings scheduled from now until next year, maybe longer.

§ § §

Jim picked me up two hours before my scheduled hearing. My hands shook, but not because of the hearing. I had an assignment for him.

I did not put on my best dress because I didn't want to seem too eager. Instead, I put on clothes I deemed presentable. My jeans didn't have holes in them, and I had on a nice long sleeve button-up shirt to hide my stitches. I found myself in the passenger seat of Jim's car. He drove up to headquarters, and we got out and went to his office.

"You realize this has to happen. Right?" Jim said carefully.

Tears started to fall, but I wiped them away as I nodded. We walked into the office. "The moment I created him with the ability, I knew how it would end." The stitches itched, but I tried to pay them no mind.

Jim frowned. His office computers were hooked up to the narration device. My story was frozen on his screen. Dr. Webb sat in a corner and gave me a small nod when we sat down.

"Are you sure you want to be here, Junior?" Jim asked.

I nodded. Jim didn't want me to come thinking I was too unstable, hence his invitation for Dr. Webb to be present. However, with what Jim needed to do, I had no choice. I handed him a notebook of my ideas.

He glanced through it and turned to me. "Are your other characters going to be okay?"

"They'll cope. With time."

Jim sat down and put on the headset. He glanced at Dr. Webb, who nodded. I knelt in front of the two screens, watching. Jim pulled the microphone to his mouth. With one last look at me, he whispered, "Resume."

§ § §

"Thank you," was all Bree could say as she hugged Josh tighter.

Allen approached, seeming hesitant. "Is she gone?"

"Yes." Josh closed his eyes. "We're safe."

Bree didn't want to let him go. She continued to embrace him until he groaned. As she broke away, Josh gripped his stomach. "Josh?" Bree asked. The others gathered around him. "What's wrong?"

He didn't answer. His breathing got more unnatural. Allen came to Josh's side right before his knees gave out.

Bree screamed in shock. Her mom and Allen eased Josh into the melting snow, his face twisted in pain. "Josh?" Bree placed her hand on top of his.

The smallest smile flickered across his face. "She was true to her promise. She's given me enough time to say goodbye. Now I must go."

"No." Bree shook her head. "No, it's not fair."

"It is fair." Josh squeezed her hand. "I didn't destroy the story, and neither did she. The price tag for this is my life."

"But you just came back." Bree's voice cracked with emotion.

"We still need you." Her mom knelt next to Bree. "She'll give us more time."

Josh shook his head. "I have to follow the law."

Allen placed a hand on her mother's shoulder. Bree made one last attempt to deny what happened before her eyes. She opened her mouth to say something else, but nothing came out.

"This was my purpose from the beginning. I don't regret a moment of it." He looked at her mom, then at Allen. He smiled, his face filled with peace. Bree heard him take another breath and waited for him to take another. He didn't.

His eyes went vacant, and his fingers relaxed in her hand. She pressed his hand against her face and began to sob.

§ § §

I knelt in front of the two screens, watching it all play out as tears fell. I bowed my head when Allen reached over and closed Josh's eyes. His soul hovered over his body. Jim awkwardly put a hand around my shoulder in a half hug as he lifted the microphone. I couldn't speak.

"Junior, it's okay. When the story is over and they enter the database, they'll meet up. Bree will live a good life, and she will see her uncle again."

I wiped the tears from my eyes. "I know," was all I could say. In a way, Josh saved me too. He was dear to my heart.

My chest felt cold as I breathed in more air, then slowly let it out. Jim was right, of course. Bree would see her uncle again, but the pain she felt was so raw I couldn't help but cry along with her. If I was going to take someone away, then I had an obligation to feel what they felt.

Jim handed me the microphone. "Narration code 2089. Narrator accepts Josh's death." My voice was quiet but confident. Josh's soul opened his eyes and grinned at the screen. He flew into the chilly spring sky until he was out of sight. I wiped my eyes. When would I be done crying?

"Stop." Jim placed the headset on the table. Dr. Webb nodded at Jim before she slipped out. He touched my unhurt arm. I turned my head to let him know I was still listening, but I didn't want to meet his eyes.

"He was amazing," Jim said.

I nodded. "I'm going to miss him. I'm going to miss all of them. I'm afraid I'll never see them again." I knew they'd be uploaded in the database, but the Guardians determined whether I could visit them or not.

Jim gave my arm a pat. "Don't give up hope yet."

I stopped and peered into his eyes. "But I'll only be able to see them if the manuscript gets published."

He smiled. "You're right."

"Mine breaks every rule the Guardians uphold. Vince will never allow it to see the light of day."

"We'll see. However, every book needs the members of the Guardians approval, and it already has mine."

I didn't dare hope. What he said was too incredible. Jim led me out of his office and closed the door.

"Come on." Jim checked his watch. "We'll be late for the Rogue's hearing."

§ § §

I sat between Lydia and Kyle, who put his crutches under the seat. Drake attended the hearing, too, but he sat a few rows back. The place was packed with journalists and other spectators. Even though it was a warm day, I didn't dare move the sleeves up my arms.

The Rogue and Devin both stood before the Guardians, their hands cuffed behind them. Vince read out loud a list of rules Devin and the Rogue broke, both narration as well as civil. Vince finished with the law of forcing a junior narrator to enter her own story.

"We heard your pleas, took them into account, and as the Guardians, we decree you are guilty of these narration charges. You are now in the hands of the civil judicial court to stand trial for those crimes. Whatever sentence they give you, we add twenty more years."

The Rogue laughed and I shivered. Kyle glanced at me. "This isn't the end, Vince. You can't destroy an idea once it's begun."

"Take them away," Vince said to the officers. The Rogue turned, and a dark, twisted sneer played across his face. He met my eyes, and I squirmed in my seat.

Kyle glared right back at the Rogue, and Lydia placed a protective arm around my shoulder as the Rogue passed. "He won't bother you anymore, Junior." I nodded and stared at the ground.

"This hearing is finished." With a *thunk*, Vince dropped the thick file to his side. My hearing was next, but Vince wanted to give time for the news crews and journalists to leave so they could attend the civil hearing.

I swallowed. Last night, the Guardians listened to me as I explained everything. It took over an hour. Vince told me they would have a conference to discuss my fate. Since it dealt with my future as a narrator, I didn't have to go through the civil judicial system. Kyle and Lydia stayed. Drake got up to leave. He turned toward us and gave us a nod before joining the throng leaving the room.

Lydia kept a happy smile aimed toward me. I felt like Kyle wanted to hold my hand but didn't know if it would be okay. The Guardians chatted among themselves while I sat stiff in my chair. Time stretched on as most of the audience left the little room.

"Junior, come up here please," Vince said.

I stood up and made my way to the front. My lungs needed way more air than what the room had to offer, and I struggled to keep my breathing steady. An officer came over with handcuffs. I lifted my hands, but Jim cleared his throat. "Those won't be necessary, officer."

I gave Jim a grateful smile, and he winked at me. Vince pulled out my file. A fair stack of papers rested in the folder. I had more of a record than I thought.

"I will now read through the crimes."

My nerves kept my mouth shut, which I'm sure Vince loved. He started reading through my list of crimes. It wasn't nearly as long as the Rogue's. I felt conflicted about the laws I broke, especially when Vince read off about ignoring the Guardian's request to get rid of Josh.

At the end of the list, Vince straightened the papers, interlocked his fingers, and placed them on the desk. It was like our first meeting, except no condescension. "This is a gray area for all of us, Junior. You broke many rules, some I once considered unforgivable."

I chewed on my bottom lip and glanced at the ground.

"But we have taken into consideration the pressures the situation placed on you and the fact breaking these rules helped capture the Rogue. The Guardians have decided the following for your sentence. First, you will be placed under Dr. Webb's care for needed therapy."

No surprise there. Even if they sentenced me to prison, I'd still have some sort of therapist.

"We will listen closely to Dr. Webb's analysis of how you're doing. When she thinks you're ready, we will hold a conference to assess your progress to see when you may continue narrating." My eyes widened. "Every time you narrate in the future, you will be in one of our housing units, close to the headquarters and to Dr. Webb. Estimated time until you narrate again: five years."

My jaw dropped. They were far more generous than I ever expected. Jim and Grace beamed at me. "Thank you, sir."

"It won't be easy, but after what you went through, we think you can handle it," Vince said.

"I'll try hard never to get on your nerves again."

He chortled as he began gathering his things together. Lydia was there, hugging me. "You should trust me more. I promised you didn't need to worry."

Vince stood up. "Is your story finished? The Guardians need to study it and see if it's publishable."

"Not yet sir. There's one last scene Jim needs to narrate."

Vince nodded. "Send it in as soon as you're done."

"Yes sir."

The Guardians had finished all the hearings for the day. Vince left for a press meeting. Jim and Grace came to congratulate me. Kyle grinned as he shook my hand. Overall, I felt like I could get used to smiling more.

CHAPTER 31

BREE PLACED SOME flowers on Josh's grave. It had been a year since he died, and though it didn't hurt like those first couple of months, part of her still ached like a muscle pushed to its limit. Other flowers were placed on his grave from well-wishers. The entire world owed their lives to Josh, but few knew the actual story. Josh was a humble man, though. He didn't need his grave covered in flowers.

Looking behind her, Bree saw her mom and Allen holding hands. Her mom let go and extended her arms out. Bree walked into her hug, holding her tight. The ring on her mom's left hand sometimes got caught in her hair, but it was a pleasant inconvenience to get used to. Allen placed his hand lightly on her shoulder. Bree may have lost her uncle, but because of him, she got a father. She never realized how big of a hole there was in her life until Allen came to fill it.

"Let's go home," her mom said.

Sandwiched between her mom and Allen, they turned and walked out of the cemetery. Bree turned one last time to see the grave and smiled.

"Thanks Josh."

§ § §

My hands clung together to keep them from trembling as I awaited Vince's verdict. When I stepped into his office, he told me he needed to finish reading an email, and then we'd talk. The chair opposite Vince's desk, despite its comfort, did nothing for my fidgeting.

It didn't take long for him to finish the email, but it lasted an eternity for me. My fingers turned in until I felt a pinch. All the moisture headed for my mouth redirected to my forehead as sweat, leaving my mouth stone dry.

Vince shuffled through the loose-leaf pages of my story, and I tried to swallow. Air sucked up any moisture left in my throat. Jim and Grace had emailed Vince their opinions of whether they should publish it. It didn't need to be unanimous, but as Chairman Vince had veto power if he wished to use it.

Why didn't he say anything? The pinch on the back of my hand turned to pain, and I breathed the minimal amount to keep me alive. Vince didn't know how much his silence caused me to suffer.

He scanned the first few lines of my story before he looked at me as a businessman. "It's good."

I cleared my throat to make sure it worked first. "Thanks, sir." He sounded sincere, and while he didn't say no, he also didn't say yes.

He picked up the stack in both hands and wiggled it. "It's short."

There was little I could do about the length. Of all people, Vince knew my predicament best. Vince tapped his fingers against his desk. "The public has a right to know what happened."

I blinked a few times. "So, what are you saying?"

"We'll publish it on one condition."

My brain ordered my breathing to normalize. Hallucinations appeared with unusual oxygen levels, and I didn't want to confuse them with what Vince actually said. "What do you need me to do?" I asked.

"This is only half your story." He touched the small stack of papers on his desk. "Write your experiences of what happened in between. All those times you stopped to rest, what happened with the Rogue Narrator, everything you feel comfortable sharing. This fortunately doesn't take a narration device. We'll let you borrow an old typewriter while we finish uploading your characters in our database."

My jaw fell open. Vince? Asking me to write my side of the story back to back? I found my voice when I began to understand the idea. "Sir, it's cool, but it breaks major laws. Like how the narrator is to be heard but not seen."

Vince nodded. "I will personally check the writing you do. You must follow *some* rules. I don't want your name mentioned at all. No physical descriptions of yourself. No family or close friends mentioned. Don't even mention this city by name. Be as ambiguous as possible."

"Okay." I released my death grip on my hand and rubbed the marks. "I guess all the phone calls I made to my sister aren't allowed?"

"No. Mention briefly you have a sister, but don't name her. Stick with what happened."

"Well, with no sister, that cuts at least a hundred pages," I mumbled. Vince smiled. He looked more relaxed with a smile on his face.

I gnawed on my bottom lip before getting the courage to ask *the* question. "Sir, why are you letting me do this?"

Vince looked away, troubled. "I'm worried about what the Rogue said at his hearing. A few people are sympathizing with his ideas without realizing the consequences of them. To fight against the Rogue, we have to show them our side too."

I nodded and touched my bandaged arm. I didn't expect my story to turn political. A part of me resisted the idea of my story being used in this way, but I couldn't deny the Rogue had power. Lots of it. He could make people sympathize with him and make the craziest ideas sound normal.

"Being completely ambiguous will be hard. Can I have two or three physical descriptions about myself?"

Vince studied me close. "One, since I'm feeling generous."

I rolled my eyes. "You don't make this easy."

"I trust your skills."

A stray strand of black hair waved in front of my face. I pushed it back. "Should I make up a name for myself?"

Vince shrugged. "Junior is your nickname, not your true name. I'll let it slide." I took the pen from behind my ear and wrote the name on my palm.

Fulfilling Vince's wishes would require me to expose my weaknesses. I might as well publish my personal diary for everyone to read. However, people needed to know exactly what the Rogue meant when he wanted complete, unrestrained freedom with the narration device. Vince straightened the pages of my story by hitting them against the desk and handed them to me. I took them, still shocked.

"Sir, you should know that when we first met I, um, didn't have the highest opinion of you. Thought I'd warn you, since you want to check what I write."

Vince gave a genuine laugh. I sat back in my chair from the shock of it. "I'm comfortable assuming what you thought of me will be tamer than what the Rogue thought of me." A small smile appeared on my face. "I'll have Jim take a typewriter to your apartment on Monday."

"I'll start drafting my side of the story." I stood up and slipped out of Vince's office, hugging my manuscript.

I walked down the stairs to the main floor. A Saturday afternoon brought about a quiet headquarters. My mind reeled with ideas after my chat with Vince. I opened the door and walked outside. It was still summer, but a chilly breeze picked up and rustled my hair, promising autumn was on its way.

"Junior!" someone called.

I turned and saw Jim, Kyle, and Lydia waiting in the parking lot. Jim wore jeans and a polo shirt instead of his business suit. I almost didn't recognize him.

I walked over to them. "This is new."

Jim placed a hand around Lydia's shoulder. "It's Saturday."

Lydia smiled at Jim. "First Saturday we've had in a long time."

"I mean your clothes. I've never seen you in jeans."

Kyle laughed as he balanced on his crutches. "Jim has no sense of style. The reason he dresses so classy is because Lydia shops for him."

As Jim pushed Kyle's shoulder playfully, his cheeks turned red. I giggled as I tucked some hair behind my ear. Jim noticed the story in my arms. "What did Vince say?"

"He wants me to write my side of the story and place it back to back with the narration. It's a clever idea."

"Wow." Jim nodded, impressed. "That's a huge step for Vince."

"I know. I don't think I've been more surprised. Well, not until I saw you in jeans." Kyle and Lydia laughed. Jim rolled his eyes.

"We're going on a picnic. Do you want to join?" Kyle asked.

I tucked my manuscript into my bag. "Sounds wonderful."

"Excellent." Kyle rubbed his hands together. "It's insufferable being their third wheel."

I laughed again as Kyle and Lydia turned toward Jim's car. Kyle gave me one last grin as he opened the door for me. I slid into the back seat and he joined me. Jim started the car and drove toward the park. I leaned against the seat with a content smile, hugging my bag with my manuscript tucked safely inside.

Also by Divertir Publishing

The Entropy of Knowledge
Mark Dellandre and Britton Learnard

We've all had moments when we felt like we were surrounded by idiots…Babylon Briggs feels that pain every day because his town, his planet, even his galaxy, is jam-packed with the most thick-headed simpletons imaginable. When his home world is invaded by a group of equally clueless conquerors, it's up to Babylon to save the day. The only question:
Is he smart enough?

The Adventures of New World Dave
Chris Cervini

In the spring of 1519, Hernán Cortés arrived at the shores of Mexico to conquer the Aztec Empire and claim its gold for Spain. That's what the history books tell us. But sometimes, right in the middle of the history we know, somebody goes and does something to change one important detail, and the world is never the same…